# Get Bloody Stuck In

# Larry Jeram-Croft

Also by Larry Jeram-Croft:

*Fiction:*

*The 'Jon Hunt' series about the modern Royal Navy:*

Sea Skimmer
The Caspian Monster
Cocaine
Arapaho
Bog Hammer
Glasnost
Retribution
Formidable
Conspiracy
Swan Song

*The 'John Hunt' books about the Royal Navy's Fleet Air Arm in the Second World War:*

Better Lucky and Good
and the Pilot can't swim
Get Bloody Stuck In

*The Winchester Chronicles:*

Book one: The St Cross Mirror

*The Caribbean: historical fiction and the 'Jacaranda' Trilogy.*

Diamant

Jacaranda
The Guadeloupe Guillotine

Nautilus

*Science Fiction:*

Siren

*Non Fiction:*

The Royal Navy Lynx an Operational History
The Royal Navy Wasp an Operational and Retirement History
The Accidental Aviator

# Introduction

In my previous two books in this series, I have given an explanation of the title. In this one, I am not going to. Please read the book and you will see why.

**Again, this book is dedicated to the memory of**
**Lieutenant Commander Dennis M Jeram Royal Navy.**
**World War Two Fleet Air Arm Fighter Ace.**

# Prologue

The whole of the City of Winchester was full of happy people. As was the rest of the country. It was a beautiful Spring day. Unlike the previous five years, there was now hope and rejoicing. The man who had been responsible for the deaths of millions of innocents had died and it hadn't taken long for his lackeys to give in. Today was the day when Great Britain celebrated the end of the war against the Third Reich. Everyone knew that things would take a long time to get back to some sort of normal but just for today they could let their hair down and celebrate,

Heather Hunt, her parents and those of her husband John's greatest friend, Freddie St John-Stevens had decided to go into town to join the throng. They walked arm in arm through the smiling crowds down towards the great Guildhall at the bottom of the town. Somewhere a band was playing. Then, as they arrived, a parade of soldiers from several of the barracks in the town marched proudly up past the imposing statue of King Alfred the Great situated further on. There were many servicemen in the crowd as well; soldiers from the barracks and sailors from the nearby naval air stations of Worthy Down and Flower Down in their bell-bottom trousers and flat hats, even a sprinkling of the light blue of the RAF.

The pubs were all doing a roaring trade and it was clear that many in the crowd had been using their facilities to good effect. The pinched, weary faces had all disappeared to be replaced with smiles of hope.

'This is a day to remember,' Heather's father said to no one in particular as he looked around. Heather didn't feel quite the same joy that seemed to be everywhere else and her mother saw the look on her face. 'It won't be long dear,' she said.

Heather just nodded. 'It just doesn't seem fair. They've done more than most and now they can't be here for this. They deserve it more than anyone here.'

'We know that but there's nothing we can do, so just enjoy the day for what it is.'

She gave her mother a wan smile and nodded. Just then a sailor who had obviously been in the pub rather too long saw Heather, who was dressed in her Air Transport Auxiliary uniform and clearly decided to try his luck.

'Hello darling,' he said with slightly slurred speech. 'Fancy a dance to the band? It's all over now, it's finished and we can celebrate.' He made a grab for her arm which she shook off.

'No it's not all over,' she almost shouted in the man's face. He took a step back at the vehemence in her voice. 'Some people are still fighting. For many it's not over at all.' And she burst into tears.

Seeing what had happened, her father pulled her close and then turned to the sailor. 'While you lot are drinking and celebrating her husband and friends are thousands of miles away fighting the Japanese. It's not over for them. Not over at all.'

# Chapter 1

*Two years earlier.*

Lieutenant Commander (Acting) John Hunt looked up at the sign over the entrance doors to the Naval Fighter School at Yeovilton. It was the same sign he had helped put up two years earlier when the school was established. Things had changed in the interim. The airfield was littered with fighters of all sorts most of which John had flown and often in combat. There were Sea Hurricanes and Martlets as well as a few Spitfires and he could even see a couple of the old Skua fighters parked over to one side. The airfield circuit was full of machines coming and going.

Before he could reach it, the door opened and there was his old friend Freddie St John-Stevens his Senior Pilot and second in command, grinning and giving him a salute which, as he was still a Lieutenant, was correct. John knew damn well it was more to wind him up than to offer any real respect.

'Good honeymoon Sir?' Freddie asked with a straight face.

'You've no idea,' he replied with a grin. 'And don't you dare call me Sir when no one else is around.'

'Yes Sir,' Freddie couldn't help replying but he held out his hand and John shook it warmly.

'Come on in, let me show you around.'

An hour later and John was sitting behind his desk taking the weight off his damaged ankle. He had lost the whole of his right foot during Operation Torch when attempting to silence a shore battery of massive fourteen inch guns. He had achieved some success but in the process, his Martlet fighter had been blasted out of the sky by the concussion of the guns. In the subsequent crash, the foot was so damaged that there had been no recourse but amputation. He was slowly getting used to the prosthetic but it still chafed on the stump a little. It had taken some fast talking but he had convinced the doctors that he would still be able to fly and now had his full medical category back. Later today he was determined to prove that he was fit physically and also mentally to cope with the rigours of flying a modern fighter.

There was a knock at the door and Freddie put his head around. 'They're all waiting for you in the briefing room Boss.'

John nodded. Freddie's use of the word Boss brought back memories of the previous year when at one point he thought he might have to take over as the CO of his squadron, something he really wasn't prepared for then. Well, he was damned well going to have to get used to it now.

He walked into the briefing room and everyone stood up for him. If anything was needed to convince him that he was the Boss now that was it. He waved for everyone to sit down and made his way to the lectern at the front of the room and turned to face the assembled officers. The first couple of rows contained the instructors, he recognised several faces and the rest of the room was full of the students who were currently on course.

'Good morning everyone. I won't introduce myself as I'm sure you know all about me, if for no other reason than Freddie over there will have spread malicious stories to anyone who would listen.' A ripple of laughter went around the room and Freddie just nodded and smiled.

'So you probably know I've been around a bit, in fact, I was one of the first instructors here when we set up this school. So I have just one message and it's about what this is all about. Even though we are not having to rush new pilots into the front line as we did a few years back and they are coming through with good hours and excellent training. That training is only about how to fly. This school is the only way we can prepare people to learn to fight and that is a very different matter.' He could see heads nodding in agreement in the front two rows. 'Teaching students how to fight does two things, it makes them dangerous to the enemy and safe to themselves. I've lost too many friends to stupid accidents and enemy action. We have to get that message across.' Once again he could see heads nodding. 'Now I am definitely not going to come in like the proverbial new broom. The last Boss here seems to have done a fine job. It's a shame we weren't able to manage a handover, I was very sad to hear about his accident but I'm afraid naval aviation is not risk free. So carry on as you were and any changes will come gradually as I get myself up to speed. I'll be talking to all the instructors individually over the next few days but my door will always be open if you need to see me. Thank you.'

He gestured for Freddie to follow and left the room. Once again everyone stood as he walked out. When back in his office he sat down again.

'Right, now tell me exactly what needs changing.'

They talked for the rest of the morning and by the end, John had a good idea what needed doing and it was remarkably little. The place had clearly been well managed by his predecessor.

'By the way Freddie what actually happened? I know he had an accident of some sort but no details.'

'No one is quite sure,' Freddie replied. 'He was flying a Hurricane and doing some mock combat with a student and suddenly the aircraft just went out of control, it went into a spin and never recovered. Most of us think he blacked out. But I guess we'll never know.'

'Well, that's behind us now. What have you got for me this afternoon?'

'Your choice, a Wildcat or a Hurricane.'

'Wildcat? Since when did we start calling them that?'

'Oh their lordships issued an edict the other day. All American aircraft are now to be known by their American names. Makes sense really.'

'Fair enough, the Yanks always seem to pick good names and then we change them to something far less war like.'

'By the way, what's happening with you and Heather now? Are you going to be accommodated here?'

'Nope, she's still flying out of Hamble and I am here during the week so we've agreed that we will meet up at weekends in Winchester at my parent's house. It's the best of a bad deal I suppose. So I'll be living in the mess during the week. And what about you? I'm sure there's at least one lady around somewhere.'

'Actually, the same one. Remember Sarah the Third Officer who was working in the Captain's office when we arrived here in nineteen forty one? Well, she's a second Officer now and is still at Yeovilton. In fact, she's not here today as she had to go down to Portsmouth on urgent business but she's your staff officer.'

'You sly sod. Please don't tell me you didn't have a hand in arranging that?'

'You'll never believe me I know that but actually, I didn't, although maybe she pulled some strings of her own.' Freddie replied.

'Alright, so here's what I want to do. I'm going over to the tower now to get an airfield brief. I called on the Captain and Commander (Air) yesterday so that's out of the way. Then you can give me a brief on SOPs for the school and then we are going to get airborne and see just how much I've forgotten. After that, it looks like I have a mountain of paperwork to plough through but I intend to fly most days if I can.'

'I'll make sure Sarah keeps the paperwork to a minimum,' Freddie replied with another grin.

'Oh and I still haven't heard how you got back from Portugal you know.' John said. 'You seem to have been stuck there for some time.'

'I'll tell all in the bar tonight,' Freddie replied.

That afternoon, John finally felt he was back at home. Despite his confidence with the doctors he was still apprehensive as he climbed into a Wildcat. Could he still fly? More importantly, could he even get into the damn thing with his missing foot?

He needn't have worried. Getting into the cockpit had proved quite simple. There had been a small moment of panic when he remembered the last time he had been in this cockpit with the water flooding around him and his head throbbing in agony. Then it melted away as the engine fired into life. With Freddie on his wing, they had climbed away to operate over the Bristol Channel area. After getting the feel of the machine again with a few aerobatics he told Freddie to climb clear and try to attack him. They then both did repeated attacks on each other. After an hour John called to knock it off and they headed back home. He was pretty sure Freddie would claim more success when they were in the bar that evening and he would probably be right but by the end, John felt he had been more than holding his own. It felt really good to be back.

# Chapter 2

That evening, as he showered and changed in his cabin, John wasn't quite so content. He may have been back in his flying world but he was missing Heather more than he thought he would. The honeymoon had been brief, only a few days in a hotel in the New Forest but it had been all they had been hoping for. Not the least because they put the war away and ignored it. It was Heather's employment that had limited their time. She had to get back to her ferrying work. The ATA was always short of pilots, especially now as production was ramping up significantly. She had passed her multi-engine qualification recently and was now flying everything from single-engine trainers to twin-engine bombers like Beauforts. She confessed her ambition to have a go in a Lancaster and be the first female to fly one but the chance had yet to come up.

The few idyllic days had gone in the blink of an eye and as John was still technically on medical leave, he had gone home to his parents. At least that way Heather could be there on a reasonably regular basis. But after Christmas was over the doctors finally signed him off and here he was now even further away. Changing into uniform and heading towards the bar, he realised he needed company.

The bar was full and soon he was chatting to old acquaintances many of them his instructors. Freddie and Sarah were also there and it made for a convivial evening. He was pleased to see that after dinner many of the pilots drifted away, clearly late nights were not too usual here and he said so to Freddie.

'Don't be so sure,' Freddie said. 'The last Boss made it clear about having a good break between bottle and throttle but stand by for Saturday nights as we tend not to fly on Sundays.'

The three of them, John, Freddie and Sarah were sitting in old, comfortable, leather arm chairs after dinner, having a last drink now that the bar was quieting down.

'So Freddie,' John said looking at him. 'We only got a chance to chat briefly at my wedding. What was the real story about you losing your ship and having to scoot off to Portugal?'

'Yes,' Sarah said. 'You've never given me the unexpurgated version either.'

Freddie thought for a moment. 'Alright, it wasn't that interesting mind you.'

'I think we'll be the judge of that,' John said as Sarah nodded in agreement.

'Right then. As you know, Audacity was torpedoed off the coast of Portugal but well offshore. I had been airborne for about an hour and a half looking for the bastard who eventually fired the torpedo but never saw a thing. I had been patrolling ahead and luckily was on the eastern leg of my search when I got a brief radio call telling me not to try and land back on. I was on my own. So I climbed up to about ten thousand, leaned off the mixture and headed east. Actually, more like east south east, I had no desire to accidentally cross over Spain's northern border. I reckoned I had about three hundred miles to go and maybe just enough fuel to make it. I saw land in good time although it was starting to get dark and then my engine stopped. The fuel gauge had been showing empty for some time. So I glided down and crossed the coast with about five hundred feet to spare. There was bugger all choice on where to go so I just concentrated on doing my best. I didn't put the wheels down because the ground look very rough and I didn't want to end up on my back. That worked well because that's exactly what happened. I got her down and then bang, the next thing I know I'm hanging from my straps upside down. I suppose with virtually no fuel there was no risk of fire but that didn't stop me from panicking. The hood was jammed in the ground so I had to undo my straps and kick the side glass out which is no fun when you're lying half upside down believe me. Anyway, I got out and then hadn't a clue what to do next.'

'Were you hurt in any way?' Sarah asked.

'Nope, not a scratch although I did bang my head when I undid my straps and fell onto the cockpit roof.'

'Lucky it was only your head Freddie or you could have been seriously hurt,' John observed.

'Thank you for that John,' Freddie replied. 'So where was I? Oh yes standing in a muddy field next to an upside down Martlet. You know it was all very strange. One minute I was flying well out to sea looking for submarines and hoping for a good night's sleep to come and then I was in a bloody field in the middle of nowhere in a foreign country and had no idea what to do next. Luckily my crash must have been heard because just as I was dithering about, two old people came up to me. I found out that they owned the farm I had crashed on. Neither of them spoke English and I'm rubbish at languages at the best of times so it was all sign language. They seemed quite happy to see me and eventually, I got the message that they wanted me to go with them. At first, I felt I shouldn't leave the aircraft but quickly realised that was just daft. What could I do with it? There wasn't even any fuel left in the tanks to set it on fire so I went about half a mile away to their little farmhouse. They seemed quite poor but were more than happy to offer me some sort of local hooch and some basic food. God knows what was in the booze because after two glasses I just zonked out. The next thing I know is it's morning. The farmer points down the road and pulls my arm. So off we go. It's not far to a small town and he takes me to what looks like a municipal building. Thankfully someone who I think was the Mayor spoke some English. Once he had got the message, he gets on the phone and the next thing I know is I am talking to the Air Attaché in our embassy in Lisbon. He tells me to hang around and someone will come to get me. While I'm waiting I seem to become a bit of a local celebrity. It seems they all like the British, so much so that they take me to a café and ply me with more booze so by the time a car arrives for me I'm really quite tight.'

'So basically you crashed your aircraft and spent the next day boozing with the locals?' Now that's style,' John said.

'Yes, although the Air Attaché who was a very dry old stick of a Wing Commander didn't seem too impressed when I got to Lisbon. Then I stayed there for what seemed like forever. There were quite a few of us by then. Some were escaped POWs from France some like me had been survivors from sea. They put us all up in a converted department store. It was very strange as being a neutral country all the lights were on and although there were some shortages in the shops it was nothing like at home.'

'Weren't you confined then? Surely as prisoners of war, you couldn't just roam around as you liked?' Sarah asked.

'Ah, you see, we weren't POWs merely internees or Prisoners of Portugal and as such, it was up to the authorities how to manage us which in the main was to ignore us and just let us get on with waiting to get home. The embassy provided funds, it was actually rather fun if rather frustrating. The locals all seemed very friendly so in some ways it was more like being on holiday than being a prisoner.'

John had a pretty good idea that his friend was glossing over some interesting stories at this point, knowing as he did how sociable Freddie could be, especially when it came to the opposite sex. He refrained from any comments with Sarah there. He would get the unexpurgated version later when they were alone. 'So why did it take so long to get home and how did you manage it?'

'Priorities really, the best link was by air at night but flights were limited and they were operating a first come first served system which was pretty silly if you ask me as there didn't seem to be any thought about who was more needed for the war effort at home. Also, there seemed to be a great deal of civilian traffic. Presumably, these were intelligence guys. The whole place was a hot bed of spying. That was what we were told, not that we saw anything obvious. Still, I managed to get onto a Wellington bomber after about two months and make it home. It was only when I got back I discovered that they had made a cock up with my surname and no one knew I was alive for ages. I blame that silly old Wing Commander but I guess we'll never know. Then I got sent here as Senior Pilot and the rest you know.'

'And there was me being shot at all over the Mediterranean and you were holidaying in Portugal. Some people get all the luck,' John said.

# Chapter 3

A month later and John was up early and walking over to the fighter school from the wardroom. He was saluted by the sailor on the main gate to the airfield and smiled as he always did when he saw the painted sign in the window of the guard hut exhorting him to 'Fear God and Honour the King'. A worthy thought at any time. The main road led up through the completed airfield past rows of Nissen huts towards the hangars at the end and then the hardstanding which was covered in aircraft. Parked outside the hangers were more aircraft which were being worked on by an army of fitters and armourers many of whom were girls. The Navy was more than happy these days to employ female WRNS on shore side maintenance work.

'Good morning Sir,' he heard a chirpy girl's voice call over to him. He looked and saw a rather pretty Wren with bobbed blonde hair and shapeless overalls who was working on a Hurricane which he recognised as his own.

'Just getting her ready for you Sir,' she said.

He went over and looked up at the girl who was standing on the wing by the cockpit. 'Any problems Wren Stevens?'

'Just finishing the before flight inspection Sir, then she's all ready for you.'

'And fully armed I hope?'

'Always Sir. Are you going to shoot down a Jerry today?'

'Hah, they're not coming over here anymore but you never know I suppose. It's better to be safe than sorry. I'll be ready for her for a ten o'clock take off.' He waved as he went into the hangar and she waved happily back.

The hangar was also a hive of activity but in here many of the aircraft were in bits, missing engines or other critical parts. He stopped to take in the sight. The previous year he had been worried that he would have to take over the role of Senior Pilot of his squadron or even the CO if things had gone wrong. Now here he was in charge of all these ratings as well as his aircrew. It didn't seem like the burden he expected it to be. In fact, he now realised that it was actually something he revelled in. Yes, he had to make sure it didn't get in the way of flying but Sarah had proved very adept at keeping the routine paperwork away from his desk. He even suspected she had become quite good at forging his signature. He wasn't going to ask and he was damned sure she wasn't telling.

His thoughts turned to the future. After Operation Torch and the battle at El Alamein, Rommel had been kicked out of Africa. With the allied invasion of Sicily and then Italy, the Allies were at last making progress against the Germans. Hitler had learned the lesson that Napoleon had learned the previous century and was having his backside handed to him by the vengeful Russians and in full retreat. Last summer, the Americans had all but destroyed the Japanese carrier fleet that had attacked Pearl harbour at the Battle of Midway and were now inexorably closing in on that fanatical empire. Maybe it would all be over soon? If so what the hell was he going to do with his life? It was something he had parked at the back of his mind. Previously, the dangers of the present were just too serious to allow any glimmer of hope. But now there was hope and he was going to have to contemplate the future. Once again he looked around the hangar and suddenly realised that maybe this was what he wanted. Maybe a full career in the navy was the answer. Just then the door in the side of the hangar opened and Sarah put her head around,

'Ah there you are Sir, they're all ready for you in the main briefing room.'

'Thank you Sarah,' John replied and made his way to the large room at the end of the main corridor. Today was the start of yet another training course and it was his job to make the new pilots aware of what he expected of them.

As he walked in, Freddie who was waiting for him called everyone to attention.

'Sit down please,' John said as he went to the front of the room and turned and surveyed the new intake. God how young they looked. At least half were wearing the white tabs of Midshipmen and looked as though they should still be at school. He had to remind himself that he wasn't that much older, merely far more experienced. They all looked eager and excited, knowing that they were immortal and ready for the day they could go into combat. He was going to give them a few home truths.

'Good morning everyone and welcome to the fighter school. You are all well qualified as pilots and have been given a good education so far. You probably think you know it all. You don't. If you were to go into combat tomorrow half of you would be dead within the week.' He stopped to let his words sink in. He could see smug smiles on several faces. 'During what they are now calling the Battle of Britain, young pilots just like you were joining operational squadrons with half the hours that you have been lucky to receive. Most of them died. The average life expectancy of new pilots in those days was less than two weeks. Think about it.'

He could see that his words were hitting home. 'At the school, we have two priorities only. The first is turn you into killers. There is no glory in aerial combat despite what you read in the newspapers and novels. The best fighter pilots fight out of ambush and then run away to ambush again. And that is our second priority, to teach you how to survive so you can get up the next morning and do it all over again. It's going to be hard work. There will be no flat hatting and fooling around, that's the quickest way to be thrown off the course and end up flying target tugs for the rest of your career. Is that clear?'

There were several rueful nods but he noticed several faces that were clearly not convinced. They would either pass the course well or be out within the week. Time to be more positive.

'That's not to say we don't enjoy ourselves here. The mess is very friendly and I expect you all to socialise not that I doubt you will anyway. But whatever you get up to in your spare time you will be here on time and in good shape to fly. Is that understood?'

Again there were nods but far more this time. 'Good. I'll leave you to your instructors who will now outline what you will be doing over the next weeks. I look forward to seeing you all in the air some time and you will have the chance to show me what you are really made of.'

As he left the room he was accosted by Sarah who had an odd smile on her face. 'Sir you've got a visitor,' she said. 'I've shown him into your office. He's a commander from some Admiral I've never heard of.'

Intrigued, John followed Sarah into his office where to his annoyance a slim, fair haired, regular naval commander was sitting at his desk. He at least had the grace to stand when John came in.

John's cheerful mood evaporated as soon as he saw the man. 'Sorry Sir but that's my chair. Why don't we sit here around my table and you can tell me what this is all about.'

'Yes, they said you spoke your mind,' the commander said as he came around the desk and offered his hand. 'James Cameron, FOCTA.'

John shook the hand. 'I take it you know who I am but who or what the hell is a FOCTA?' He asked as they sat.

The commander looked amused. 'Flag Officer Carrier Training and Administration, your new boss.'

'News to me,' John said. 'As far I know I answer to the Captain of HMS Heron.'

'Well, that's all about to change. A new Admiral has been appointed to manage all operational training which includes this Fighter School.'

'When I get official notification of that Sir I'm sure I will be happy to comply. Until then, if you'll excuse me I am programmed to fly.'

'Actually, I'm sorry to say but you will have to pass that task on to your most senior chap because as of this moment you have been relieved of command.'

John looked completely nonplussed. 'You bloody well can't come marching in here and say that. What authority do you have? I've no idea who you really are or where you've come from.'

The commander handed over a piece of paper to John who reluctantly took it and read it. He was silent for a moment and then went to the door. 'Sarah,' he called. 'I need Freddie in here now and then tell Tom to take shareholders and take both of our names off the flying programme for the rest of the day.' He remained silent until Freddie knocked and came in.

John handed him the piece of paper and let him read it.

'This can't be right,' Freddie said after a few minutes. 'We can't just up sticks and leave.'

The commander spoke. 'Gentlemen that letter is signed by the Chief of Staff to a Rear Admiral and as you can see, has been endorsed by the CO of Yeovilton. Look, I'm truly sorry this has come around at such short notice but there is a matter of real urgency to this task.'

14

'That's all well and good,' John said. 'But this operation order doesn't even say what the task is, just that the two of us are needed urgently to go to London for a briefing.'

'And that's all I know,' the commander said. 'Look, you two are far too experienced to be wasted on a second line teaching job. There are plenty of people who can take over. John, you've been here a month. Is there anything serious you want to change? I know you and Lieutenant St John-Stevens helped set this place up early last year.'

'Well not really,' John said, 'It seems to be running pretty well especially now we have some decent aircraft to use.'

'Right you are then. What I can tell you is that once you've been briefed you will be abroad for some time. I know you are married John so you will need to tell your wife that you will be away for several months but that is all. You've got today to pack and are expected at the Ministry of Defence at nine tomorrow morning. I'm sorry but I have to leave you to it, good luck.' And he left the room.

'What the hell?' Freddie said when they were alone. 'Sorry but why should we take any notice of that stiff necked sod?'

'Because of the signature on the bottom of that order,' John said. 'Take another look. Do you remember that name?'

Freddie looked again and his face cleared. 'Well, he's a pretty good sort maybe this isn't quite what we thought.'

# Chapter 4

The pair of men stood at the main doors to the Ministry of Defence Building. It could hardly be seen for the piles of sandbags surrounding it and the two armed policemen wearing tin hats who were guarding it. However, it seemed that naval uniform was all that was needed for the two of them to be able gain access. Inside the reception area was crowded and they had to wait in line until a harassed looking woman looked up at them. John showed her his letter and she simply grabbed a telephone and spoke briefly.

'You're to go on up, floor three, room three seventeen.'

John could see she thought she had finished. 'A little more information would be helpful,' he said. 'We've never been here before.'

The woman sighed. 'The stairs are behind you over there. Third floor and the office you want is on the left hand side of the building. All the doors are marked.'

However, their worry disappeared at the sound of a familiar voice.

'Ah, there you two are. I thought I'd come and see if you had arrived. This bloody place is like a labyrinth. Didn't want you wandering around lost for hours. Welcome.'

John and Freddie turned to see the beaming face and outstretched hand of Captain Mike Tucker, the man who had arranged their entry into the navy and who John had last seen as the Commanding Officer of the Air Station at Lee on Solent.

The captain could see the war on the two younger men's faces. Should they shake his hand or salute him? They were all in uniform after all. He decided to put them out of their misery. 'No saluting in here chaps we're all far too busy with real work to worry about all that bull. Come on follow me, we've got a busy morning ahead of us.' He turned and led them to the stairs. They chatted amiably as they went up various stairs and along gloomy corridors.

'As you can see, I escaped Daedalus only to be incarcerated here,' Captain Mike said. 'But actually, it's damned important work and I know you two will be dying to know what is going on. Just humour me a little.'

They stopped in front of a nondescript wooden door just like all the others down the corridor and went in. The room inside was larger than they expected with a small conference table and two other men sitting. One was a slim naval commander sporting pilot's wings and an impressive chest of medals. He had a sharp nose and piercing blue eyes but smiled as he stood up as they entered. The other man was small and mousey haired with round thick lensed glasses. His hair was receding and by the pallor of his skin, it looked like he rarely got outside.

'Right, introductions are in order,' the captain said. 'Commander Peter Lethwaite here is actually Chief of Staff to the naval attaché in New York and has come over to discuss things with us. And this is Thomas Forrester from the research people at Farnborough. He's our boffin for the day.'

If the scientist resented the captain's remarks he gave no sign. He simply shook the two pilot's hands as did the commander before they all seated themselves just as a pretty young Wren came in and put an urn of tea and plate of biscuits on the table.

'That'll be all Julia,' the captain said. 'Make sure we're not disturbed for the next couple of hours please.'

When they were alone again the captain spoke. 'Now you two must be burning up with curiosity but before we tell you what this is all about we want you to design the perfect carrier aircraft for us.'

'Sorry Sir, could you be more specific,' Freddie said.

'Yes of course. Look, you two are probably just about the most experienced naval fighter pilots we have at the moment. You both flew with the RAF in nineteen forty then went off to help develop naval fighter tactics before going on to fly off various carriers with some success I might say. We want your honest opinion on what is wrong with our current aircraft and so what you would want to see in their replacements.'

Fighter or attack aircraft Sir?' John asked.

'Both but in one machine. A fighter that can also bomb and strafe. Rather like our old Skuas were meant to do and singularly failed to manage. What are the key characteristics? Have a second to think while Peter there pours us all a cup of tea.'

John and Freddie exchanged glances and Freddie indicated that John should start. 'Well Sir, the machine needs to be fast. Something close to four hundred would be good. It should have good firepower but personally I don't like cannons, you can never carry enough rounds. Half inch machine guns, six if possible to give a good punch but also have plenty of ammunition.'

'What about manoeuvrability,' Peter asked. 'Should it be a good dog fighter?'

Freddie answered. 'If you get in a dog fight you're half way to losing already. You're much better to go in fast, attack and then get the hell out of it. You can then always come back and do it again. Higher speed and rate of climb compared to your adversary are your real advantages.'

'And then good endurance,' John said. 'These land fighters we are trying to convert just can't carry enough fuel. The Wildcat we both flew had four hours endurance which meant you could carry out effective long range patrols and engagements. Frankly, the Seafire is just a fleet defence asset as it can't go anywhere. Oh and why carry extra crew? An Observer and Gunner just reduce the aircraft's performance.'

'Hang on you want good endurance for long range work but don't think you need a navigator?' Thomas the scientist asked.

'Never did in the Wildcat,' Freddie said. 'Look, if we're in the vicinity of the fleet we will always know where we are. If we conduct long range work it will be as a number of aircraft together, either escorting other strike aircraft or going to attack a fixed position ashore. In both those cases we either have navigators in the other aircraft or the navigation is really quite simple.'

The scientist and commander looked at each other. 'Something I've been saying for ages.' Peter said. 'The problem has always been what their lordships really thought their aircraft should be doing. Between the wars when I was flying, we were often considered just the eyes of the fleet, not the main armament. That has changed totally now of course but even so we are designing aircraft like the Firefly with a crew of two. Mind you once we get radar into our machines that will be a different story.'

'You mentioned an attack role,' Freddie said. 'I would hope the machine would be capable of carrying bombs or rockets and maybe have some sort of dive brake to allow for dive bombing. It's a far more accurate and survivable tactic rather than dropping from level flight.'

'Then there is the other issue,' John said. 'Operating this hypothetical aircraft we're designing at sea has other requirements. It will have to be rugged and reliable. When we put Wildcats on the carriers like Audacity with no hangar, their serviceability was dreadful. And then of course there is the issue of landing them safely and easily. Take offs are not too much of a problem with these new accelerators and rocket packs but getting back on board has always been the issue. You need an aircraft that can generate a great deal of drag. That may sound odd but when you cut the throttle you want to stop flying very fast. I was talking to a friend the other day who had been flying Seafires and said the real problem with them apart from weak undercarriage was that they had a tendency to float. This isn't a problem at an airfield but when you only have a few feet of deck to play with it'll put you in the barrier in an instant.'

'Yes we know about that,' Thomas said. 'The obvious thing to do is to give it much larger flaps, even air brakes but the wing just isn't large or strong enough.'

'But it also means that the undercart has to be very tough,' Freddie said. 'Again the Wildcat is an example. It could take really rough impacts, mind you if the wheels had been further apart that would have helped as well.'

'So to sum up gentlemen,' the Captain said. 'You would like to see a four hundred mile an hour machine, armed with machine guns or bombs that can fly for four hours or even more with only a pilot. It has to have a strong undercarriage and a flap system that means it has to approach with power so that when the engine is cut it can use its strong undercarriage to thump down in a short distance.'

'Yes Sir,' John said. 'Give us an improved Wildcat, capable of four hundred that could carry more ordnance and with wider undercarriage and we would have something pretty effective.

The captain looked at his other two guests and smiled. 'Well you two are clearly the men we want. You're booked to go over to America with Commander Lethwaite. You sail in two days' time from Liverpool on the Queen Mary. When you get to America we want your opinion on not one of the aircraft you just designed but two.

# Chapter 5

John lay back in bed and stared at a beam of sunlight coming in through the window by the bed. Little motes of dust were glinting in the shaft of gold generated by the early morning sun. Next to him, Heather was snoring gently, something she always refused to accept that she did.

He rolled over to look at his watch, it was coming up to seven. In several hours' time, he would be meeting Freddie at the train station for the long trip up to Liverpool. He pushed the thought out of his mind. One thing he had learned very quickly was to make the most of the time you had and not worry about the future, even one that was only a few hours away.

Heather must have heard him as she rolled over, opened her eyes and smiled at him. 'Good morning Darling,' and then as if reading his mind. 'How long have we got?'

'Long enough,' was the reply as he dived below the covers to repeat what they had been doing the previous night. She didn't object.

Sometime later on, lying side by side in comfort she rolled over and looked at him. 'America? You lucky sod. Come on tell me what you're really going to do over there.'

'I told you and everyone else last night as much as I've been allowed,' he replied. 'The Americans want to talk to us about our experience and compare notes. We should only be away for a couple of months.'

'And that was good enough to remove you from your command at the fighter school? It seems rather draconian to me.'

'I can't really go into it anymore but believe me it is worthwhile and I'll be home before you know it. It's only meant to be for a couple of months.'

'Well, you can damn well bring me back some good presents. I haven't had any real nylons for over a year.'

'Of course I will.'

'And keep clear of all those American girls.'

'Of course I will.'

'And don't drink too much, I know what you and Freddie are like.'

'Right that's enough,' he said and made another grab for her which only made her giggle before she became too busy to nag him anymore.

Later on, John reversed the subject. 'And are you going to keep on flying as much as you have been?'

'Good question,' she replied. 'And the answer is hopefully not so much. I'm hoping for promotion to First Officer soon and if so I'll be doing more admin than flying.'

'Good, you work too hard and some of the wrecks they make you fly are really not safe.'

'I know what risks to take but you're right and I really could do with more time on the ground.'

'Good, well I suppose we'd better get up. I'm already packed so let's have some breakfast and you can drive me to the station.

And then all too soon John was watching the train come into Winchester station. Freddie was also there with Sarah and so it was yet another war time parting for all of them, something they were getting used to but never enjoyed. Freddie was now also sporting the two and half gold stripes of a Lieutenant Commander in his jacket sleeves. He was due promotion anyway and it had been brought forward to ensure that the Royal Navy's new ambassadors were of appropriate rank.

The trip to Liverpool was slow, uncomfortable and crowded. There were a surprisingly large number of naval cadets who they soon found out would be travelling with them across the Atlantic.

'Towers scheme lads,' Freddie said to John when he realised who they were.

'No idea what you are on about Freddie old chap,' John replied.

'Oh maybe you hadn't heard. Last year it was realised that most volunteers to fly were going to the RAF. The glamour of the Brylcream boys I suppose. Anyway, we needed to do something about it and a Captain Towers was given the job. Recruitment was stepped up and also all training shifted to Canada or the States. Much better weather and less crowded skies. It's been quite successful as you can see by the number of lads here. I've heard that the courses are quite tough but at least when they get to the front line they will have far more hours than most of us managed.'

'I guess I should really have known about that,' John said. 'But being in the Med and then hospital trying to learn to walk again sort of took my mind of that sort of thing.'

'Yes and getting married probably gave you other things to think about as well,' Freddie said with a grin.

'True. Very true.'

'Talking of hospital, how's the leg, you don't seem to be limping too much at all these days.'

'Much better although I still feel it at night even though I know it's not there. I was lucky in a way, at least it was only the foot, not the leg. I wonder what the Yanks will say when they find out.'

'They will probably say you're not fit to fly their new wonder aircraft and the whole trip will have been a waste of time,' Freddie said with a grin.

'I sincerely hope our good commander has cleared that with them,' John replied. 'I'm not going to waste my time when I could be doing something useful over here.'

'Not even to see the bright lights and acres of willing young girls?'

'Hah, maybe that's great for you, I'd rather be home for obvious reasons.'

'Well, we'll be able to ask the commander when we get on board, he came up yesterday.'

The rest of the journey dragged on. There were no refreshments to be had but both men had managed to get some sandwiches when they transferred trains in London and both of them also had full hip flasks. They were fast asleep as the train pulled into their destination. John woke and looked blearily out of the window. He remembered the last time he had been here. It had been in the Invincible, embarking Spitfires for the trip down to the Mediterranean. But the most vivid recollection was being landed as a survivor from the destroyer Tempest after Audacious had been sunk. With a mental shudder, he prayed that this forthcoming trip into the Atlantic didn't end up the same way. Being sunk once was more than enough.

Reaching over, he gave Freddie a shake. 'We're here old chap, rise and shine and all that stuff.'

When they emerged onto the crowded and smelly platform, they joined the throng of passengers who were almost completely military heading towards the exit. Once outside, they saw a pretty young leading wren standing by a car painted dark blue. She had blonde hair tucked up under her cap and was scanning the crowd. Then she spotted them. 'For the Queen Mary Sir's?' she asked.

'That's us,' Freddie said. 'Are we the only ones?'

'Yes Sir, my name is Carter, the cadets will be going by bus but Commander Lethwaite thought that wasn't appropriate so here I am. If you'll just give me your bags?'

It wasn't long before they were driving through the docks. They were packed with ships all painted in rusty wartime grey. There were merchantmen and warships seemingly mixed up in the various basins but it didn't take long to spot the stately lines of the massive passenger ship. She might also have been painted grey but she was by far the biggest ship there and towered over all the rest. The car drew up alongside and the three of them got out.

'Don't worry about your bags Sir,' the Wren said. 'I'll make sure they get on board. Officers use the gangway over there.'

'Hang on,' said Freddie. 'Are you coming with us?'

'Yes sir, I'm going out to work at the embassy but I've also been detailed off to write up your reports. I'll get your bags on board and then I have to return the car to the pool.'

When she had left Freddie turned to John. 'I suppose we had better get on board but suddenly I'm looking forward to the trip a little more.'

John decided to hold his tongue.

# **Chapter 6**

The officer's mess room was almost empty even though it was breakfast time. There were plenty of military officers on board. The first evening out from Liverpool, the bar had been quite crowded but it hadn't taken long for the ship to round the top of Ireland and head out into the Atlantic. A big swell was running and even a ship as big as the Queen Mary was feeling the effects, especially as the Captain clearly had no intention of slowing down. Speed was their major defence against U-Boats.

John was just about to take a mouthful of scrambled egg when the ship slammed into the next wave. The jolt caused his fork to miss his mouth much to Freddie's amusement.

'Bloody ship,' John cursed as he grabbed the edge of the table for support. 'Invincible never bounced around like this.'

'Never had to go flat out to avoid submarines. Don't forget we've got no escort, unlike the carriers.'

'Oh well at least we're not throwing up the contents of our stomachs like nearly everyone else seems to be,' John said as he looked around the almost empty dining area. I wonder when we'll see the good commander again?'

Before Freddie could answer, the good commander appeared at the door and made a slightly staggering approach to their table as he tried to counter the movement of the deck beneath his feet.

'Good morning gentlemen,' he said as he managed to gain the relative safety of his seat. 'Would either of you care to tell me why I gave up the sanity of the Royal Air Force and put on a dark blue suit and joined the navy?'

'Because the navy's far more fun and we get all the girls,' Freddie replied. 'Oh and the suit is black, not blue.'

'Thank you for that Freddie. Now, what's for breakfast?'

'Actually Sir, why did you transfer to the navy,' John asked. 'I know many did of course.'

Just then a waiter came over with the practised gait of someone totally used to the movements of the ship and took the commander's order who then turned back to John.

'I joined up in nineteen twenty,' he said. 'I wanted to fly and at that time the RAF was the only guaranteed way to do it. I specialised in naval flying and had some great fun but it was a complete nightmare in many ways. When we were at sea we were subject to Admiralty rules and regulations and when ashore the RAF equivalents. The problem was that they were totally different in many respects. Frankly, it was a complete mess and then it was clear we were never going to get the latest kit. I blame the Admiralty for a lot of that. They really didn't know what they wanted and the Air Force took advantage. It was such a shame as it was clear to many of us that naval aviation was a potent weapon. Look at us now and imagine what things would have been like if we had the ships and aircraft we have now at the start of the war.'

'Yet we're going to the States to look at more American machines.' John said with a frown.

'Correct, because they didn't neglect things between the wars and have designed aircraft specifically for the job, something we're only starting to do now. You two should know after all you've been flying Wildcats for some time.'

'So what did you fly Sir?' John asked.

'Oh, I'm a biplane man. Various types but I ended up as CO of a Sea Gladiator squadron up in Scapa Flow before their Lordships decided they wanted to give me a third stripe and that's just about ended my flying career. Then, for some reason, they seemed to think that coming out to the States was a good idea.'

'You sound a bit disappointed Sir,' Freddie said.

'Funny you know, I was at first but now the Yanks are in the war and they've developed some really good kit it's been quite a challenge trying to get hold of some. This lend lease arrangement is helping of course. Which is where you two come in. You'll get a detailed briefing at the Embassy. Oh and John please don't mention your foot to the Americans. I see you walk quite naturally but I really don't want to get into an argument about your medical fitness.'

'Understood Sir,' John replied.

Three days later the ship entered New York. With just about all the other passengers, they were standing at the ship's rail taking in the view, or goofing as the navy would have it. The weather had improved. The wind had dropped to nothing and the sun was shining.

25

'My goodness that really looks as big as the pictures show,' John said as they watched the Statue of Liberty glide by on its own little island.

'Donated by the French, in the last century I believe,' Freddie said. 'They couldn't afford to put it up at first and only had that hand with the lamp on a plinth somewhere but in the end they raised the money for the whole thing from private subscriptions.'

'Goodness, what a mine of useless information you are this morning,' John said. 'But just look at the harbour.'

There were ships everywhere, many in wartime grey but also many in the bright colours of a country unthreatened by war and John commented on it just as the commander joined them.

'They had their own U boat scare you know.' He said, as he also gazed over the crowded harbour. 'Once they declared war on Germany a handful of U boats came over and had a very happy time off the American coast. We did warn them to start convoying but it took a great deal of persuasion and quite a few losses before the penny dropped. The Americans are rather like the RAF. As individuals, they are very likeable but as a nation, they can be quite arrogant and pig headed. So just be aware of that.'

John snorted with laughter at the analogy. 'Don't know about the Yanks Sir but I do know the RAF and thanks for the warning.'

A few hours later, they were in one of the famous Yellow cabs and heading through the city to the Embassy. The city teemed with life. It seemed very strange that there was not a sand bag in sight and nor were the windows taped up against possible bomb blast. All the people looked prosperous and well clothed. Although there were some servicemen to be seen, the vast majority were civilians. John commented on this to Freddie who was sitting next to him.

'So that means the night life should be of similar quality,' Freddie said.

'You, my friend, have a one track mind,' John replied. 'But a few beers would definitely go down well.'

'Nice to see the Fleet Air Arm maintaining their priorities,' Commander Lethwaite said. 'I don't think you'll find a shortage of evening entertainment. We will go to the embassy now and I'll introduce you to the Naval Air Attaché. He will have a few things to say to you about your forthcoming task. The US navy has allocated you a liaison officer who will accompany you while you are here.

His name is Hank Bertelli and he's also a pilot. I think you will all get along quite well. He was at Pearl Harbour and one of the few that managed to get airborne, although far too late of course. The embassy is rather full at the moment so you will be staying at a nearby hotel and as it's only Thursday today and your task starts on Monday you can have the weekend to acclimatise. If that's the right word for it of course.'

Freddie's eyes lit up at the prospect of a free weekend. They hadn't really been expecting it. Weekends in England were very much optional.

A few days later, John was not so sure. Their new best friend, Hank, had taken them under his wing and seemed to have made it his mission to convert the two Limeys to the American cause. John had lost count of the number of bars and night clubs they had visited each evening. During the days, if you counted daylight hours after midday, as days, they had toured the city and seen all the famous sights. Freddie was in his element and he and Hank had really hit it off. John had just decided to follow the whirlwind. At least today was Sunday and they could get back to some real work tomorrow. As long as his liver lasted of course. John was sitting at a table in a fairly quiet night club. Freddie was on the dance floor with yet another pretty female and Hank was approaching with yet another round of beer.

John reached over and took a beer as Hank plonked the rest down on the table. Hank was nothing like John had expected. They were about the same age but it looked as if the slightest breeze would blow Hank away, thin and tall, he had a shock of black hair and a very prominent nose and despite his surname, he was actually Jewish. He had indeed flown at Pearl Harbour but his subsequent flying career had been far more impressive. His last action had been at the battle of Midway where the US fleet had effectively crippled the Japanese carrier force. He had been lucky enough to be flying a Wildcat. Many of his friends were still in the old Brewster Buffaloes and most had not fared well. Although he did talk about his experiences he had been very eager to hear about the two Englishmen's combat time. By now there was a great deal of mutual respect between them. It was clear that they talked a common language when it came to air fighting.

'Looks like Freddie had made yet another conquest,' Hank said as he plonked himself down. 'Not making any efforts in that area yourself John?'

John waved his left hand at Hank. 'Married man old chap as you well know. I leave all that to Freddie these days.'

'And I hear she flies as well?'

John explained about the ATA. 'She's got more hours than me on far more types, she's even qualified to fly multi engine machines now. I've never flown anything with more than one propeller.'

'She sounds like one hell of a girl. When this is all over I'd love to meet her.'

'Our pleasure, the invite is there whenever you want it. Now what time are we off tomorrow?'

'Transport picks us up at nine. We'll spend the day briefing and then you two have the rest of the two weeks to play. I'll be flying too so we can maybe do some adversarial encounters as well, once you're up to speed.'

John looked at his watch. Midnight was approaching fast. 'In that case, I think I'll turn in Hank.'

'What should I do about Freddie?' Hank asked.

John looked over at the dance floor where his friend seemed to be attempting yet again to cement Anglo-American relations, literally. 'Oh don't worry about him. He's got two loves in his life. One is what he's doing now and the other is flying. He'll be there.'

# Chapter 7

The next morning, precisely at nine, the three men were met at the hotel entrance by a larger grey US Navy car. True to predictions, Freddie was on time and looked refreshed and eager. John, as always, was amazed at his friend's capacity for late nights which seemed to have no effect on him the next day.

Hank was also impressed and said so. 'Good morning Freddie. All ready for a day's hard work?'

'Never better old chap,' Freddie replied. 'Up and at em I say.'

John and Hank exchanged looks but refrained from saying anything more.

'We're off to Roosevelt fields today gentlemen,' Hank said. 'It's not too far from the city and used to be a civilian field but was taken over by the military last year. Today we will go over our radio and air traffic procedures as the place does get a little crowded. Then we will do cockpit and pilot's notes briefings followed by ground familiarisation. The next two weeks are for flying. I suggest a day to get familiar with the machine and then we can move on to some tactical and ground handling assessments. There will also be a representative from each of the manufacturers for you to talk to.'

'Sounds good to me,' John said. 'We're in your hands. However, I suggest we each take one machine for a week and then swap over.'

'Yes that was my thinking too,' Hank said.

It didn't take long to get to the field and Hank looked at his watch as they drove through the gates. 'We've got time guys, fancy going over to the hangar where you can see the beasts?'

'Absolutely,' Freddie said.

The car pulled up outside a small hangar off to one side of the main field. Inside they could just make out the hulking shapes of two aircraft. They climbed out of the car and walked into the hangar.

'Well they said it was ugly,' Freddy said as he looked at the machine on the right. 'They weren't wrong.'

'Beauty is in the eye of the beholder,' John said. 'That just looks like it's ready for a fight. And the other looks like a Wildcat that's been overeating.'

Hank laughed. 'Well, guys you'll be getting to learn all about them very soon. The Vought F4U Corsair often known as the 'bent wing bastard' and the Grumman F6F Hellcat or the 'Wildcat's bigger brother'. Both have the same two thousand horsepower engine and six, fifty cal machine guns. You're gonna have a lot of fun.'

They did. For the first week, John flew the Corsair and Freddie the Hellcat. By Friday they were both well conversant with each aircraft and were able to try some 'one on one' combat against each other with Hank appearing in a Wildcat to enliven the situation. Part of one of the runways had been painted to represent a carrier deck and they were also able to practice deck approaches and landings.

Another boozy weekend then occurred before another week flying where they swapped aircraft. On the final Friday, the pretty Wren they had met on the dock at Liverpool came with them and started to type up their notes so they could put a final report together for the Naval Air Attaché.

It wasn't long before the three of them were back at the embassy in front of Commander Lethwaite and his boss Captain Michael Smythe.

The captain greeted them warmly and indicated to take seats around a small table. An amiable looking man with thinning red hair streaked with grey, he had a chest full of medals from the last war and pilot's wings on his sleeve.

'So gentlemen, I kidnapped you from your rightful employment in England and set you the task of telling me what you think of the two machines. I am in the process of negotiating with our American colleagues over getting more fighters under the lend lease agreement. I've already gone out on a limb with promises to the Americans so I wanted real experienced combat veterans hopefully to back me up. I know your written reports will be with me soon but I want your verbal findings as well. Words on paper are fine for an audit trail but it's your impressions that I want. So first question. If you had to go to war in either machine which one would it be?'

John looked at Freddie then turned to the captain. 'In the air, the Corsair Sir. On the deck of a ship, the Hellcat. Sorry if that's not a clear answer but Freddie and I have been talking about this all week and there's no simple answer.'

'Go on, start from the beginning. John you first.'

'Right Sir, the Corsair is the faster of the two but not by that much. It makes a difference if you are up against other machines that are about the same speed but frankly rate of climb is probably more important. Dive on your enemy, blow him to bits and get out of it. If necessary climb away and do it again. Dog fighting is for suckers and should be avoided. That said, both machines are pretty good at it. The Hellcat has spring loaded flaps that will come down automatically below a certain speed like the Wildcat does. This means if you are in a turning fight then as the speed comes off your rate of turn increases. I caught Freddie out with that the first time we tried mixing it. But there's a real problem with the Corsair.'

He remembered back to when he first climbed into the massive machine. The cockpit was extremely far back along the fuselage, apparently so that an extra fuel tank could be shoe horned in to give the necessary endurance. This meant that ground taxying was even more difficult than with normal tail wheel aircraft. Basically, when on the ground you could see absolutely nothing ahead of you. Once in the air, it wasn't an issue. His first landing attempt had been easier than he expected as the view to one side was good enough to judge height and see enough of the runway. However, on his second trip, he returned to the field to attempt a landing on the painted dummy deck. He aborted his first approach as soon as he turned onto final approach. Yes, he could see the runway in the distance but absolutely nothing of the painted area that simulated a carrier deck's landing space. Thinking it over as he flew around the circuit, he realised he needed to do a curving approach to keep the landing zone in sight all the time. It seemed to work quite well even though the cooling flaps around the engine cowl which had to be open at slow speed effectively reduced his field of view. He came in slowly with gear down and full flap so needed a fair amount of power to maintain speed. This augured well for when he cut the throttle to land, although he was still flying much faster to avoid a stall than the older Wildcat had needed. At the appropriate moment, he shut the throttle and as expected the machine made solid contact with the ground and then all hell let loose. Instead of settling firmly down, he was suddenly flung back ten feet in the air. There he was with not enough airspeed to fly and dropping back down fast. He forced himself to resist the temptation to slam the throttle open. So close to the stall, the torque reaction from the massive propeller would flip

31

him over on his back. All he could do was ease the stick slightly and wait. He hit the ground hard again and bounced again, not quite so violently this time but ended up porpoising down the runway like a student in basic training. When he got back to the hangar, Hank was there grinning like a Cheshire cat. Apparently, he had discovered the aircraft's Achilles heel. It was only then that Hank admitted that the US navy had decided that the aircraft was not suitable for ship operations and only the Marines would be using them from shore bases.

John explained this all to the captain. 'Sir, the view from the cockpit is terrible but that can be overcome but unless the undercarriage is redesigned somehow, it's absolutely useless as a carrier born aircraft. After a week of flying it, I probably only managed one simulated deck landing where I wouldn't have ended up in the barrier or even over it and into the aircraft deck park.'

Neither the captain nor the commander looked surprised. John realised they must have known about this issue from the start.

'And the Hellcat?' the Captain asked.

John turned to Freddie who answered for them. 'Lovely machine for deck work sir. The view from the cockpit isn't good but you can see over the nose and it lands like a Wildcat but better as the undercarriage is much wider. In the air, John summed it up quite well. It's slower than the Corsair but not by much. It's pretty manoeuvrable and more importantly, its's built like the proverbial brick shithouse. Whoever designed it must have listened to Wildcat pilots very carefully because it addresses all the issues of the older machine. Even the cockpit layout is well thought out. Whoever designed the Corsair cockpit wasn't worried about pilot work load, it's a mess.'

'Thank you gentlemen,' the captain said. 'Now supposing I were to were tell you that the Americans are prepared to let us have a few Hellcats but as many Corsairs as we can accommodate. What would you say to that?'

John spoke first. 'Sir, clearly the major issue with the Corsair is the undercarriage. Solve that and adopt the curving approach and it would be fine, more than fine in fact.'

'I agree Sir,' Freddie said. 'But for me, I would still prefer to go to sea in a Hellcat.'

'Thank you gentlemen. I can now go back to the War Office and Admiralty with recommendations backed up by two of our own pilots who know exactly what they're talking about. I think I can safely say that a great number of these machines will soon be sent across the Atlantic. Now as a reward, how would you like to go on holiday?'

# Chapter 8

Heather put down her empty cup of tea and looked around the crewroom. As duty officer she had to stay here and man the phones but everyone else was out on deliveries which was quite unusual. Normally someone would be in even if they were only transiting through. Still, it had given her time to relax for a change and read the paper. She missed John and now it appeared that he would be delayed for several weeks in Canada of all places. It hadn't helped that the previous week they had been turfed out of their comfortable little airfield at Hamble and had been moved up to RAF Aston Down in Gloucestershire. None of them had been surprised. The south of England was soon going to be used for thousands of troops and their equipment now making their way across the Atlantic from America. Their ATA unit's job here was to support a massive aircraft Maintenance Unit which repaired a wide variety of aircraft. Either collecting any wrecks that were flyable or returning the refurbished ones back to their owners.

She had sent John a letter explaining that their cosy domestic arrangement with his parents in Winchester was now not going to work but as he had no idea where he would be appointed when he returned from America, they would just have to wait and see what their Lordships decided. Meanwhile, she was staying in the officer's mess and routinely fending off the advances of various young men. She was getting quite good at making sure her wedding ring was clearly visible.

The phone rang and startled her out of her contemplative mood. She went over and answered it. She listened for a few moments and noted down the next day's tasking with a sense of mounting excitement. Mainly routine deliveries but the Maintenance Unit had just expanded the types they were repairing and the first of a new one was ready for delivery. Once she had the complete list she put the phone down. As Duty Officer it was her perk to assign pilots for the next day's tasks. There was no way this was going to anyone else. She spent the rest of the day reading pilot's notes for the aircraft from the large library they kept to hand.

The next morning she was dropped off outside one of the hangars where her new type was waiting. She went inside to see the engineers and got the usual double take from the senior engineer. It was something she was so used to now she barely noticed it. And once she had made it clear that, yes she was the assigned pilot and yes, she was qualified, then she just got on with going over the paperwork and then working out her route plan. While she was looking at the paperwork someone plonked a mug of tea down next to her. She turned to see a very good looking RAF Sergeant smiling at her. He looked much older than the young boys she was used to seeing. He must have been in his thirties which was positively ancient for aircrew these days.

'Jack Thomas,' he said holding out his hand. 'I'm your flight engineer for the trip.'

'Oh, yes of course,' Heather said in reply as she shook his hand. 'I'm First Officer Heather Hunt.' She had completely forgotten that she would need crew. She noticed that Jack seemed to have a rather odd accent. He was quite short with piercing blue eyes and very dark hair. There was something Mediterranean about him although she couldn't work out why she thought that.

'The squadron sent me as I was in the crate when she got shot up. Rather appropriate for me to be to help return her.'

'Oh goodness,' Heather said. 'Was everyone alright?'

'Well no, the pilot got hit and it was me who actually landed the aircraft when we got back. There is always someone in the crew trained to fly them albeit only in an emergency.'

'So you don't really need me then?' She said. 'Presumably, if you can land one then you can also take off.'

'Hah, no way maam. Most of the damage to her was done on the ground when I tried to taxy clear of the runway. One thing they don't teach us is how to steer the ruddy things on the ground.'

'Please call me Heather,' she said. 'I'm not a commissioned officer, really just a civilian in uniform. Anyway, all the paper work looks good so why don't we go and get ready then we can chat more when we are in the air.'

The two of them went outside to where the Lancaster was parked ready to go. Although she had seen them many times now that she was actually going to fly one it seemed even bigger than she remembered. The four Merlin engines and massive wings towered over her. She clamped down on a sudden attack of nerves. She'd flown many twin engine types, this was just bigger with two more engines.

'Got many hours on the Lanc?' Jack asked as they approached the boarding door in the fuselage.

Dare she tell him? She wondered and then decided that honesty was the only sensible option. 'In the ATA we qualify on types based on the number of engines and weight. I've flown Wellingtons, Beauforts and Blenheims amongst others. But to be honest this is my first time in a Lancaster. As far as I know, no female has flown one ever but don't worry I've been here before, climbing into a machine for the first time. I've got thirty seven types in my log book and in only three of them was I given any instruction.'

Jack looked startled for a moment and then grinned. 'Well, as long as you can get us in the air I can always get us down. After all I've done it before and clearly have more flying hours than you on the Lanc.'

'Good point, let's see if we can muddle this through together then.'

Once in the cockpit, Heather went through her checks with Jack's help. 'You know with one pilot, it doesn't feel like a heavy bomber,' she said at one point, just before starting the first engine.

'Actually, that's because it isn't really,' Jack said. 'It started life as the Avro Manchester, a medium bomber with two engines which were underpowered and unreliable. So they decided the best thing to do was put on a bigger wing and give it four Merlins. That worked very well and it made it far simpler that the Stirlings and Halifaxes which were designed as heavies from the start. And the single pilot was a simple solution to increasing the number of available pilots. Before the war, they always flew with two but by going to one they doubled the number of aircrews they had at a stroke.'

Heather thought about that for a moment. 'It must be hard work for the pilot having to stay on the controls for hours. Some of the trips must last a long time.'

'Which is where I come in, at least in my crew. When it's quiet I can take over and give the pilot some rest.'

'Oh well our trip should only be a few hours and hopefully no one will be shooting at us. So let's get the beast started.'

Half an hour later, they were cruising at five thousand feet heading towards East Anglia. Heather had flown many types with a

Merlin engine and so starting four instead of one or two was just a little more time consuming than usual. Taxiing had been relatively simple but she had needed to use the throttles more than the brakes to get it to turn. Once lined up on the runway the take off had been straightforward although she was surprised at just how much effort was needed to operate the controls. The aircraft had leapt into the air with a surprisingly good rate of climb but as Jack pointed out there were no crew or bombs on board. Apparently, when setting out for a mission they often struggled to just clear the end of the runway.

'So excuse me for asking Jack,' Heather said as she settled down. 'But you seem much older than the normal lads I see flying.'

'Yes well, I'm actually a pilot. I am half French and lived near Paris where I ran a small business and flew at weekends. When the Bosch came, I decided to stay but it was never going to work. I saw too many things that the Germans were doing. I have no family, so about eighteen months ago I managed to get to Normandy and come over by fishing boat. I applied to join the RAF as a pilot, as I have dual nationality but they turned me down saying I was too old which I found strange. However, they offered a non commissioned job as a flight engineer. I decided to accept, it was the best on offer and I needed to make a contribution.'

'And then you were attacked and ended up flying anyway?' Heather said with a smile.

'Yes, we were coming back from a trip and almost at the coast. It was starting to get light and we were off course. A coastal battery opened up on us and we were hit. Not badly but the pilot was badly wounded so I took over. I had some time on the controls as one pilot can't sit behind the controls for ten hours or more and our chap was quite happy to let me fly when we were well away from any action. As I said, flying was easy and the landing was good enough but I knew there would be other aircraft behind us. When I tried to turn off the runway I completely misjudged it and went over a ditch which made the undercarriage collapse which is why the aircraft was taken in for repair. It was funny, the CO called me in and gave me a commendation for the landing and rollocking for the accident. But enough about me. How did a lovely girl like you end up such an experienced pilot?'

Heather immediately recognised a bit of Gallic charm being turned on but was totally used to ignoring such things. She told him the abbreviated story about how she and her husband had grown up around aeroplanes and how they had both flown before the war and how he had joined the navy and she had got into the ATA. She emphasised the word husband several times just to make sure Jack got the message and explained that he was abroad at the moment but expected back soon.

They chatted amiably as the Lancaster droned on over the skies of England. The weather was fair with only a few broken cumulus clouds below them. As they approached the bulge of East Anglia, Heather started to get concerned. She knew which airfield she was going to. The problem was that there were so many others all over the landscape. Luckily, there was an area control frequency she could talk to and the helpful controller along with advice from Jack allowed her to pick the right one. She wondered what would happen to them all after the war. It was true in many ways that England was turning into one giant aircraft carrier. Landing was remarkable easy but the machine did have a tendency to swing about and she could easily see why Jack had trouble controlling a shot up machine in the dark.

Once they had parked up, Jack insisted on taking her to see the squadron CO and she went through all the usual reactions to her presence. She was even invited to stay over in the mess and join everyone for dinner as the squadron was currently stood down from operations. A pretty female Lancaster pilot was very much a novelty.

# Chapter 9

The room was large, draughty and crammed with about two hundred British student pilots. John looked down from the stage at a sea of expectant faces and thought how young they all looked. He then had to remind himself once again that he wasn't that much older than them. He was tempted to use the same speech he had given to the students at the fighter school back at Yeovilton but decided that would not be fair. These chaps were only half way through learning to fly and the risks and pressures of that were more than enough. There would be time to teach them the realities of combat once they had their wings.

John wondered how Freddie was getting on. When they had finished with their assessments in New York they had been instructed to split up and go and tour the two main training camps for British pilots on the Towers scheme. The idea was to talk to them, lift their morale and provide encouragement. John wasn't sure he had that much to say in that regard. One base was in Florida the other in Canada. John had seen Freddie's eyes light up at the thought of Florida so he hadn't objected and had volunteered for Canada. So here he was in Kingston on the banks of Lake Ontario not far from Ottawa and very close to the American border. It was the main training base for the Royal Canadian Air Force and had been massively expanded in the last year. Here students were taken from basic training and taken through to when they would get their wings. His old friend the Harvard was used and he had already been up in one just to get the feel of the machine again.

When he arrived a couple of days ago, he was met by a British Lieutenant Commander called Harry Paterson. Harry had been a Swordfish pilot and had taken part in the attack on the Toronto some years previously. He was now in Canada to mentor the naval students although there were just as many RAF students and quite a few Canadians as well.

He had met John off the train from New York and drove him up to the Kingston base.

'I guess you could call me their Sea Daddy,' he explained. 'It's quite a culture shock for them. Most haven't been out of the country before and have had very little flying experience just basic

39

Elementary training in England. Believe it or not, the biggest problem, when they get here, is stomach upsets. The food is a little richer than at home and no matter how much I tell them to take it easy they hit the ice cream and burgers and then reap the rewards. You know sometimes I feel just like a housemaster at a public school.'

'Hmm, but how are they taking to the training?' John asked. 'I understand that the curriculum is quite intense.'

'Well compared to the Canadian chaps they're not as good when it comes the practical stuff like engines and airframes. Washout rates are higher too, we've got very little time to repeat training if they don't pick it up first or second time. Nobody's really sure why. My theory is that we've dropped our intake standards just to get pilots in cockpits whereas the Canadians are far more picky. There's no real proof of that of course. The other thing we are seeing is a disturbing number of cases of the twitch. The pressure is pretty high and we've had our share of accidents which really doesn't help.'

John remembered when he lost his friend Sparky in a horrific Harvard crash while he was undergoing the same sort of training. 'I suppose it's better to find your limits during training than when you get to sea.'

'Maybe but it's not normally a reason to chop a student. However, I do spend quite a deal of my time talking to them.'

John mentally filed that remark away. If a pilot couldn't handle the pressure of training, then he was the last person he would want on a squadron.

'So what line should I take with my chat to them?' He asked.

'Oh, just lots of encouragement and how important it is that they pass their training and get to sea, that sort of thing. I expect most of the time will be taken up by questions. I was going to introduce you by giving a potted history of your achievements if that's alright.'

And that was what Harry had done. Even John was impressed by the man who Harry introduced although he wasn't really sure it was him at all.

'Good morning gentlemen,' he started. 'And thank you Harry for that modest introduction. Yes, I've clocked up a few hours and a few kills. But the first thing I would say to all of you is that getting a so called score is not what it's about, it really isn't. Yes, you read the newspaper reports about fighter aces and all the glamour. Frankly, that's all propaganda. Yes, a pilot's job is to do damage to the enemy but also and probably more importantly, to stop him doing damage to you, your ship, your fleet or even your homes. But to do that you need to be able to fly. You have to do it instinctively so that your brain is ahead of the machine. You may have heard of the old story of the instructor saying to his pupil that he was the safest student pilot he had ever met because he was so far behind his aircraft it would have crashed, burned and the fire would have gone out before the student caught up with it.'

A titter of laughter swept the room.

'Yes but there's a hard kernel of truth there. You chaps are at the stage I was only a few years ago. Once you've got your wings you can then go on to learn how to fight and even manage to land back on your ship which is definitely not as easy as it looks, or even find the damn thing for that matter. Many will tell you that the greatest lie in the world is 'your cheque's in the post', trust me it's not. You will no doubt all find out at some time or another that it's 'the ship's position is.''

More laughter.

'So what can I tell you that can help? Well, when I was training I knew I was immortal, I knew that I was the best pilot on the course and I knew that I could fly lower and do better stunts than anyone else and I'm pretty sure you lot all think the same. But be in no doubt, you're as wrong as I was back then. The best pilots are those that are careful and think things through, that have taken time to study their machines and how to get the best out of them. You also need to know when to back off. One spectacular sortie that ends up in your death is of absolutely no value to anyone. That's not to say that being damned good behind the stick isn't also important because of course it is but being able to think and weigh up the odds quite often in a very few seconds is just as important. The old saying that there are old pilots and there are bold pilots but not many old and bold pilots came out of the last war and is as true today as it was then. Now I've been told that we should leave plenty of time for questions so over to you.'

Several hands shot up and John pointed to one dark haired young man in the front row. 'Yes.'

'Sir, if I understood you correctly you've just told us to be cautious surely that's exactly the wrong thing to be in a fight.' The lad turned and grinned at several of his colleagues as if to say 'look how clever I am'. John recognised the type.

'When did I use the word 'caution', young man? What I said was 'careful' they're not the same thing at all. Let me give you an example. Last year I was mixing it with a French fighter off the coast of Algeria. The chap bounced me. He was in a faster machine, I was in a Wildcat but he was clearly inexperienced and a lousy shot but I bet he didn't think that. He came at me from height with plenty of excess speed, opened fire from too far away and then went straight past me. What he then should have done was keep going at full throttle and get out of range of my guns before pulling up and either heading home or having another go. He did neither, he wasn't being cautious he was being stupid. A careful pilot would have known what to do. So instead of scarpering after missing me, he pulled into a tight turn right in front of my nose and I gave him the benefit of four, half inch Brownings. He didn't go home that night, I did. Do you see the difference?' John didn't add that he went home by boat, with a missing foot which would have spoiled the story somewhat.

There was a few seconds of silence, then the questions started coming thick and fast. John noted that the original questioner didn't ask anything more.

He stayed at Kingston for a few more days and met up with some of the students in a more informal manner and even managed a few sorties in the Harvard with a couple of them but then news of a passage home on another liner, not the Queen Mary, unfortunately, came through and it was with a great deal of happiness that he made his way to Halifax to get on board. He would be with Heather again soon but even as his thoughts turned to their reunion they also turned to wondering exactly what the navy would want of him now.

# Chapter 10

John woke up slowly and for a few seconds had trouble remembering exactly where he was. Then it all came rushing back. He rolled over to see Heather lying on her side and snoring gently. It was something she flatly refused to accept that she did and he had given up teasing her over it. The small hotel room was quiet and a shaft of sunlight was spearing through a small gap in the curtains. Motes of dust were catching the light and glittering like fine gold dust. He lay back again feeling the best he had for months. Even his phantom foot had decided to take the morning off.

The trip back on the crowded troopship had been uncomfortable but he hadn't minded. Even the loud and arrogant American officers who he had shared accommodation with didn't upset him. They were all sure they were going to win the war in what they seemed to think would be weeks. He had kept his council, knowing they would soon find out what war was really like. Mind you he had enjoyed it when once again they hit rough weather and all the armchair warriors took to their cabins. When they finally arrived, Liverpool looked no different but at least this time he was arriving in comfort, not as the survivor of a sinking.

Whilst still in Canada he had been told he needed to report to Lee on Solent for debriefing and to discuss his next appointment. However, the dates he was given meant he would have at least a week to go over to Aston Down and meet up with Heather and he had no intention of letting their lordships know he was back in the country early. He had written to her and suggested she try to get the week off and they could have a quiet time away in a hotel somewhere. As soon as he got ashore, he found a phone box and called her.

She had been successful and had met him at the train station in his old Austin which she had been using while he was away. She had planned everything and booked them a hotel in Tetbury not too far from the airfield but far enough to be able to forget it was there. They had a week on their own together, something they hadn't experienced for far too long. Even their honeymoon hadn't been that long.

Heather gave an unladylike snort and then rolled over to see John looking at her.

'Morning, what time is it?' She asked sleepily.

'Absolutely no idea,' he replied. 'And I've no intention of finding out for that matter. But there's plenty of time for this.' As he slid down and put his arms around his naked wife.

Later, they went down for breakfast, being in the country, the hotel had access to farm produce and was able to rustle up a pretty fair meal. While they ate, they discussed what to do for the week. In the end, they decided not to plan at all just take the days as they came.

Their time together passed in a happy blur. They went for long walks and explored the beautiful English summer countryside. The owner of the hotel had a Golden Retriever that they offered to take on walks with them. They both agreed that after the war they would get one of their own. They also drove further afield and discovered places to explore. In the evenings they found various pubs that still managed good food as well as the hotel and then it was almost always early to bed. They talked, John was fascinated to hear about Heather being the first woman to fly a Lancaster as well as the party the squadron threw for her that evening. He was also grateful when she told him she was being promoted again and would be spending far more time on administration than flying. He had never been totally happy with some of the machines she had to fly. When he said so she scoffed saying that the flying he did was far more dangerous than hers. At that point, they stopped talking about flying and the war and agreed that it was a subject for another day.

In retrospect, John always looked back at that week as one of the happiest of his life. It had been an oasis of calm in what had become a mad pressure cooker of a world. Sometime later, he would drag the memories out carefully and go over them in detail as one of the main ways of retaining his sanity.

But it had to come to an end and on the Sunday they parted. Heather back to Aston Down and himself back to Lee on Solent. They stood at the train station and hugged each other oblivious to the looks of the other passengers and then he had to board the train and wave goodbye. What was to come next?

In fact, the answer to that question was that nobody knew. When he reported to headquarters it was clear that no one was expecting him. He even had to explain where he had been. He made an appointment with his appointing officer who seemed surprised to see him. Apparently, he had been seconded to the US embassy staff and no end date had been stated. John quickly pointed out that Freddie would be in the same position. He left the office with a promise that something would be found but it didn't fill him with confidence.

He decided that a phone call to Mike Tucker would be a good idea and managed to get a call through. When he explained what was going on Mike was not surprised. 'You were appointed to the Embassy Staff and we weren't sure how long we would need you for,' he said. 'They must have arranged your return and no doubt the letter got lost in the post or something. Don't worry, I'll sort it out. I have a report from the Air Attaché though and it seems that you two did a good job. I'll speak to your appointer but how do you feel about carrying on with the good work you and Freddie did in America? We've got a couple of Corsairs over here now and they are being worked on by the boffins at Farnborough and some experts from one of the aviation companies. They could do with another pilot and you've got current first hand experience.'

John needed no further encouragement and so he was told to wait where he was and Mike would arrange things.

And so it was that two days later John drove through the gates of the Royal Aircraft Establishment at Farnborough in Hampshire. In many ways, it was the home of military aviation. It was here before the Great War that the American Colonel Sam Cody used to tether his famous 'Army Aeroplane Number One' to a tree to measure its power and went on to develop several aircraft and win numerous awards. If military aviation had a birthplace in England this was it. John wondered what it was like now. He would soon find out.

# Chapter 11

Farnborough was a mad house, there were people bustling everywhere and the continual sound of aircraft overhead. When he reported to the main gate, he was directed to a row of Nissen huts next to a large hangar in the distance around the perimeter track of the airfield. He parked up along with several other cars and went inside. This was definitely not a military installation, not the least because of the motherly looking woman in a twin set and pearls who was sitting at what he took to be a reception desk. He went up to her and explained who he was.

'Lieutenant Commander Hunt reporting. I believe I am expected.'

The woman looked at a list on a clipboard on the desk. 'Goodness you're early young man, we didn't expect you until next week.'

'Oh, I was told report on Monday, maybe I should have asked the actual date,' John replied. 'Still, I'm here now, what should I do?'

'Why don't you go over to the Officer's mess and see if they can arrange accommodation and then come back here afterwards. I'll let the director know you're here early. I'm sure he will be able to use you.'

He got directions to the mess and was glad to find that there was indeed room for him although no one had actually informed him he was coming. He really wasn't surprised. His appointment to Farnborough had been arranged by Mike Tucker with just a couple of phone calls after all. Then it was time to head back to the experimental flight section. When he arrived, the receptionist, who he discovered was called Gladys, told him the Director would see him. John knocked on the door he was directed to and went into a cluttered office. Technical drawings covered three of the walls and the other was completely covered by a large bookcase stuffed to overflowing with what looked like aircraft manuals. There were two men in the room. John immediately recognised Thomas Forrester, the scientist who had been at the briefing in London before he and Freddie had gone to America. Next to him was another man with greying hair and round glasses. His face looked familiar but John couldn't quite work out why he thought he recognised him.

'Good morning Sir,' he said to Mister Forrester, falling back on the tried military routine of calling someone 'Sir' until he knew their real status.

'No 'Sirs' here John, just Thomas please,' he replied. 'And I've read your reports from America. Damned good work I must say although I wasn't quite expecting you so quickly.'

'Only obeying the last order Thomas,' John replied. 'You know us military types.'

'Indeed I do. And may I introduce a friend of mine who is hoping you might be able to help him out with some work he's doing at the moment? You being here early is actually a bit of a Godsend as we've no spare pilots and your Corsair won't be here until next week at the earliest anyway. So, this is Mister Barnes Wallace. You might have seen his name in the press recently to do with a certain raid in Germany.'

Suddenly, it all clicked in John's head. Yes, everyone had read the reports of the bombing of the damns in the Ruhr and this was the man who had invented the amazing bomb that had done the damage. There had been a photo of him in the Times which was why he had seemed familiar.

John shook his hand. 'Honoured to meet you Sir,' he said. 'Damned successful raid.'

'Thank you,' Barnes replied. 'I just wish more of those brave young men had come back.'

Just then Gladys bustled in with a tray of tea and biscuits. She cleared a space on the cluttered table, giving Thomas a disapproving glance as she did so and then left. The three men then sat around the table.

'I'll be mother,' Thomas said as he started to pour. 'Barnes why don't you tell John here what you want him to do.'

Barnes looked over at John. 'You can fly a Hurricane I am led to understand?'

'Yes, I flew them in the Battle of Britain and recently as CO of the Navy Fighter School at Yeovilton.'

'And what was the biggest threat to your airfield while you were there?'

'Well I was at Exeter and then Tangmere. We were bombed from high level several times but with a grass airfield it was pretty easy to repair the runways.'

'What about low level attacks?' Barnes asked.

'Yes, they happened, particularly at Exeter and probably did just as much damage in some ways. We had some barrage balloons but they can hardly cover the whole perimeter and the attacking pilot can see them so can avoid them.'

'Exactly,' Barnes said. 'And no doubt you had gun emplacements but they got very little warning before the attacking aircraft were overhead.'

'I suppose so, it's not really my area of expertise,' John said.

'So what airfields need is a defence system, that can react very quickly and in exactly the place the aircraft are coming from.'

'I suppose so but what has this to do with me?' John asked in a perplexed voice.

'Well, in the past, people have tried to use simple rockets trailing a wire to get in the way of attacking aircraft. These systems haven't been very useful because there was no way of firing them at the right time and in the right place. We have been working on solving that problem and are now in a position to try it out for real.'

'Hang on, you want me to deliberately fly into a wire that's been towed into the sky under a rocket? I'm sorry but that sounds suicidal to me.' John said.

Barnes smiled. 'Not at first. The system works by using sound to detect the incoming enemy. Microphones around the perimeter hear the approaching aircraft and use the Doppler Effect to measure when it's overhead.' He stopped as he saw the look of confusion on John's face. 'Doppler is when the sound changes from when the aircraft is approaching to when it's flying away. You've probably heard the effect when an express train goes through a station. They also compare how loud the sound is between microphones to work out its location. What we want you to do is fly in on various attack profiles so we can see how the system responds. If things are successful then we will actually use live rockets to see how accurate the system is and we may do one live wire firing at the end but we've had the leading edge of the wings of the Hurricane especially strengthened to keep you safe. Also, we will use a much lighter line

48

than the operational system. As a final demonstration to the Minister that will be quite important.'

John nodded and decided not to point out that the wire could also go through his propeller as well and that would not be much fun. 'So it's mainly flying low level attacks to see if the system is working?'

'Exactly old chap. We're just about ready to go so how about we start tomorrow?'

John looked over at Thomas who was smiling encouragingly.

'Fair enough but I haven't flown a Hurricane for a while. Will it be available for me to take up this afternoon to get the hang of it again?'

'I'm sure that can be managed,' Thomas said. 'Get Gladys to show you to the hangar and they will sort it out for you.'

'And then we start with briefings tomorrow at eight in the morning,' Barnes said. 'I'll see you here. Now if you'll excuse me I need to chivvy up my chaps and get everything ready.' So saying, he left the room leaving John with Thomas.

John turned to him. 'This sounds interesting Thomas but not particularly safe.'

'Oh don't worry John, we do lots of mad things here but we keep it under tight control. Now go and get yourself settled in. I believe your machine is ready to fly so please take her up this afternoon and re-familiarise yourself, I think you've got a busy week ahead of you.'

That evening John met up with several other pilots in the bar. They were all RAF and involved in various trials. When he told them he thought he had been there to do assessments on a new American fighter but then seemed to have been hijacked at least temporarily, there were amused glances all around. It seemed that working for Mister Wallace was something everyone tried to avoid.

# Interlude

The summer sun shone through the windows of the Oval Office in the White House. Around the table were the president of the United States, Theodore Roosevelt and his military advisors. In particular, there was Admiral Ernest J King Commander-in-Chief of the United States Fleet and Admiral Chester Nimitz the Commander-in-Chief of the Pacific Fleet. King had a reputation as a 'Formidable old Crustacean' who allegedly shaved every morning with a blow torch. More importantly, he was not a great fan of the British Royal Navy. This was going to make the meeting interesting because the final person at the meeting was Winston Churchill the British Prime Minister with his military staff. This was not the first time they had all met and the tension in the atmosphere was high. Today they were going to have to make some serious decisions.

With an end possibly in sight for the European War, Churchill was now thinking about the Far East where Britain had lost so much to the Japanese. His initial thoughts about waging an amphibious operation to regain some of their lost territory were proving futile. They just did not have the resources to make such an attack, at least until Hitler was defeated. However, supporting the Americans in their efforts to directly take on the Japanese Empire was definitely something they could do, especially now that the latest aircraft carriers were becoming available. He felt it was imperative that Britain was seen to support the Americans both to keep relations between the two countries on a good footing after the war was over and also to make negotiations of the pay back of the massive war loans America had granted much easier. The meeting was going to be critically important.

Churchill stood and addressed the meeting. He started by outlining the gains that had been achieved in Europe. He then went on to give some detail about the bloody Burma campaign and how they were fighting the Japanese with some success. He made it very clear that Great Britain would be part of the continued fight against the Japanese Empire.

When he sat down there was silence for a moment then Admiral King spoke. 'With the greatest respect to our allies. The war we are fighting in the Pacific is totally different to that in Europe. It's

50

mainly conducted by ships and aircraft carriers and then short fights over the various islands that we are retaking. The Royal Navy is an Atlantic force not designed to fight our way.'

Everyone could see Churchill bristling at King's patronising remarks. He stood before King could continue. 'May I remind the meeting,' he said in a deceptively calm voice. 'That we declared war on Japan before the United States when Japan attacked Malaya, Singapore and Hong Kong. This was before Pearl Harbour. Pearl Harbour was a tactical loss to you but that is all. We have had vast areas of our territories invaded and occupied, you have not. In fact you've lost no territory to the Japanese at all. We are actively fighting the Japanese on the ground in Burma you have no land battles with them apart from a few small islands. So with respect to everyone here, the British Empire has lost more and has at least as much if not more reason to be in this fight than you have. You may feel it is your war to fight. It isn't.' He looked directly at Admiral King as he spoke.

Several of the American officers nodded in agreement but not King.

'I'm sorry Prime Minister,' King said as if he had not been interrupted at all. 'To fight over the thousands of miles of the vast Pacific you need supply bases and massive logistical train of supply. If some of your ships come and join us then how will you supply them and from where? The US cannot give you some of our effort as it will only reduce our own capability. Even as we speak, a discussion paper on the subject has been written and is being studied. At the very least we should wait until the results of that are known.'

Churchill snorted in derision. 'You can study all you want but we can replace some of your battle worn ships with new ones of our own and as to the logistics, I'm assured we have the support vessels we need. Oh and of course we have a supply base.'

'Where Mister Churchill?' King said in a withering tone.

'Admiral King, surely you've heard of Australia?'

Several smiles appeared around the table and King was starting to look red in the face with anger or was it embarrassment? Then the President spoke. 'I think that's enough gentlemen,' he said forcefully. 'I happen to agree totally with Prime Minister Churchill on this matter. If anyone has as much grievance with Hirohito as us, it is the British and they have every right to join the fight at sea in the Pacific. I also have faith in the strength and depth of the Royal Navy. So tell us Prime Minister do you have a concrete proposal to make?'

Several people around the table exchanged knowing glances. This looked very much like something that the two Heads of State had already cooked up between them.

'Yes Mister President,' Churchill said. 'I'm offering you a British Fleet to fight alongside yours but under overall American control.'

'Accepted,' Roosevelt said.

Admiral King looked ready to explode. He clearly hadn't been consulted on the issue. Admiral Nimitz looked pleased and Churchill who had also been getting very angry suddenly looked relieved.

# Chapter 12

John had been having great fun. Despite the dire predictions of the other pilots in the mess, the flying had been simple and exciting. The scientists had him conducting low level attacks against the airfield. At first, they had been straight flights over specific positions to calibrate the system and set everything up. Then slowly they asked him to be more aggressive and come in lower and provide as little warning of his presence as he could. This meant flying as low and fast as possible from varying directions. Screaming along at rooftop level or even lower was every pilot's idea of fun. If they didn't want him back for a while he could land on or nip up to height and do some aerobatics or skid along between the clouds before coming down again.

His machine was in good condition. It had been used exclusively for trials flying ever since it was built so had never suffered the ravages of fighting and actually had less than a hundred hours on it. That said, there were many non standard items fitted most of which John ignored, primarily because he didn't have the slightest idea what they did. The one major modification that he had to take notice of and which actually had some effect on the Hurricane's aerodynamics was the solid strip of steel fitted to the leading edge of both wings. It should have caused more problems but as the guns had been removed, all it meant was that he had to trim the aircraft more tail heavy than normal.

However, the trials had taken longer than expected. Something that was not unusual apparently but as the Corsair had likewise been delayed at the depot where they were doing the modifications it didn't matter. So this was the end of the second week now and the final proving flight of the whole programme. The day before they had used live rockets for the first time. After he had landed, John had suggested that they didn't need the wires as the shock of a barrage of fiery missiles appearing from nowhere was enough to put even the best pilots off their aim.

But all good things must end and if this flight was successful he should be able to get back to his real reason for being here especially as the Corsair was being delivered that afternoon.

53

'Baker Charlie, you're cleared in for final hot run, over,' the radio said. He was several miles to the east near the town of Basingstoke. He acknowledged the call, opened the throttle fully and dived down to the deck. Navigation was simple as he had done this run many times from various directions. Once clear of the airfield at Odiham he turned further right and headed for Farnborough. There was a particular wooded area he was looking for then he would jink left and aim for the main runway. At three hundred miles an hour, it didn't take long. Suddenly, the airfield boundary was swiftly approaching. Although he knew what to expect, it still made him jump as the trail of several rockets reared up ahead of him. There was a sudden shock through the airframe and the aircraft tried to turn right. He corrected automatically and also pulled up to gain height. What had happened? He looked along his right wing.

'Bloody hell,' he muttered as he saw that the leading edge protection had not really done its job. A wire was clearly visible embedded in the wing, it had penetrated back almost two feet. He just prayed that the main spars were intact. The broken ends of the wire were whipping violently in the slipstream.

'Baker Charlie, wing damaged landing immediately,' he called. They had chosen this general approach direction to allow him plenty of airfield to land on in just such a situation. Luckily, the machine took to the ground with no problems and he was able to taxi back to the experimental hanger before shutting down. It wasn't quite like coming back from a combat mission but not that different. As he climbed down from the wing and went around to inspect the damage, he met Barnes Wallis walking over, clearly intent on doing the same thing.

'So will that convince the minister Mister Wallace?' John asked as he looked closely at the damage. 'Without that strengthening, I reckon the wing would have just been sheared off. Looks like you have a viable system.'

'Yes John and thank you for your efforts although I have to apologise as I was sure the modified wing would be strong enough.'

'So is that it for me? I understand the Corsair should be here today.'

'Er yes, I suppose so, we will have to write up all the trials reports now of course and I will have to call on you to provide your input but that can be done in slower time. So you go off to your next job. Oh and if you should ever want a recommendation for more experimental flying work don't hesitate to use me as a reference.'

John thanked him and headed back to sign the aircraft back in and discuss what had happened and the damage with the engineers. Barnes Wallace's remark about further test flying stuck a cord with him. Maybe it was something he should think about? Mind you he was not too sure it was any safer than actual combat. There the enemy were trying to kill you. If this programme had been anything to go by it would be the boffins trying to do the same damn thing.

Later that afternoon he heard the distinctive roar of a large radial engine and he went outside to see a Corsair fly overhead and then turn to land. It didn't seem any different from one he had flown in America, he just hoped it actually was.

In addition to the Hurricane test work, John had also been working up a test programme for the Corsair based on what he had learned in the States and what he had been told about the modifications made to the machine. He went to greet the company test pilot as he climbed out.

They talked for a while and he was shown all the changes but he knew that it was one thing to see the modifications and quite another to find out whether they actually worked in the air and on the ground.

The next few weeks were intense. He flew at least twice a day establishing a full flight envelope for the aircraft. One of the modifications that had been made was to trim eight inches of the wingtips. This was to allow the aircraft to fit into the hangars of British carriers when the wings were folded up above the fuselage. It had seemed a good idea at first as John quickly discovered that the aircraft had lost all tendency to float as it approached the ground. If the throttle was cut just above stalling speed the only way the aircraft was going was straight down, exactly what you needed in a naval aircraft. However, what he hadn't expected was its effect on the aircraft's stall characteristics. It was well known that the gull wing design of the Corsair would make it unpredictable at the stall and he had found this to be true when flying in America. But this machine was even worse. When approaching the stall it felt quite benign right up until it would viciously drop a wing. What was worse was that there was no way of predicting which wing would drop. Added to that, the massive torque from the enormous propeller and two thousand horse power engine meant that if the throttle was slammed forward at low speed it could easily spin the aircraft into the ground or if done at altitude it could induce a spin which could be very difficult to get out of. It was quite clear to John that training on the machine would have to be carried out with care and spinning should be banned in normal service.

However, the other modifications, especially to the undercarriage which now had double acting oleos that damped not just the compression of landing but also the rebound stroke, were going to make the machine much more suitable to operate at sea. Unlike his first attempt at a deck landing profile in America, you could dump the Corsair down on the runway and it would stay there. It no longer bounced along, much to the amusement of any spectators. He spent many hours in the circuit practising various approaches to a section of runway he had painted in the exact size of a carrier's landing area. The cowling flaps had also been modified now. Normally when opened they formed a ring around the engine to allow air to circulate and cool the machinery when at slow speed. However, there was now a second setting that opened all the flaps except for those on the top left of the nose. He now found that if he carried out a continuing curved approach of the right shape he could keep the deck in sight at all times. He even got one of the other pilots to act as a batsman to confirm he would be able to see him when he gave the signal to cut the engine. It was all looking good. There was still the final test though. Landing on an airfield was a good start even if it was marked like a ship's deck. However, there was no barrier to crash into if you got it wrong. The only way to really prove the aircraft was safe to operate at sea was to go to sea. Also, although John had done all the initial assessments he was just one pilot and he strongly felt that a second opinion would be needed. He knew that Freddie had returned from Florida so he made a few phone calls and got him to join him for the final tests. He gave Freddie an abbreviated session with the Corsair and then it was off for the final validation.

HMS Formidable was working up in the channel so it wasn't hard to arrange half a day to test the Fleet Air Arm's newest and finest fighter. As he approached the ship from several thousand feet up, he once again got the feeling that the deck was just too small but brushed the thought aside. It wasn't the first time he had felt that and it probably wouldn't be the last. What he did decide to do was to show the ship just how fast this machine was. So he manoeuvred himself astern of the carrier and descended to fifty feet with the throttle fully open. At over four hundred miles an hour, he shot past the flight deck and pulled up to enter the circuit and then it was time to concentrate on getting onto the deck. His hours of practice paid off. He started to turn when half a mile astern of the ship and continued his turn right up until the LSO signalled to cut the engine. The Corsair dropped to the deck with a firm thump. For the first few attempts, the deck was clear and the barrier was down so he was able to open the throttle and take off again. This he did for three more landings before asking for the barrier to be raised and lowering his hook. Once again he made a near perfect touchdown and the hook caught the number three wire and came to a halt. Once the hook was disengaged, he taxied to one side and shut down. Freddie, who had embarked in Portsmouth the day before, then came over.

'That looked pretty straightforward old chap,' he said. 'They're just going to refuel her and then it's my turn.'

'She's all yours old chap. I just can't wait to get back into the fight in one of these. Neither the Jerrys nor the Japs have anything to touch her.'

# Chapter 13

John always found the view from the lounge bar of the Osborne View Hotel to be relaxing. The sun was setting and the wind was calm with the surface of the Solent almost mirror like, it was so still. Orange streaks of cloud, coloured by the setting sun covered the sky. His second pint of beer, which was already half empty was also contributing to his mellow mood.

Freddie was sitting opposite and also admiring the view. 'Remember when all we had to worry about was who was going to win the next dinghy race? He said.

'Oh I never worried about those,' John replied. 'Heather and I always won.'

'Really? I seem to remember crossing the line before you many times.'

'Ah but we won the important races,' John said. 'And I guess now we have another competition to consider.'

'Well not quite, it's no competition as such just a decision we have to make.'

'I suppose so, I just wish they hadn't left it to us. Sometimes it easier just to be told what to do. You know it's only four years ago we joined up and only three years since we joined our first squadrons and got stuck in. Now look at us, both, Lieutenant Commanders and both about to become commanding officers.'

Freddie nodded and raised his glass in salute. 'Dead men's shoes. Here's to absent friends.'

John nodded in agreement and took another pull at his pint. 'So what are we going to do?'

After the Corsair trials were over and all the reports had been written, John and Freddie had been recalled to Lee on Solent. They spent the morning chatting to old acquaintances before being called into a Captain's office who wanted to know all about the Corsair. They were then told to report to their appointing officer after lunch. Strangely, they were told to see him together which was unusual to say the least. Not only that but instead of one Lieutenant Commander there was also another officer present. He was a tall thin Commander with an impressive row of medal ribbons and pilots wings who looked vaguely familiar to John. He introduced himself as Simon Peters but initially said little more.

'Chaps,' the appointer, Sam Jones said. 'I know it's a little odd asking both of you to attend at the same time but Commander Peters will explain the detail. On my side, I just need to tell you both that you are to be offered command of your own squadrons but because of the timing, we thought it best to talk to you both at the same time. Commander Peters over to you.'

'Right gentleman,' he said. 'Firstly, well done on your trip to the states, we've had very positive feedback, both on your evaluations of the new fighters but also on your trips to talk to the trainees. Secondly, well done on the testing of the modified Corsair, especially you Lieutenant Commander Hunt. It seems Mister Wallace was also very impressed and even made an application to try and get you permanently assigned which we very much had to decline. Pilots of your operational experience are getting far too rare and we need you back in the front line. And this is what your appointer was alluding to. We've been commissioning new squadrons over recent months as our numbers of new aircraft have increased. Corsair squadrons are forming up in the states and conducting initial training over there before coming back to have the machines modified and completing their work up. However, we also have a relatively limited number of Hellcats already in the country and those units will be working up at HMS Gannet which if you didn't know is near Londonderry in Northern Ireland. The aircraft are one thing, the pilots quite another. We simply don't have enough experienced men to man them and will be relying on the chaps coming back from training in the US and Canada. We will also have a limited time to prepare them for next year when there are a large number of operations in the pipeline as we move towards invading France amongst other things. So any thoughts?'

'How long will we have Sir?' Freddie asked.

'We're hoping for three months from when a squadron is fully manned and equipped. Oh and they won't be going to the Fighter School as you chaps have the necessary experience to teach them yourselves. So that is fully qualified on type and also deck qualified.'

'That'll be tight Sir but it's a lot longer than we got in nineteen forty,' John said. 'But of course, that was far too short. Will we get any experienced pilots to help?'

'Yes, at least one as your Senior Pilot and possibly one more. We really are short of people with this rapid expansion. The squadrons will have ten aircraft and ten more pilots plus yourselves. Oh and I will be your Wing Commander, both your squadrons are earmarked for the Tenth Naval Fighter Wing which I will command. Don't worry, I won't be breathing down your necks, especially for 1855 Squadron as they will be in the States to start with. The other squadron will be 1854 by the way. So all it requires is for you two to decide which squadron to take. I thought it only fair to let you decide as you have experience of both types of fighter and will probably have your own opinions. Don't choose now let me know in the morning. Now, I have to go and call on the Admiral so I'll see you tomorrow at nine. Good day chaps.'

When the Commander had gone John and Freddie looked at each other but before either could speak Sam Jones pre-empted them. 'Go on you two, bugger off now will you, I've got a busy day and you've been very lucky to be allowed to decide where to go and I'm not jealous at all.'

The two men took the not so subtle hint and left.

'Any thoughts John?' Freddie asked as they walked down the corridor. I know you've always liked the Corsair. I could put up with Northern Ireland.'

'Let me think on it,' John replied. 'In fact, give me a couple of hours will you. Let's meet up at the Osborne this evening, away from all the chaps in the mess and we can discuss it in peace.'

'Fair enough,' Freddie said. 'See you about eight.' He had a pretty good idea what John wanted to do and could wait.

So that evening they had met up to talk it over.

Freddie answered John's question. 'What we are going to do is make a decision. How about we toss a coin?'

'Ah actually I've got a different idea,' John said. 'Look I'll be honest, Londonderry is much closer to Aston Down than Florida and who knows what next year will bring.'

Freddie chuckled. 'It's alright old chap, I was pretty certain that was what you would say. I assume you were on the phone to Heather this afternoon?'

'How did you guess? Is this alright with you though?'

'Of course it is. Remember while you were freezing your backside off in Canada I was in the warmth of Florida. I'm more than happy to spend a few months back in the sun.'

'And no doubt the American girls were quite warm as well.'

'You got it,' Freddie replied with a grin.

# Chapter 14

John looked out of the window of the twin engine Anson he had cadged a lift in to get to RNAS Eglington or HMS Gannet as it was more properly known. It was funny, he mused; when he took off from a ship, flying over the water wasn't even an issue but when flying from land and then coasting out over the sea there was always a slight apprehension. They had just left Liverpool behind them and would soon transit the Irish Sea. He turned his thoughts to the job ahead.

He had been given a detailed briefing at Lee by the various staff officers but that only gave him numbers and names. He knew that the real job would involve a great deal more. The aircraft had apparently already been delivered and were sitting in his hangar waiting to be used. The majority of the maintenance ratings were also there and had been working on the Hellcats to get them fully ready. The only officer ahead of him was Tom McDonald his Senior Pilot. John knew Tom from his days flying Wildcats in Invincible and knew he was a steady hand and an excellent pilot but as for the rest of the aircrew, all he had at the moment was a list of names. Six would be arriving from Canada next week. After his visit there earlier in the year at least he had a good idea of the standards they would have had to meet. In fact, it was highly likely he had lectured them as they would have been training there at the time. The final three were from the American training school in Florida and they would arrive a week later. From his discussions with Freddie, he was confident that they too would be well trained.

The problem was that they were now going to be presented with a two thousand horsepower, four hundred miles an hour fighter, with six fifty calibre machine guns. They were going to have to learn to fly it, then learn to fight it and then finally how to get it safely on and off a carrier's deck. It was John's responsibility to make sure that was achieved in three months. To say he was feeling challenged was no exaggeration. And then what? The war in Europe was very much a land battle now. The U-boat menace was still causing problems but had largely been contained. The Mediterranean was now a 'British pond' so whilst nothing was being said openly, the general consensus was that the Pacific was where the next naval aviation battles would take place. They could either be in support of the land war against Japan in Burma or help in retaking such places as Singapore or maybe even joining in with the Americans in directly taking the fight back to Japan. Either way, he knew there was a big fight in the offing and the squadron would probably be away for some time. He didn't mind for himself but knew he was going to miss Heather dreadfully. Still, at least for the next few months, she wasn't too far away and where there was a will there was a way.

They landed at Eglington just before the airfield closed for the evening and John jumped out with just a suitcase, the rest of his possessions and uniforms would follow later but he had all he needed for now. The aircraft was staying overnight at the station flight so John went into the office by a small hangar. A Chief Petty Officer was there behind the flight line desk.

'Any chance of some transport Chief?' He asked. 'I need to go over to 1854 and then the wardroom.'

'Sorry Sir, who are 1854?' the Chief replied with a puzzled frown.

The question caught John off guard for a moment and then he realised that as the squadron had yet to fully stand up maybe no one had been told of its number. 'It's the new squadron of Hellcats Chief, I'm the new CO.'

'Ah, right you are Sir, they're in a hangar over the other side of the field. Hang on a second,' and he turned and called out to someone behind him. 'Wren Jenny, got a job for you.'

A rather well built but attractive young Wren appeared. Her hair was tied up in a bun and she had a rather unfortunate case of acne but a wide smile.

'Jenny take this officer over to the new Hellcat squadron and when he's finished, off to the wardroom and then your day is over.'

'Thanks Chief,' she said with a grin in a strong local accent. 'If you'll come this way Sir.' And before he could stop her she had grabbed his suitcase and led him out of the building to a car park at the rear.

'Sorry I didn't quite catch your name,' John said as they went over to an old Austin painted black with the letters RN pained on the side.

'It's Jenny Wren Sir, really it is. So I'm Wren Jenny Wren. I often wondered why I joined up. Maybe I should have joined the WAAFs. I certainly wouldn't have got the comments I do all the time.'

They climbed in and chatted as they drove around the airfield. Jenny was a mine of information and he learned quite a lot about the local goings on. It didn't take long to arrive at a classic looking hangar with a two storey building built onto one side facing a large area of tarmac. There didn't seem to be anyone around, there were certainly no aircraft in sight and the building looked closed up. He directed Jenny to drive around to the hangar doors which he could see were still partly open. Asking Jenny to sit and wait, he got out and went into the hangar. It was eerily quiet and there, parked in two rows of five, were his aircraft. He went up to the first one and looked at its massive two thousand horse power, Pratt and Whitney R-2800 Double Wasp engine. He suddenly realised that although he had been apprehensive about the challenge ahead, he was also incredibly excited. The previous year there had been at least one instance where he might have had to stand in as the squadron CO if things had gone wrong. He had not been enamoured with the idea, all he wanted to do was fly. But now looking up at these beasts it came to him that he really wanted to make the squadron work. Dammit, this could be hard work but also enormous fun.

His musings were interrupted by a voice from behind him. 'Excuse but who are you and what are you doing in my hangar?'

He spun around to see a Lieutenant approaching him. The man had a shock of red hair but looked to be well into his thirties. He also had spoken in a strong Irish accent.

The Lieutenant had clearly seen the two and a half stripes on John's jacket as his demeanour quickly changed. 'Sir, sorry didn't see your rank stripes. Can I help you?'

'Probably,' John replied. 'Lieutenant Commander Hunt the CO of 1854 squadron, I take it that this is that squadron? I've literally just arrived.'

'Goodness Sir, we weren't expecting you for a few days yet. Yes, well welcome to your squadron. I'm Lieutenant Sean McGuire, I'm your AEO.'

'Sorry 'AEO'? John asked puzzled.

'Air Engineer Officer,' Sean replied. 'I'm in charge of getting the aircraft rebuilt and flight tested then I will stay on to manage the maintenance team.'

'Oh, they didn't mention you when I was being briefed.'

'Not surprised Sir, it's a new idea to have officers in charge of maintenance. I was a Chief myself until last year then I was commissioned.'

That explained why Sean was so much older John thought. 'Well I'm glad to meet you, I'm sure we will be working closely together over the coming months. So as we're here, tell me about the state of the aircraft.'

'All ready to go bar one Sir and all that needs is a flight test tomorrow. I sent all the lads home early today as we're well on schedule. In fact I was just about lock up. It's lucky I spotted you or you could have been stuck here all night.'

'No, I've got a car waiting outside I'm sure the Wren driver would have worked it out. In fact, can I give you a lift to the wardroom as well? I assume it's quite far away.'

That's alright Sir I've got my bicycle. We all use them here, I'll arrange to get you one. By the way, your senior pilot arrived last week. It's him who's being test flying the aircraft. He'll be in the wardroom.'

'Right thanks for all that Sean. I'll probably see you and SPLOT in the bar later this evening once I've unpacked. We can chat a bit more about where we are and where we're going for that matter.'

The two men left the hangar and Sean looked over to the car and waved cheerfully to Jenny who smiled and waved back.

'You two know each other?' John asked.

'Everyone knows Jenny Sir. Actually, she's a distant relative of mine. Mind you most people in Derry seem to be related in some way. There's not many girls on the base and she's by far the most helpful. Her family live locally and she's a fount of local knowledge.'

'Yes, I got quite a lot of that on the drive over here.' John said with a smile.

The one thing John had been careful to do was telephone ahead to the wardroom and tell them of his arrival so when he arrived they already had a cabin allocated for him. After a shower and change of clothes, he made his way to the bar. Most of the faces were new but he quickly spotted Tom McDonald and went over the greet him. Tom was a small and energetic man with a black beard and a mischievous grin. They had both served in the same squadron and knew each other reasonably well. John had made a point of not getting too friendly with his colleagues. It was a policy he had slowly taken up as time passed. The pain of losing friends could never go away. Now he needed to get to know him intimately. They would be working hand in glove for some time.

'John, you're early,' Tom said as he spotted John walking towards him. He stood and proffered a hand. 'Didn't expect you for some days yet. Can I get you a drink?'

'Large scotch would go down well Tom,' John replied. 'And I'm going to break the 'no talking shop in the bar' rule as we have a mountain to climb and need to get started as soon as we can.'

# Chapter 15

John was having fun despite the sore head from spending too much time in the bar the previous evening. At least he had got to know the two most important officers on his squadron a little better. Or as he corrected himself, the only other two officers on the squadron at the moment. The pure oxygen he was breathing had largely cleared his head and the view from the cockpit of the Hellcat did the rest. He had taken up the final machine for its test flight and one of the requirements was to ensure it could climb to its service ceiling of thirty seven and half thousand feet. In fact, the machine had clearly wanted to go higher so he had coaxed it up to almost forty thousand and the view was staggering. The weather was crystal clear and the whole of the northern part of Ireland was in view. Eglington was in the north west part and right next to a large body of water, Lough Foyle, which had a small opening to the open sea and provided a handy navigational reference point at this height.

Despite his stated preference for the faster Corsair, John was starting to get to grips with this powerful machine. It climbed like an angel and handled like a sports car. It also had a cockpit which had clearly been designed by someone who wanted to keep the pilot's workload to a minimum. The Corsair seemed to have instruments and gauges scattered almost at random, not so the Hellcat. Everything was placed logically and fell immediately to hand. It was also extremely strong. Having proved that this particular machine could easily achieve its ceiling, he decided on another test that was not in the book and pushed the nose forward and dived vertically. The old Wildcat would only manage about four hundred and fifty before the airframe drag stopped it from going any faster and it seemed it was the same with its successor. This was very useful to know in combat when trying to lose an enemy and also a good omen for using it in the dive bombing role. Levelling off at twenty thousand he tried some aerobatics; snap rolls, a split S, even a loop and roll off the top, all the manoeuvres needed to shake off an enemy and it performed them like a trooper. Having noted all the readings needed on the test flight proforma, he decided it was time to go home and called the field who gave him joining instructions and told him that the circuit was clear. The temptation to do something spectacular was almost impossible to ignore but he put it aside. He didn't know the machine that well yet. Instead, he lined up downwind and made a curved approach to land as if approaching a carrier. Full flaps and plenty of power to keep the aircraft above the stall and then when he estimated the batsman would have told him to cut the throttle he did just that and thumped down with no bounce and was able to pull up in a remarkably short distance.

He taxied in and climbed out. Sean was there to meet him. 'All working Sir?' He asked.

'Yes, she's fine. Climbs like an angel, in fact can you assign her to me as my own machine please.' John said as he handed over the completed test flight proforma.

'Certainly can,' Sean said. 'Oh and while you were up, there was a message for you. Would you call on the Captain and Wings this morning rather than this afternoon.'

'Yes of course I'll go over now.'

'In that case Sir you'll be needing your new transport,' Sean said, pointing proudly at a rather splendid looking bicycle. It was painted a shiny blue and had the words '1854 CO' painted in gold lettering along the frame. Just for a second, John recalled the two airmen who had painted both his Hurricanes during the battle of Britain. He knew that nose art was very much frowned upon these days but maybe just some small pictures could be managed. He had always thought that sort of thing was good for morale. He made a note to talk it over with Tom at some time. So thanking Sean, he set off for the main administration building on his new steed.

Captain Patterson seemed a pleasant enough man. The interview didn't last long. John got the impression that he was more than happy for John to manage the squadron as he saw fit. Commander (Air) was a different matter. When John knocked a strangely familiar voice called him in. As he entered the room John saw a man turned away from him facing the window overlooking the airfield. As he turned, John immediately knew him. Just a little older than John they had shared time together in Invincible. Dennis Lawrence had been the CO of one of the Barracuda Squadrons and he and John had developed a friendship for a while based on a mutual interest in sailing before the war. John also knew he was dead. Indeed judging from the scars on his face and the way he limped John wasn't sure that just for a second he seeing an actual ghost.

'Yes it is me,' Dennis said as he limped over and held out his hand, which John shook. 'Don't look quite so surprised, the rumours of my demise were premature, to misquote someone or another. And before you ask, yes I did prang a Barracuda when we got back from the Med. Bloody hydraulic pipe in the cockpit burst and sprayed into my face. They dragged me out of the wreck and everyone thought I was a gonna. I was in a coma for two weeks but I'm also a tough old bird and they put me back together. Only got one real leg now. Mind you I hear you're missing some body parts as well. Something to do with trying to attack a shore gun position I heard?'

'Something like that,' John replied. 'But only one foot and they've signed me off to fly as you must know.'

'Yes, unfortunately, they reckoned I was too bashed up so to shut me up they promoted me instead, so here I am. So what about your lovely wife is she coming to join us?'

'I wish. No, she's based not too far away on the mainland. I've got a few ideas about that though, maybe we can talk about it some time.'

'Sound interesting but first let's chat about your new squadron and what you intend to do to get them operational. You will be the first outfit to work up here but as I'm sure you know several more are planned to follow. I know our erstwhile Admiral and his staff have given you some guidelines, but let's face it, you will be the one making it work and I can hopefully offer some advice as well.'

'That would be accepted most gratefully,' John said. 'I will be starting today to work out a programme with my Senior Pilot but I would really value your input as well.'

'Excellent, now, it seems to be lunchtime so let's carry on this chat in the bar and you can introduce me to this Senior Pilot of yours.'

Later that afternoon, John cycled back to the squadron wishing he hadn't had that third pint of beer but it would have been rude to refuse. When he arrived, he entered the eerily silent building and went to look for Sean. He found him in the hangar along with several of the squadron Senior Rates. He was introduced to them all and realised it would be more than just the pilots that he need to get to know. These people would be just as important to the smooth and safe running of the squadron as the aircrew. He made mental note to get Sean to let him see all their papers so he could start to familiarise himself with them all.

When he had a moment he pulled Sean aside. 'Sean I have another task for you. I need more aircraft.'

'Sorry Sir what do you mean?'

'We're going to have to do a great deal of air to air combat training and for that we will need target tugs and also aircraft that can act as aggressors. I know we can call on the other training facilities when they are available but that may not be when I want them. So we need to see if there are any surplus machines around. I'm going to put you in contact with Heather, my wife. Before you ask she is also a pilot and flies with the Air Transport Auxiliary and she delivers machines all over the country so she knows where many of the older machines are kept. I was thinking of a couple of old Skuas as tugs and maybe a couple of old Hurricanes or Wildcats as aggressors. Commander (Air) is happy with the idea as he will get the station to take them on when we've finished. Also, another Hellcat squadron is forming up here next month so we can come to some sharing arrangement. I hear you are rather good at acquiring things. What do you say?'

Sean's eyes twinkled. 'Leave it to me Sir and how about I get us a twin of some sort for local communication work? Maybe one you could use at weekends?'

'Sean you just read my mind.'

# Chapter 16

Nine young expectant faces looked at John. Despite the predictions, all his aircrew had arrived at the same time. Tom had got them organised while John had made a start going through their training records. They made for varied reading although none were bad and several were well above average. However, John was of the opinion that reports on people often reflected as much on the writer of the report as the person being commented on. He had made some notes but very much intended finding out about each of them as soon as he could. This morning was their first time together where he could at least start to assess them. Earlier that morning he had what the navy called a 'clear lower deck' which meant getting the whole squadron of maintainers and aircrew together so he could see them and probably more importantly they could all see him. He kept his speech brief, there was going to be far too much going on to waste time on pep talks. In fact, that phrase had been his opening remark.

However, now it was time to get on with the real job in hand. There were three midshipmen and six sub lieutenants. He already knew their names but that was about all.

'Gentlemen welcome to His Majesty's latest and best Naval Air Squadron. For that is what I intend us to be. We have three months to get to know one another and for you to get to know that beast there out on the hardstanding. By the end of that time, I will expect you to know them inside and out and have learned what it will be like to fight with them. It was only three years ago that I was in your position except that I trained on a Spitfire and then went to a Hurricane squadron and my learning curve was far steeper than the one you have to climb. I was in actual combat within a month of joining my squadron. So I want absolute commitment from all of you. That doesn't mean we can't enjoy ourselves socially but the more training we all get, the greater the chance that we all see the end of this war. I'm going to hand you over to SPLOT in a minute who will go over the training schedule in detail with you. The first few weeks will simply be learning to fly a Hellcat but it won't be long before you will have to learn to land it on the deck of a ship as well as take it into combat. One final note, you are all wearing the uniform of the Royal Navy. When we get to sea, you will be part of the ship just as much as any of the other ship's officers. You will also act as Divisional Officers for a number of our ratings. The point I'm making is that you don't just need to learn to manage the Hellcat but you've also got to learn the basics of the navy. We have allowed some time in the programme for that and I expect you to take it seriously. Tom will now take over but I will be asking each of you to come and see me over the next few days so we can have a personal chat. Thank you very much.'

Two weeks later, John and Tom got together to review progress. 'Right Tom, let's see where we are. I know everyone has managed to get airborne and back again several times so that's a start. I've already got some initial impressions but I'd rather hear what you have to say first.'

'Right you are Sir but please bear in mind it's very early days yet. Starting with Midshipman Neville Parsons, his birthday is in a couple of weeks so he'll be putting his stripe up then. He's probably the best pilot of the bunch. His flying generally agrees with his training assessment. Seems very quiet when on the ground and doesn't seem to mix in that much.

'That's fine, if he flies that well that's all I ask.'

'Then there are the two Sub Lieutenants, Brian Steele and Malcolm Patterson. I understand they went to school together and have trained together. I've overheard some of the others calling them the twins although they look completely different. In flying terms, they seem to be in the same grade, above average.'

'Alright, next.'

I would then say that at this stage I would put the next four, that's Paul Markham, Dennis Soper, James Trent and Peter Robinson in the same category. They've all got to grips with the aircraft. All four were in Canada and seem like good solid material.'

'That leaves two Tom.'

'Indeed it does Sir. Hamish Gregory, the red haired Midshipman, if he's eighteen I would be very surprised but he got through training. He seems to have struggled a little and his first landing in a Hellcat was rough to say the least but he's very keen.'

'Yes his training report had a few negative remarks but apparently he was top of his class in several subjects as well. You know, when I was with the RAF we had a pilot who was bloody dangerous in a Hurricane when near or on the ground. But it worked both ways because when he was airborne he had eyes like an eagle and was the best shot we had. So let's keep an open mind.'

'I know exactly what you mean Sir. I've come across the type before as well.'

'So Tom that leaves one name,' John said. 'Mark Hanson.'

'Yes. Very much the extrovert, he's several years older than the others. His father is quite rich I believe. Very much a line shooter and the others seem to have noticed. He has a much higher opinion of his flying ability than I or the other pilots do. He's one of the Florida trainees. I think we need to keep a close eye on him. He could be very good for the squadron if we can get him to be less arrogant and more of a team player.'

'Hmm, well we are possibly going to need one of them to become a Flight commander. I've no problem with arrogance if it's effective. Let's keep a close eye on him for all those reasons.' John then looked at his watch. 'And now Tom it's Friday late afternoon and it's time to initiate our young airmen into another Fleet Air Arm tradition. Let's see how well our new pilots cope with the rigours of Friday happy hour.'

John quickly realised he need not be worried about the new officers' social skills. The first happy hour went well. He was able to relax and assess the pilots without the formality necessary when in the squadron. He was starting to realise how clever Sydney his last CO had been in trying to lead his pilot astray. Applications of booze immediately brought out different aspects of people's character. Neville Parsons the quiet Midshipman was blossoming. Not the least because he was sitting in front of the wardroom piano and singing some quite disgusting songs which somehow he seemed able to do without upsetting anyone, including the Commander, which was quite an achievement. The twins were leaning on the piano singing along, so clearly this was not an unusual way they spent their time. He had managed a chat with them all at one time or another but was now propping up the bar talking to Tom.

'Did I just hear our piano playing Middy sing something about a Hippopotamus?' He asked Tom.

'Yes, apparently, he was revelling in the joys of fornication. The Hippo that is, not Neville,' Tom replied with a grin. 'A regular

Noel Coward in the making. I think we might have underestimated him.'

'I agree and even Mark Hanson doesn't seem quite so obnoxious. Mind you, it could be because I've had one beer too many.'

'I've probably had too much beer as well Boss, but there is one thing you need to know,' said Tom. 'Not only are you their first CO but your reputation had preceded you. I think they're all a little in awe of you.'

'What? Come on Tom, I've had my successes but also had my bloody foot shot off. I'm hardly a good example. Dammit, I'm only a year older than a couple of them.'

'It's not age, it's experience as you well know Boss.'

'Right there's one way to make them realise I'm just human,' John said. He went over to the piano and said leant over to the pianist. 'Do you know the Ball of Kerriemuir?'

# Chapter 17

Two Fridays later, John was talking to Sean in his office. 'We're going to need those extra aircraft soon old chap. Any news?'

'I've managed to acquire two Skuas as you asked,' Sean replied. 'They should be here any day, they've been modified to be target tugs but so far I've drawn a blank on getting any old fighters. But there might be a way around that.'

'Oh? Go on.'

'Well, the new Hellcat squadron is standing up now, why don't you do a deal with them? They will have the same problem and you could borrow each other's machines when needed if we can't muster enough serviceable ones ourselves.'

'I suppose that could work, their CO is due here this week and I know all their machines are here, some of the chaps have been doing the acceptance test flights for them. And actually although the Skua is an old dog nowadays and may be relatively slow, I reckon I could still teach some of my guys a thing or two. Right, let's go with that.'

'And one more thing Sir. I've had a word with your wife as suggested and she says twin engined aircraft like the Anson are in high demand but a load of Stinson Reliants have been sent over as part of the lend lease agreement with the Yanks and no one is really sure what to do with them.'

'Never heard of a Reliant, what is it?'

'Single engine high wing monoplane Sir. Can carry up to four plus the pilot and cruises at about one eighty.'

'Now that sounds ideal. I wonder why she didn't mention it to me when I rang her last night.'

An amused smile crossed Sean's face and immediately, knowing his wife, John had a pretty good idea why not. 'When is she due?'

'She said about midday Sir.'

'Right, hang on a second, I'll ring air traffic,' John said as he looked at his watch and realised it was almost noon. He spoke briefly on the phone and then turned to Sean. 'Why don't you join me in the crewroom Sean, this could be interesting.'

The two men went along the corridor to the crewroom. It was like any crewroom anywhere John thought. Some old tattered armchairs that had been purloined from God knows where and some old upright chairs. A large tea urn was off to one side with a sink full of dirty cups. Several tables covered in old magazines mainly about aeroplanes as were the posters decorating the walls. As it was almost lunchtime, the morning sorties had finished and so most of the pilots were lounging around, although four of them were clustered around a table with an Uckers board on it. Uckers being a rather vicious navalised version of Ludo. John could see the looks of intense concentration on their faces. John had made it very clear that there was no rank in the crewroom and even though some of the chaps straightened up a little, no one said anything.

'Cuppa, Sean?' John asked as he made his way over to the hot water urn and dredged through the sink looking for two of the least disgusting mugs.

'Yes, thanks Boss,' Sean replied just as an unusual, high wing, monoplane could be seen touching down on the main runway.

John managed to make two cups and handed one to Sean as they watched the Reliant taxi towards their hard standing.

'That's an interesting machine,' someone said. 'Wonder what it's doing here.'

One of the Uckers players looked up. 'That's a Yank Reliant, saw them in Florida,' he said. 'Might be delivering something I guess.' And he turned back to the game and everyone else also seemed to lose interest.

It soon changed. A few minutes later someone else called out. 'Hang on chaps just take a look at the pilot getting out. What a corker. She must be one of those girl transport pilots I've read about. Goodness I would fly with her any day.'

At the word 'girl' all faces turned and looked out of the window, even the Uckers foursome. Several rather inappropriate remarks were then made as she made her way towards the squadron. John decided he'd better step in before someone said something they would regret.

'Gentlemen,' he announced to the room,' You are correct, the lady is an ATA pilot, she has more hours on more types than any of you and in fact, more than me and I should know as she is my wife.'

Silence greeted his remark. 'Don't worry. I'll go and get her and introduce her to you lot. I'm sure you could learn a great deal from her.'

That evening, in the bar, John realised he had lost Heather. Not only were his chaps fascinated by a pretty girl but one who had been flying since the start of the war and was qualified to fly anything with up to four engines made her a goddess.

Tom came up to him at the bar. 'Seems your wife has a few admirers Boss.'

'You could say that Tom, even Mark seems happy to be on the sidelines for once. My big problem will be rescuing her at some stage. She's flying back on Tuesday so I spoke to little Miss fix it, in station flight and she's arranged a cottage for us for the weekend. So once I manage to extricate Her you're in charge and I'll see you on Monday morning.

'Fair enough, have a good weekend.'

'Oh, I intend to old chap.'


Monday came around far too soon. The weekend had been very pleasant, there was a delightful local pub just down from the old cottage Jenny had arranged for them. It belonged to a cousin apparently. John suspected that most people around here were probably cousins of some sort. At one point when they were out for a walk he had an idea and when he explained it to Heather she was all for it. So on Monday, both of them walked into the briefing room for the morning 'shareholders' meeting. John had already told Tom and Sean what he wanted so once the briefing was over he and Heather put on their life jackets and went out to two Hellcats parked on the line. Heather already had over twenty hours on the type as she had been ferrying them from near Liverpool where they were being reassembled after crossing the Atlantic.

The two machines took off in formation and climbed into the pale autumn sky. As John had explained, this was probably the first time that a husband and wife had flown modern fighters together. Once at twenty thousand feet, they split up and then tried to get on each other's tail. If John thought he had an advantage and it would be easy, he was soon put in his place. Heather was clearly a natural, he just hoped his pilots would prove to be as good. So for half an hour, they chased each other around the sky. He couldn't remember when he had had such fun. From sharing an old Gypsy Moth biplane only four years ago here they both were in the latest state of the art fighter.

Eventually, they had to stop. 'Two this is One,' John called on the radio. 'Time to go home. This is what we are going to do.'

Back in the crewroom, there was quite a lot of banter about husbands and wives flying together. It ranged from whether Heather would actually shoot down the Boss, to what sort of marital row they would have over the radio. It all stopped when someone called saying that they were back. Two Hellcats in very close formation could be seen at the downwind end of the main runway and very low. They roared along the runway at almost four hundred miles an hour and then pulled up into a vertical climb wingtips overlapping. One then half rolled and pulled inverted the other continued in the opposite direction also pulling inverted. For a few seconds, they carried on and then dived to the opposite ends of the runway pulling out once again at low level but this time heading directly towards each other. There was a collective silence in the crewroom as the two machines hurtled seemingly straight towards each other at over eight hundred miles an hour. They passed each other in a flash. The one heading down wind then pulled up in a half loop and rolled upright while the other machine climbed more sedately. They joined up again, turned downwind, slowed down, and lowered their flaps. They turned onto their final approach, once again in close formation and touched down before gently taxiing back to dispersal. As they climbed out they were met by the pilots who had come out to greet them.

'Right gentlemen, you have two months to be able to meet the flying standards my wife can set. Any questions?'

# Chapter 18

The briefing room was full. All his pilots were seated looking expectantly up at John as he stood in front of them.

'Well done chaps,' John said. 'We've reached the end of working up to becoming operational except for one thing. Today I will be reporting that we are operational for land based work. We've covered everything from navigation and formation flying to aerial gunnery and even Mister Parsons finally worked out that I was pulling the target in the Skua not pushing it.'

A ripple of laughter went around the room as they recalled the famous sortie where Neville Parsons had managed to put a bullet through the tail of John's aircraft as he vainly tried to shoot at the target being towed well behind.

'So now we have one last hurdle to contemplate, if that's not a dreadful mixed metaphor. But as you all know there is one lever in the cockpit that none of you have operated, at least not intentionally. I'm of course referring to the arrestor hook. It's Christmas in a fortnight and, weather permitting, we are going to spend that time and some weeks afterwards doing Airfield Dummy Deck Landings, ADDLS. You will all get to fly plenty of trips but will also be required to carry out the duties of the Landing Signals Officer and also learn all the ins and outs of ship operations. As of yet, I don't know which ship we will then go on to conduct real deck landings but that will be some time in February. Then we will probably be going on real ops.'

He could see several hands about to go up. 'And before anyone asks, the answer is no. I really do not know where we are going to be deployed, although I'm sure we all have our theories. I will let you know when I know and I just hope that the book Mister Steel has running can pay out.'

Just then the door at the back opened and Wren Jenny put her head around and signalled to John. With a little connivance from Sean, he had managed to 'borrow' Jenny to act as his assistant. She was as brilliant with paperwork as she was in arranging things with the local community. He was going to miss her when they went back to sea.

'Sorry chaps, I have a meeting now with our Wing Commander and who knows maybe I'll learn something about our future. So I'll hand over to the Senior Pilot who'll continue with the brief.

When John got to his office Commander Peters was waiting for him.

'Good morning Sir. I hope your trip here was alright, I take it you didn't fly in?'

'No, came by train from Belfast. No flying today, the weather is bloody awful.' He replied. 'Oh and when we are alone, please feel free to drop the rank, my name is Simon.'

'Certainly Sir, sorry Simon, can I get you a tea?'

'That would be most welcome, there was nothing on the train.'

Jenny had managed to purloin a small urn for his office so he proceeded to do the honours. When they were seated again, Simon spoke. 'To business John, firstly I've read your reports but please give me your assessment of where you are with 1854 as of today.'

Operational Sir apart from becoming deck qualified. We've trained in navigation, low flying, formation flying, aerial gunnery and combat to a level that I believe is more than satisfactory. You can only train so far before you really need to go out and do it for real. And speaking of which is there any news of our future deployments?'

'We'll come to that in a moment. But first, tell me about the accident the other day,'

'Ah yes, Sub Lieutenant Hanson. He was on a cross country exercise and returning from Aldergrove. The aircraft crashed into rising ground near Ballymena. There was a witness, a local farmer. He was certain that the machine was on fire before it hit the ground. If it wasn't for him we would have assumed it caught fire as it crashed. The Board of Enquiry concluded it was some sort of engine failure although my engineer couldn't find anything obvious. And I had to write my first letter to grieving parents.'

'Not your last,' Simon said. 'That's not one of the perks of command I'm afraid. And how was his loss taken?'

'Surprisingly well, if I can put it that way. All of my chaps had experienced accidents during training but of course it's different when you've come together as a tight knit squadron. Hanson was a bit full of himself but had started to mature and he was one of my likely candidates for Flight Commander. I don't like to talk ill of the dead but the weather wasn't good that day and it looked like he was pressing on when it would have been more prudent to turn around. If he had been flying higher he would have had time to bail out.'

'Still, I am assuming that his replacement will be your new Flight Commander?'

'Johnny Preston? Absolutely, he's been a godsend. Someone with his experience on Sea Hurricanes is exactly what we need here. I'll be honest, forming up with no one in the crewroom with any combat or operational time hasn't been easy. SPLOT and myself have to keep some distance, it's not easy to pass on the little details and experiences whereas someone like him is one of the boys.'

'So when do you think I can count on you ready to deploy?'

'As we agreed. We're starting ADDLS over the next few days and should be ready for deck qualification at the start of February. So fully operational a few weeks later. Do we have a ship?'

'Yes and I think you'll be happy. It's your old steamer the Invincible. She's just finishing a refit. By the time you're ready for deck qualifications she should have finished her work up. This is all assuming everything goes to plan of course.'

Both men smiled at the remark, they had plenty of experience of exactly the opposite happening.

'And after that? Any idea what's in store for us?' John asked.

'Yes but I can't be exact at the moment. Suffice it to say that once ready you will be deployed to Scotland for some specialist training but that is not to go any further please. However, I'm pretty sure you have all worked out that in the longer term it will be the Far East but I have no details yet and once again we keep that to ourselves.'

John nodded. He wasn't surprised at the information, it was what everyone was expecting, although this specialist training seemed to infer something more local. He kept his council but had a strong suspicion he knew what it was all about.

# Chapter 19

Heather knew all good things come to an end and the last few months had been pretty good. They had managed some time together at Christmas and regular weekend trips had continued with the Reliant fulfilling its primary role of getting John to her. However, everything was now changing. John was at sea with his squadron, teaching his chaps how to land on a carrier and she really wasn't sure when they would be able to meet again.

Still, she had a job to do and needed to concentrate on that. Today she was at RAF Manson at the bottom right tip of the country. It wasn't a delivery trip she would normally have taken on but everyone else was already on other tasks and it would give her something to keep her busy and her mind occupied. It was pretty straightforward. A Beaufort bomber had landed here a few weeks before with an engine problem which had now been fixed. All she had to do was fly down the coast and deliver it to Southampton. It wasn't required anymore and was going to be stripped for spare parts and then scrapped. As she walked around and inspected it, it seemed that the process had started already. The engineer who accompanied her explained that all the weapons and radios had already been removed along with the compass, none of which she would need on her short hop down the coast.

It was a Friday and she was keen to get away. Getting back to base from Southampton was going to be a chore unless anyone was flying that way and she could scrounge a lift. She might even be able to meet up with the Anson that had dropped her here earlier if she was quick. It didn't help that the weather forecast wasn't good with a warm front due to arrive mid afternoon which meant that cloud base would be dropping all day as the weather approached.

She clambered in and went through the pre-start checks. The Taurus engines fired up well, the starboard engine was the one that had given trouble but she had been assured the problem had been diagnosed and repaired. It all seemed to be working well now.

The control tower knew she had no radios so she just taxied out to the main runway and waited. They quickly saw she was there and a green light appeared telling her she was cleared to take off. Watching her engine gauges carefully she lined up and opened the throttles. Take off was normal and all seemed good as she climbed away. All she had to do was follow the coast to the Solent and turn right at Southampton Water.

For the first fifteen minutes all was normal. The cloud was at about fifteen hundred and the visibility was several miles. The Beaufort was reasonably fast and cruised nicely at two hundred and fifty. Her mind started to wander. She wondered when she would see John again, he had been very vague about what he would be doing over the next few months, probably because he really didn't know that much himself. With a start, she realised the world had gone grey. She had entered cloud. Not to worry, she throttled back and started to descend. The cloud cover broke but now she was below a thousand feet. Looking ahead she could still see the coastline. If it got really bad she could always turn around so she pressed on. Minutes later, she realised it had been the wrong decision and decided to return to Manson. She then made her second mistake and turned to port, out to sea. When she expected to see the coast again there was nothing just grey sea and cloud. She was down to three hundred feet now and didn't dare go any lower because if she was heading towards land she wanted to fly over it not fly into it. Her big mistake she now realised was taking the aircraft with no compass. Had she turned through one eighty or not? Either she had or she was heading towards land or out to sea and she had no way of knowing which. Keeping the turn going, she just prayed something would appear to give her, her bearings. It didn't, the cloud was getting lower and it was starting to rain heavily. Cursing herself for making stupid mistakes that would have had her thrown out of training, she realised she needed to make a decision quickly. Ditching was an option, the loss of the aircraft would be no loss to anyone but she had no idea if there was a dinghy on board and anyway, how would anyone even know she needed rescuing, she had no radio and even then couldn't have told anyone where exactly she was.

No, she opened the throttles and started a steep climb. The flight instruments were all working and she was qualified and experienced in blind flying. If she got on top of the cloud she would be able to see the sun and orientate herself. She might even spot another aircraft and get close enough to make hand signals to explain her plight. It was the only sensible thing to do. Except it wasn't.

If the met forecast had been right she should easily have broken the cloud tops at a reasonable height. She was technically limited to ten thousand feet as there was no oxygen on board. At twelve thousand she was still in thick cloud with no sign of it getting lighter above her. This was not going to work. Her fuel gauges were reading low. Plenty to have flown down the south coast but not nearly enough to stay airborne for long when she had no idea of where the hell she was heading. So now she was running out of choices, in fact, she only had two. Throttle back again and pray she was over land and she saw it before flying into it or the sea for that matter. Alternatively, she could use her parachute. Neither filled her with any optimism. Suddenly she felt totally alone she really needed John by her side but he wasn't there. She had to work this out for herself.

She had always hated the thought of having to use the parachute. Many of her friends had 'taken to the silk' but she had always managed to avoid it. No, she would try one more time to find what was below her. She throttled back again. At first, she let the aircraft descend quickly but when the altimeter was reading fifteen hundred she slowed it down, gradually letting the height decrease as she peered desperately through the windscreen. The rain had stopped now so maybe the worst of the weather had gone through? If so the cloud base might well have come back up. Her altimeter was set to read the height above the sea so she knew she would have to be very careful because the land could well be much higher. Five hundred feet, nothing. Four hundred still nothing and then just as she approached three hundred she saw something and then she broke out into the clear. Land, beautiful land. Fairly flat with a few trees but only less than a hundred feet below her. She made an instant decision and put down full flap but left the wheels up. The throttles were slammed shut and she kept the nose rising as the speed washed off. She hit the ground at less than eighty and bounced back in the air before thumping down again hard. The cockpit windows were getting covered in mud and grass as the nose churned into the soggy ground. She was hurled forward in her straps as the aircraft came to a shuddering halt it half spun around as one wing impacted a large tree. Then the lack of noise was what first made her realise she had made it, just the ticking of metal cooling, no engines nothing.

Desperately unstrapping, she clambered out of her seat. There didn't seem to be any sign of fire but that didn't mean there wouldn't be. With the aircraft so close to the ground as the wheels were retracted she was able to open the side cockpit window and drop to the ground, landing with a thump on the wet grass. Without hesitating, she ran for a good hundred yards before stopping and turning to look behind her. The visibility was poor and the bomber looked almost as if it had been dropped there in one piece.

So where on earth was she? Looking around she could make out what looked like a small county road off to her right. It must lead somewhere so if she followed it she should be able to get help. As she walked down the road in a randomly selected direction she realised she was shivering and suddenly felt weak. Delayed shock no doubt. She sat down on the grassy kerb and took a deep breath. She fumbled in her jacket for a packet of cigarettes and lit one. She rarely smoked but if ever one was needed it was now.

Suddenly, there was a sound and looking up the road to her left she could make out the lights of a car approaching. She stood and waved as it pulled up and stopped next to her. She opened the driver's door only to find it was empty and the driver sitting on the other side.

'I'm terribly sorry,' she said. I'm a pilot and I've had a bit of an accident, could you take me somewhere where there is a telephone so I can call my people.'

The man gave her a strange look. She was starting to feel something was very wrong when the man replied.

'Désolé madame, mais parlez-vous français?'

# Chapter 20

John looked down at the deck of Invincible from several thousand feet. The last of his squadron were conducting their final deck landings. He watched as each one lined up and came to a safe stop in front of the barrier. When the last one was clear of the barrier and parked up on the forward part of the deck, he shut the throttle, lowered his flaps and hook and started on his final approach. No matter how many times he did this there was always that moment of apprehension as he turned in towards the stern of the ship in a gentle curve. Then he was far too busy watching the batsman, adjusting his power and rate of descent to worry any further. As the flight deck appeared below him the batsman gave the signal to cut and he shut the throttle. The aircraft dropped the last few feet with a positive thump and he was flung forward in his straps as the arrestor hook took a wire. He then followed the marshal's instructions as he taxied over the lowered barrier and parked up at the rear of the squadron. They would be striking all the aircraft down quickly because the Barracuda squadron was due on board next.

He climbed out and went into the island to sign the aircraft in and then made his way up to Flyco to see Commander (Air) and Lieutenant Commander (Flying). It was like coming home. The ship may have had a refit but it still smelled the same, aviation fuel, diesel exhausts, paint and boiled vegetables. Everything looked unchanged.

When he got to Flyco, Wings greeted him. One thing that was different was that most of the ship's officers were new. This Wings was an unknown quantity although Little F was the same man from his last time on board.

'Ah, Lieutenant Commander Hunt,' Wings called over when he saw John approaching. 'Well done. All your lot safely on board and have now completed all their training landings. I think we can declare you operational now.'

'Yes Sir, we're ready to go.'

'Yes but don't forget we aren't. We've got to get the Fisheads up to speed. So once the Barracudas are on board it's going to be a busy few weeks.'

'Yes Sir, I'm going to go down now to brief my chaps.'

Before he could say any more there was an exclamation from Little F who grabbed the flight deck broadcast microphone but it was too late. John looked aft. The first Barracuda was making a hash of his approach and had got far too low in the final few yards. Even through the armoured glass of Flyco they could hear the pilot desperately slam open the throttle and its Merlin engine roar to no avail. It hit the round down at the back of the flight deck and continued to skid along the deck on its belly, shedding propeller blades and other parts of its airframe before slamming into the barrier and coming to an ignominious halt. The deck crew all seemed shocked and no one moved.

Wings grabbed the microphone. 'Deck crew, firefighters, don't just bloody well stand there. Bloody get on with it.'

The deck was suddenly galvanised into activity. Hoses were run out and the aircrew were helped out of the wreck which luckily showed no signs of catching fire.

Just then the Captain put his head around the corner of Flyco. 'Commander (Air), a word please.'

John had yet to be introduced to the new Captain but realised this was definitely not the time. Instead, he tried to hear what the Captain was saying.

'There is no need for foul language on my ship old chap.' Was all he could make out and then Wings came back in looking angry and frustrated. Little F looked over at John and gave him a knowing smile. John decided he need to speak to F in the bar that evening.

There were no more incidents that afternoon and as soon as flying was over they headed north. The ship was programmed to work up off the west coast of Scotland.

John spent the afternoon in briefings with the ship and then the squadron. They were going to have a busy fortnight getting the ship up to speed, especially in deck operations. That was very clear from the accident that morning. He made it plain to his pilots that they would need to keep a close eye on what the deck crews asked them to do, especially in the early days. If they felt they were being asked to do anything unsafe they were not to comply. He then went down to the hangar and gave the same warnings to Sean and his senior rates.

That evening F collared him at the bar.

'Nice to see you again John,' Mike Collins said as he saw John approaching. 'Pink Gin or scotch?'

'You know me Mike, scotch always. Anyway, how are you?'

'Oh same old but I was surprised to see your name on the squadron lists. I would have thought losing a foot was enough for most men.'

John laughed. 'No, you can't keep an old aviator down for long.'

'And that lovely wife or yours. Please tell me you've managed to keep hold of her?'

'Yes, she's fine. Still flying but not so much these days. Now look before it gets busy in here, what's going on between Wings and the Old Man? Captain Johnson seemed more worried about Wings swearing than the fact that we had just had an aircraft crash.'

'Chalk and cheese old chap. Wings is a bit of a firebrand and he's very protective of the air department but also makes quite a song and dance with the ship's officers. Don't get me wrong he knows what he's doing but expects everyone else to be the same. He seems to have an uncanny knack of getting on the wrong side of just about everyone. Unfortunately, two thirds of the ship's company are new and we've not had that much time to start working together. I think it safe to say he doesn't suffer fools gladly. The skipper, on the other hand, is a real gentleman and he's also a bit of a God botherer. He's made it clear he will not tolerate bad language which for a naval officer, is decidedly odd. Also, he's not an aviator and has made it clear that the air department is the responsibility of Wings and he won't interfere which in some ways is a good thing. But of course, we don't operate in isolation and it's proving difficult to get the rest of the ship to integrate with us. So we have the situation where Wings is critical of the ship but doesn't get on with the Captain. On top of that, it doesn't help that the Flight Deck Officer and Wings go way back and there is little love lost between them either. I'm afraid that by the end of the fortnight something will have to give. I'm just keeping my head down and doing my job and I strongly suggest you do the same.'

John thought about that for a second. 'Thanks Mike, that sounds like good advice. I've got my hands full teaching my lot which end of the ship is the sharp bit and how not to get lost when coming from their cabins to the bar. Oh, I was wrong, here they come, let me introduce you.'

'Later that evening after dinner John was summoned to Wing's cabin along with the Terry Donaldson the CO of the Barracuda Squadron. They were offered a seat.

'Sorry to drag you two away from the bar,' he said. 'But time is short and I need to get you two on side as soon as possible.'

John exchanged a look with Terry which luckily Wings didn't see.

'You are both highly experienced aviators and have both had extensive sea time. In your case John, in this very ship. As you probably know most of the ship's company are as green as grass and the ship's officers aren't much better so we are going to have to get them up to speed, carefully but fast. The Captain has made it clear that I and therefore my COs are responsible for safe air operations and that's fine but to be brutally honest the FDO has not impressed me so far and some of the other ship's officers are very inexperienced. What I'm saying is that you must keep your eyes out and come to me if you have any concerns at all. Luckily, we are going to operate with just the two squadrons on board for the moment but I will tell you in confidence that later we will be embarking a squadron of Seafires and another Barracuda outfit. It's going to be crowded and we will need to be on top of our game before that happens.'

'But Sir, we alone can't be responsible for safety and operations, that's a whole ship activity,' Terry said looking concerned.

'You know that old chap and so do I. I'm working on it but it's a top down problem and I've probably said too much by saying that. Let's see how the next few weeks go and take it from there.'

They chatted for a little longer and then John and Terry left. As they went down to their cabins Terry turned to John. 'Please tell me it wasn't like this on board last time. I've only operated from escort carriers up to now, not these monsters. There was no doubt that we were of one company then.'

'And it wasn't when I was here last time either,' John replied. 'The one thing I don't want to get sucked into is a fight with the command. We'd best just do as we're told and wait things out.'

'As long as I don't end up losing any of my guys in the process.'

# Chapter 21

The next few weeks were as hectic as expected but not always for the right reasons. Flying operations took place from dawn to dusk. There were no more accidents but John grew increasingly frustrated. The flight deck teams seemed to operate in slow time and everything took too long. It didn't help that every time the Flight Deck Officer or one of his senior rates started to do something, a voice from Flyco would either contradict or lambast them for doing it incorrectly. On several occasions, the ship started manoeuvring just as aircraft were being moved and one Barracuda almost went over the side. The overall effect was to make everything happen late which resulted in the next operation starting late. This could be crucial if returning aircraft, that were low on fuel, had a foul deck and had to hold off.

It all came to a head on the last day. The Admiral's staff had arrived to oversee the final exercise which included Commander Simon Peters as the Fighter Wing Commander. John had already had a quiet word with him about his misgivings. He didn't want to be disloyal to his command but at the same time, it was quite clear to him that the situation couldn't be allowed to continue. Simon had clearly heard the rumours as well but told John to concentrate on his job and let him worry about the ship.

The day was programmed to start with an all aircraft dawn strike on the uninhabited island of Barra Head, at the southern end of the Outer Hebrides. Invincible was some hundred miles to the west and the supposed enemy had radar so they would need to come in low.

John's squadron was due to launch first and take cover over the ship as the Barracudas got airborne. They would then form up and head east for the attack. The ship had landed some of their own and the Admiral's staff on Mingulay the next island in the chain the previous day and they would assess the attack itself before the ship returned to pick them up. They would be using live weapons. The Hellcats would go in first and ground strafe with their machine guns. Ostensibly to soften up the enemy defences. Then the Barracudas would dive bomb a marked target with five hundred pound bombs.

The first problem happened as they tried to range the Hellcats on deck. Someone in the hangar had parked the aircraft in such a way that two of the Hellcats could not access either deck lift. This meant that John could only launch with eight aircraft and the final two would have to follow the Barracudas. It wasn't a real problem but showed an astounding lack of foresight on someone's part. Getting his eight aircraft off the deck went reasonably well but one of the Barracuda's engines refused to start and had to be moved to one side causing another delay. By the time all machines were in the air and John's missing two had joined up, they were almost forty five minutes late. Instead of attacking at first light with the sun barely on the horizon, it was going to be full daylight.

They raced over the sea at low level with the Hellcats split into two flights on either side of the Barracudas who were leading as they had the crew to navigate.

Despite the cock ups on the ship it all seemed to be going well. Flying so fast at no more than fifty feet and in loose formation was something they had already practiced but the exhilaration never went away, nor did the need for total concentration. It wasn't long before the islands could easily be seen silhouetted against the lightening dawn horizon. Which of course meant that even though they were approaching from down sun in the semi darkness they would still be visible far too early.

It all went as planned with the exception of one Barracuda who turned back, quickly flashing his landing light to indicate engine problems. They were in total radio silence until the attack began. Once the target island became clear, the Hellcats opened their throttles and left the Barracudas behind. When he judged it the right moment John said one word over the radio 'climb'. Both flights of aircraft pulled up but only to a thousand feet and then they all started looking for their targets which should be white crosses laid out on the ground with a much larger cross in the middle for the dive bombers. Now that it was light, the crosses which simulated enemy anti aircraft positions, were easy to spot. Two flights of five Hellcats opened up with sixty half inch machine guns as they dived back down. It was over in seconds and they were streaking over the far side of the island and pulling up hard to take up a race track high over the island to give protection against enemy fighters as the Barracudas themselves now at five thousand feet started their dives.

One after the other, the ungainly machines pushed over into a near vertical descent. For a second John was reminded of watching JU 87 Stukas doing exactly the same thing to British ships in the Mediterranean. The first puff of an explosion was just off to one side of the target but soon there was virtually no sign of it. It was pretty damned accurate bombing but John wondered how accurate it would be if the enemy were firing back.

Then it was over and time to go home. Although the attack was finished they still had to assume that enemy aircraft could retaliate so it was back down to the deck and allow the Barracudas to lead them home. It soon became clear that there was a problem. Where was the bloody ship? They had only been airborne for just over an hour it couldn't have gone far could it?

The Barracuda CO clearly had the same misgivings and broke radio silence. He called the ship but no one replied. Maybe they were still in exercise mode. He pulled up out of formation to get a longer radio horizon and called again but this time made it clear he was now concerned and calling for an end to the exercise. Still nothing and then finally a terse voice came over the radio telling all aircraft to divert to RAF Stornoway some hundred miles to the north east. Stornoway had already been briefed as their diversion airfield should things go wrong so they all should have enough fuel to get there. Even so, John looked down at his fuel gauge but was happy to see he had more than enough. Hopefully, so did everyone else. Despite further requests for information, the ship seemed reluctant to say anything merely repeating the instruction to divert. They all turned north east and headed back towards Stornoway but as they approached the airfield, once again, no one seemed to want to talk to them. John wasn't too surprised as it was still early although he thought someone would have warned the airfield that they were nominated as a major diversion.

With no other option, the Barracudas, followed by the Hellcats lined up and landed in a stream on the main runway. Half way through, the radio came to life and quick explanations were given. The RAF radio operator seemed totally surprised. Yet another cock up John mused as he taxied in last and shut down behind the other Hellcats. All the aircrew gathered in a crowd and started muttering as they looked around wondering what the hell had happened on the ship and what they were going to do now.

Just then a staff car followed by several lorries drove over to them and a harassed looking Wing Commander got out, demanding to know who was in charge. John and Terry Donaldson nodded to each other and walked over.

'Good morning Sir, sorry to drop in uninvited but we had no option,' John said. 'Our ship has some sort of problem and couldn't get us back on board.'

'So it seems,' the Wing Commander said.

'Surely you knew you were nominated as our emergency diversion?' Terry asked.

'No, sorry, first I've heard of it and I'm the station operations officer.'

John and Terry exchanged a knowing glance.

'Anyway,' the Wing Commander continued. 'If your chaps want to jump on the lorries they will take them to the mess for some food and a cup of tea. Your other ranks as well but could the two COs come with me please.'

John and Terry jumped into the car and were driven quickly to the control tower and shown inside. They went into an office where a WAAF gave them cups of tea.

'Now chaps what's this all about?' The Wing Commander asked.

John let Terry lead the conversation and explain what had happened. When he had finished the Wing Commander nodded and asked them to hang on while he went to check some things. He returned looking more than a little annoyed. 'I can confirm that we have no record of either a request or for that matter an instruction to act as a diversion for over twenty aircraft. Your ship should have done that and I would appreciate you passing on my concern when you get back. Now, on that subject, we have managed to make contact with Invincible. She is making her way to Liverpool for repairs and cannot take you back for the moment and before you ask I have no idea why, they wouldn't say. They have asked us to refuel your aircraft and then you are to go to Hawarden where they will be expecting you. Sorry but after that, it's your problem.'

'Understood Sir and thank you for your flexibility in this matter,' John said. 'We'll be out of your hair as soon as we can.'

Later that afternoon, the air group flew into Hawarden and at least they were expected. John wasn't surprised when he and Terry were whisked away to the main administration building. What did surprise him was that having debriefed the station Captain on what had been going on, John was asked to stay behind.

When they were alone, the Captain handed John a telegram with the simple words. 'I'm terribly sorry old chap.'

A river of ice went down John's spine, his hand shook slightly as he took the paper and opened it. His eyes were already blurring but he could see the word 'missing' and Helen's name.

# Chapter 22

The man frowned at Heather and said something more in intelligible French. In desperation, Heather pointed over to the field behind her at the distant aircraft and said 'Pilot,' and then pointed to herself followed by 'Anglais' one of her few French words.

The man looked her up and down and back to the aircraft. Heather immediately recognised the look of incomprehension on his face.

'Can you help me?' she asked desperately.

It seemed he did understand what that meant and impatiently indicate she should jump in next to him. He quickly drove off and started talking urgently at her. At first, she didn't understand anything then, when he started making desperate hand gestures which included taking both hands off the wheel, she got the message. No one including the Germans would probably recognise her uniform jacket but even so any sort of British uniform was not going to help if they were stopped. Nodding to the man, she shrugged out of the jacket. Her hat was still in the Beaufort and her trousers were plain blue. She bundled the jacket and put it under the seat. The man nodded and said something that she interpreted as satisfaction.

He continued to talk even though it was clear he was not being understood until after a few miles they turned off the tarmac road and took a rough track up towards what was clearly a farm, with a main house and several outbuildings.

They parked in a large yard behind the farmhouse and the man indicated that Heather should stay in the car. With no other choice, she sat, waited and worried. She didn't have to wait long. Her rescuer and an old man walking with a cane came out. The old man was stick thin and quite tall, with long white hair. He came to the door and spoke to her in near perfect English.

'Madam, Henri here says he found you on the road in some sort of uniform near a crashed aircraft and claiming to be the pilot.'

'That's correct Sir,' Heather replied. 'I am a ferry pilot, in England these days, many of us are girls. I got lost in the bad weather and had to crash land. Can you help me?'

'So you are not military and not a spy?'

'No just a civilian, well sort of.'

'Very well you must come in. Henri is our vet and has come to look at some of our cows. We will let him get on with is work.'

She was led into a large stone flagged room with a massive weathered wooden table in the middle and offered a chair. An old, plump woman in a long skirt and apron came over and started talking to her benefactor. There was obviously some sort of disagreement which the man clearly won. The woman made a very Gallic shrug and went over to a shelf. She poured some sort of liquid into a glass and handed it to Heather.

She sniffed it experimentally, it was probably brandy and she suddenly realised just how much she needed it. She took a gulp and felt the fire ignite down her throat, immediately followed by her muscles relaxing just a little.

'I am sorry, I should have introduced myself,' the man said. 'My name is Nicholas. Please understand why I say no more, this is a very dangerous place to be.'

'And I'm Heather,' she replied. 'Thank you for taking me in. Your English is very good.'

'It should be, I was born in Oxford and only moved here after the last war. My parents were both French though. Now look, you can't stay here. The Germans are always around and we are both too old to risk being caught with you.'

'I understand but where exactly am I? I was totally lost when I crashed.'

'You are just outside Rouen. Not too far from the coast.'

'So what should I do? I don't speak any French and I need to get home.'

'Well, the first thing to do is get you far away from here. If they haven't found it already the Bosch will soon find your aircraft and with no pilots in it, they will assume they are on the run and will be searching everywhere. At least as a girl, they won't be looking for you but if you are caught with no papers you could be taken for a spy and the Gestapo would take you.'

'But I will have my uniform,'

'Yes but if you are not officially part of your military, your status would be very hard to establish and the Germans have a simple solution to that sort of problem.'

'So how do I get away from here?'

Just then the woman who Heather assumed was Nicolas's wife came over and they started another heated debate. This time it was the woman who seemed to have won.

She disappeared for a few minutes and returned with a suitcase which she mutely handed to Heather. Inside there was an array of female clothing and a pair of shoes.

'These belonged to my daughter,' Nicholas explained. 'They were sent back to us by the Gendarmes. There are even her identity papers and you look much alike.'

Heather was desperate to ask what had happened to the daughter but realised it was probably the wrong thing to do so kept quiet. The identity card had a faded photograph and there was indeed enough of a likeness to hopefully pass inspection.

'Take the suitcase, it will be good cover for you and you should be able to use some of the clothes. I have a car and as my wife has pointed out, the further away from here you are, the safer it is for us. I will take you to the village of Croixdale. I have a cousin there. He may have some contacts who can help you.'

Heather realised she had no choice, she was completely out of her depth. She knew that all British aircrew had some training in evading capture and even carried various maps and devices to help. She had nothing. She felt very alone but also realised just how lucky she had been so far. She just prayed the good luck would continue.

'We must go now. The Germans will be very suspicious if we are stopped at night, as you don't speak French, I will say you have a throat infection. Just croak if you have to, alright?'

She nodded and Nicholas got up to leave. Heather went up to the old woman and shook her hand. She saw there were tears in her eyes and was suddenly embraced in a hug before being shooed out of the door.

They drove in silence for some time then Nichols sighed. 'You should know about Marie, my daughter. As you now have her identity papers it would be sensible.'

Heather could hear the pain in his voice. 'You don't have to Nicholas'

'Yes I do, you need to know. She was part of the Resistance. There are many of us and England is now starting to provide help. They sent an agent over to help with training but it didn't go well. To cut a long story sort there was a raid by the Gendarmerie who seem to be more Nazi than the Germans at times. Believe me, when this war is over there will be a reckoning,' There were tears in his eyes but also a grim determination. 'She was one of the ones they captured. We never found out what happened after they were taken but we can imagine. Six weeks later, an officer came around with that suitcase. He told us she was dead but wouldn't say anymore. He was one of the good guys, he told us to be very careful as the families of those they had interrogated were now under suspicion as well. So you understand now why my wife and I can't offer you more help.'

'You've done more than enough. I don't know how to thank you.' Heather said meaning every word.

They drove on for another half an hour before entering a pretty little village. Heather was quite surprised. For a country under enemy occupation, there was almost no sign of the occupiers. But having heard what had happened to Nicholas's daughter she realised there was much more than the eye could see.

They pulled up and Nicholas told her to stay in the car while he went into one of the cottages.

He was soon out. 'You may be in luck. They have a system for getting airmen back to England. There is one more man waiting but you will have to hide out with him. He is staying in a barn not far from here. I will take you.'

They drove out of the village and turned up a rutted track. There were farm buildings in the distance and an old dilapidated barn off to one side in one of the fields.

'The farm is deserted and falling down but the barn has hay and an upper floor,' Nicholas said. 'It has been used for some time for hiding people. You will need to wait there. Someone from the village will drop food off when they can and there is a water pump just outside. You will be contacted when it is safe to move you on. I'm sorry I can do no more.'

'You've done more than enough,' Heather said and leant over and gave him a kiss on the cheek. 'When the war is over I will come over with my husband and thank you properly.'

'I will look forward to that now go.'

She got out of the car and went over into the barn as Nicholas drove off. It was very dim and smelt of hay and mildew.

'Hello,' she called. 'I'm British is there anyone here?'

A strangely familiar voice answered her. 'Good God is that Heather, what on earth are you doing here?'

She saw a man approaching in a very worn RAF uniform. 'Jack Thomas, I suppose I could ask the same question. The last time I saw you, we were in a Lancaster.'

# Chapter 23

'It should have been me. I always thought it would be me.' John said to himself for the hundredth time as he climbed into the cockpit of his aircraft. It had been a hell of a week but in some ways, it had been lucky for him as he had some spare time to try and find out what on earth had happened. The two squadrons had been told they would need to stay at Hawarden for at least a week while some sort of repairs were made to the ship. They still hadn't found out what had occurred during the exercise. With very little accommodation free at the air station, John's squadron was moved out to a nearby hotel. It would have been quite a fun week except the squadron pilots were taking the news about Heather badly and no one was in the mood for misbehaving. Over the previous months, she had become an honorary member of the squadron. John had laughingly told her that they were all in love with her and it was probably true. However, he hadn't spent much time with them at Hawarden. He left Tom to oversee them and as soon as he could, he flew down to Heather's base and even then down to Manston to try and find out what had happened.

When he got back to Hawarden a few days later he told Tom what he had found out. 'She was picking up an old Beaufort bomber from Manston to be delivered to Southampton. It was pretty routine except for the weather which was shitty.' He said. 'It was straightforward apparently although I did discover that many of the aircraft's instruments had been removed or were not working.'

'But that should have been fine for a trip in daylight down the coast surely?' Tom asked.

'Yes, except for the weather. I spoke to the forecasters at Manston and they admitted that the timing of the warm front that came in was proved to be wrong, it was at least three hours earlier than forecast.'

'So you think she was forced up into cloud? Why didn't she just turn back?'

'We'll never know. Dammit, she was so experienced she shouldn't have made a silly mistake like that. Maybe the aircraft had a failure of some sort but she had no radios so nothing was heard. If a Beaufort had crashed somewhere on land we would have heard by now. There have been no reports of anyone being picked up at sea either.'

'John, I'm so sorry.'

'Yes well, life goes on old chap. We've all been here before in some way or another. And there is still hope you know. I won't give that up. Now tell me what's been happening while I've been away.'

The answer to that had been not very much. It had been quiet without even any flying as the airfield was too busy to accommodate so many more aircraft. Tom had introduced a programme of ground lectures and other training to try to keep everyone busy which had been partially successful but the usual high spirits which could have led to problems were absent. So it was with relief all round that the signal came from the ship to re embark.

The Barracudas went first and then the Hellcats. The ship was back at sea half way between Ireland and Liverpool. As the CO, John was last to land. On more than one occasion he found he was forgetting important things. In fact, as he turned onto final approach he realised he hadn't lowered his arrester hook. Hopefully, no one had noticed.

As soon as he was on board, he sought out Sean. He was expecting an imminent call from Wings or the Captain but wanted to find out what had actually happened first. He found him in the island and they both went out on deck so they weren't overheard.

'What the hell happened Sean?' John asked. 'We've been told nothing.'

'Well, I would have come ashore to Hawarden and told you but they cancelled all leave and confined us all on board.'

'Jesus, it must have been pretty serious. We are all wondering whether it was something to do with that Barracuda that turned back during the exercise.'

'Well, you're right. I was on the flight deck when he came back. It was odd because nothing was prepared, he just suddenly appeared. There was nothing from Flyco so the FDO started to get the barrier and deck ready. The Barracuda was clearly in trouble, he was flying quite slowly and the engine sounded rough. He made straight for the deck. Then Flyco started yelling to wave him off and the ship started to turn. Can you believe it? The poor guy had no chance. He tried for the deck even with the ship turning but was never going to make it. He was far too low and crashed into the back of the ship below the round down. There was a massive fireball and some serious damage to the whole area which is what we were repairing in Liverpool.'

'So what the hell was going on with the command?'

'No one is sure but I can tell you that Commander (Air) left the moment we came alongside. A replacement arrived two days ago I think that tells us quite a lot don't you?'

John was about to reply when the flight deck broadcast came to life. 'Lieutenant Commander Hunt is requested to come to the bridge.'

John clapped Sean on the shoulder. 'Why do I think I might just be about to find out what happened.' He went into the island and up the ladder to the bridge. The Captain and a Commander he didn't recognise were there. The Commander who John assumed was the new Wings, was a strange looking man, almost as wide as he was tall and completely bald. There was a twinkle in his eyes though as he smiled a John. Also, there was John's boss Simon Peters. Terry Donaldson was standing to one side and gave John a quick smile.

'Gentlemen, my cabin please,' the Captain said and they all followed behind. Once in the privacy of the Captain's day room he turned to John and Terry. 'Gentlemen welcome back. I'm sorry you had to stay ashore but as you will probably already know we had an accident during the exercise last week and had to put into Liverpool for repairs which is why we couldn't get you back on board. What no doubt everyone is also talking about is why the accident happened in the first place. I accept part blame, my Officer of the Watch thought he saw something in the water and ordered the helm over without thinking about what was happening on the flight deck. However, there was clearly a major breakdown in communication between the Air and Seaman's departments as the bridge was not aware that an aircraft was returning. I have taken steps to ensure that this does not occur again. May I introduce Commander Desmond Harry our new Commander (Air) who has just joined us.'

The new Wings nodded to them. 'We'll talk later gentlemen.'

The Captain continued. 'Under normal circumstances, we would be carrying out a further period of working up to address the issues we've uncovered. Unfortunately, we are required to become involved in a new important operation which you will be briefed about separately. Consequently, we are going to the north of Scotland to conduct specialist training with a couple of other carriers. I'll leave you now to go with Commander (Air) and Commander Peters who will fill you in on the details.'

Later that evening, John spotted Little F at the bar and went over to him. 'Mike I've had all the stories from the new Wings. Now what really happened?'

The two men went over to a quiet corner and sat down.

'Hey, I heard about your wife old chap, what can I say?' Mike said.

'Nothing I'm afraid. Life goes on. Now you were there, spill the beans.'

'A complete clusterfuck is the simple answer,' Mike said. 'The returning Barracuda boys were sticking to the script and maintained radio silence which frankly was totally unnecessary. So we had no forewarning that they were coming back. Luckily the Flight Deck Officer spotted the aircraft and started to get things ready. Wings then blew his top because he hadn't realised what was going on and thought the FDO was deliberately ignoring him. He started cursing over the flight deck broadcast and the Captain heard. Just as Wings realised what was really happening, the Captain came into Flyco and started to have a go at Wings about his language. It was getting really heated with Wings trying to get the Captain to realise there was an emergency happening when the bloody Officer of the Watch decides to turn the ship. The poor buggers never had a chance. At that point, Wings lost it and told the Captain exactly what he thought about him, his ship and his attitude. The Captain didn't say anything until he shut up. Then he ordered him to be confined in his cabin and no one saw him again.'

'All I can say is thank God we were all ashore. Any idea why the ship wasn't where she should have been?'

'No, not really. I think the Office of the Watch wasn't really that fussed after all aircraft can see for miles can't they?'

'I'd like to meet that chap,' John said.

'Won't happen, he left in Liverpool as well. Don't forget we had the Admiral's staff on board. They probably didn't hear Wings and the Captain going for it but they were well aware of the overall situation.'

'And the new Wings? I don't think I've come across him before.'

'Swordfish man. He was on the Ark when they intercepted Bismarck. A totally different character to the last chap. Very easy going but don't let that put you off. He's already making great efforts to get us all working together. Expect many of the ship's officers to be offered rides in a Barracuda over the next few weeks. And he'll be wanting our officers to work with the ship much more closely.'

'Sounds a damned good idea so it seems we're going to be pretty busy in many ways over the next month or so. I've been briefed on the upcoming Op, I assume you know as well.'

'Oh yes. The Submarine boys have had their go at her, now it's our turn. We stopped the Bismarck for the Fisheads to sink, now we can go one step further and sink her sister, the Tirpitz.'

# Chapter 24

Heather lay on her back staring at the roof of the barn. Of all the things she thought she would be feeling hiding out in enemy occupied France, mind numbing boredom was not one of them. The only thing that kept preying on her mind was wondering what John was thinking. He would have been told she was missing by now and there was no way she was able to tell him she was still alive. It must be terrible for him. It made her even more determined to get home somehow. She had been hiding out with Jack for almost a week. A young lad of about twelve would come over early every morning with some bread and cheese even some boiled eggs on occasion but apart from him they had been on their own. With nothing to do and absolutely no sign of any enemy, all they could do was talk. She told him her story and they talked over where she had gone wrong but in the end it didn't help.

He then gave his account which was far more hair raising. They had been on a night mission to Stuttgart. The inbound trip had gone well and they had found the target and dropped their bombs. It all went wrong on the return journey.

'We were all just starting to relax a little,' Jack explained. 'Then the aircraft just seemed to explode and fall to bits. One moment we were droning along looking forward to breakfast when we got back and then the world went mad. It could have been anti aircraft fire but I'm pretty sure it was a night fighter, we were warned they are starting to use aircraft with some sort of radar. The whole tail of the aircraft seemed to have gone and we were in a spin. I was just behind the cockpit and the pilot just yelled to abandon the aircraft. I was very lucky as my parachute was right next to me. I managed to get it on but the force of the spin was pining me to the bulkhead. Our navigator was having the same problem when there was an enormous bang and don't ask me how but I found myself clear. I think the aircraft was breaking up and I was flung out. Anyway, the parachute worked and I landed in a field somewhere. I never saw any of my crew after that. Luckily, my training kicked in so I got rid of the parachute and found the nearest village.'

'And you are half French so speak the language, unlike me,' Heather said. 'Presumably, you could take advantage of that.'

'Yes I managed to make contact with someone in the resistance and they were able to get me here. I have to say though that I'm not too impressed so far. They seemed more interested in sabotage than helping escaped airmen.'

'I seem to remember that you said you had escaped from France once before. A boat from Normandy wasn't it?'

'Yes and frankly I'm inclined to try that again. I suggest we give these people a week and if there's no progress we strike out on our own. It's only about thirty kilometres that's less than twenty miles to the coast, to a small town called Criel Sur Mere. I have friends there and it's where I managed to get a boat last time.'

So now the week was almost up. Jack had a map printed on a silk sheet and some other survival gear including a small compass. He also knew the area pretty well and was getting more and more inclined to suggest that they move on when the decision was taken from them. It was sometime in the middle of the night and Heather was awake keeping watch. They had decided that someone should be awake at all times, getting enough sleep was not exactly a problem. Even so, she was having trouble keeping her eyes open when she heard vehicle engines in the distance. There was a strict night curfew in force and so anyone on the roads in the dark would be German. She rushed over and shook Jack awake.

'Something is going on in the village,' she said urgently.

They both went and looked out of the large second floor opening in the barn, presumably that was used to bring up hay but luckily overlooked the track and the village in the distance. Suddenly, they heard distant shouting and then shots being fired. Lights started to come on.

'I think my brave French friends might have just carried out one act of sabotage too many,' Jack said. 'Time to go I think.'

Heather could only agree, even if part of her felt safe in the barn. Running around the French countryside in the dark did not appeal but it was clear they couldn't stay either.

'Right, before we go, make sure we have everything,' Jack said. 'We don't want to let the Germans know anyone was here if they decide to come and check. Then we use the exit we scouted out the other day. Across the big field behind us and then into the wood. Once there we should be relatively safe until dawn and we can see if there is any more activity.'

They left the barn and went over to the overgrown field. There was very little light as it was overcast and the moon had already set. Keeping the field's hedge on their right they were able to carefully make their way towards the distant wood. It took much longer than expected not the least because it had been raining earlier and the ground was very muddy. Once safely inside the trees, they stopped and looked back. At first, nothing could be heard or seen then suddenly vehicle lights appeared.

'They're coming to the farm,' Jack said. 'They must either have known something or someone in the village has talked. We need to get as far away as we can. Are you ready for a stroll in the countryside?' He asked as he got out his compass and tried to read it in the faint light.

'No,' Heather replied. 'But we don't exactly have much choice do we?'

It took far longer than either of them thought it would to reach the coast. They could only safely travel at night and the weather was awful with regular heavy rain that turned the country side into a swamp. They were permanently wet even after they had managed to steal some coats from an isolated house when the residents were out. Heather soon dumped her suitcase but kept the identity papers just in case. If it hadn't been for Jack she would have given up but his endless encouragement and determination had kept them going. By the time they reached the outskirts of the little fishing village, she was at the end of her tether. They hadn't eaten for days and she was shivering with the cold. She was lying behind some bushes waiting for Jack to reappear. He had gone ahead to make contact with his friends and hadn't come back yet and it had been several hours. Suppose he had been taken? What should she do? She realised she couldn't stay where she was for much longer, she would literally die of the cold. Even with her identity papers, she wouldn't fool any Germans for a second. So it was go into the village and try to get someone to give her shelter or accept the inevitable and giver herself up. She was just about to get up and walk into the village and take her chances when she heard her name being whispered and Jack appeared.

'All set Heather,' he said. 'We've got shelter for the night.'

Half an hour later, she was warm dry and not a little drunk. Jack had taken her to the cellar of an old stone house only a few yards from the harbour side. It was warm, as a fire had been lit in an old stove. Two men and a woman were already there. The woman had taken her aside, given her a large blanket so she could take of her soaking clothes and dry them on a rack by the stove. She was handed an enormous glass of wine and a plate of bread and cheese. All this was done without a word being exchanged. It was clear no one spoke any English. Meanwhile, Jack had been talking in rapid fire French to the two men. To Heather, they looked like typical fishermen with weather beaten faces and scruffy but no doubt weather proof clothes. There seemed to be a lot of hand waving and exclamations going on.

Eventually, Jack came over to Heather and introduced one man while the other slipped out of the door.

'This is my friend Marcel,' Jack said and the man gave her a gap toothed smile and gabbled something at her. She smiled back and looked enquiringly at Jack.

'He says you're far too pretty to be a pilot and would you like to stay here with him until the war ends? I've already told him his Gallic charm won't work but he had to try.'

She smiled at Marcel again and pointed to the north. 'England, husband,' she said

He grinned and nodded as Jack translated. 'He says he had to at least ask. However, we have a problem. The days of the Germans letting boats come and go as they please are long over. They let the fishing boats out but only in groups and there is always an E boat or suchlike around to keep an eye on them. I've asked if they have any contact with England by radio or other means. There was a radio operator in Dieppe until a few weeks ago but they were arrested. It seems that the Germans are getting much better at intercepting their transmissions these days.'

'So, we are on our own?'

'It seems that way unless we wait here and see if we can contact England some other way. Frankly, I'm at a loss. At least we will be safe here for a while.'

Heather thought about being stuck in a cellar for possibly weeks and what John was going through even now. She looked around the little room. It was clearly used to store fishing equipment. She looked at the ceiling which was strewn with what looked like wooden spars all held up in a large net and had an idea.

'Ask Marcel what those things on the ceiling are because if they're what I suspect they are then there may be a way we can get ourselves across the Channel.'

# Chapter 25

'Operation Tungsten Gentlemen.' Wings announced to the packed wardroom. 'We are going after the Tirpitz. As you will all know the submariners did her some serious damage last year with their miniature submarines. However, intelligence now tells us that she is almost repaired and will be sailing in about a month for sea trials. The RAF bless them have said the risk to their bombers is too high as she is in a fjord in Norway that is too heavily defended so our Admirals have agreed that we should give it a go. It should be easier for us as we can hopefully sneak in low level and gain surprise. Also, the Barracudas now have the new sixteen hundred pound armour piercing bombs which if dropped from three and half thousand feet or higher should be capable of piercing her deck armour. There are going to be several carriers, notably us, Victorious and Furious plus four escort carriers as well as the usual gathering of escorts. We are working on the force mix and which aircraft will do what. However, it has been pointed out that almost eighty five percent of all our aircrew have never carried out an operation from sea. Because of that, we are going to attack Scotland, Loch Eribol to be precise as it has many similar characteristics to Kaafjord where the bugger spends her days. To do this we will fly from the ship but also RNAS Hatston in the Orkneys. Then sometime, probably early April, we will go when intelligence says it's the right time. As you are aware, we are now supplying Russia with war materials using convoys going over the top of Norway. You can imagine the carnage that would result if Tirpitz made it out and got stuck into one of those. This is a big one and we need to get it right. There will be more detailed briefings to come and we are getting a scale model of Kaafjord made so you can study the real terrain in detail. That's all for now, tomorrows flying programme is already on the noticeboard. Would the two squadron COs join me in my cabin please?'

John and Terry followed Wings up the stairs to his cabin. He gestured for them to sit down and reached into his desk and produced an illegal bottle of whisky. 'I know officers are not allowed booze in their cabins chaps but rank hath its privileges and I won't tell the Commander if you don't.' He poured them both a good measure each.

They took their glasses while John briefly thought of the bottle of scotch he had stashed in his sock drawer, purely for medicinal purposes of course.

'Now, this ship has got off to a rocky start as you are well aware. However, the Captain and I have had a heart to heart and I'm pretty sure things will start to improve and quickly. Terry, whenever you can I want you to take one of the ship's company airborne with you starting with the bridge watchkeepers. Nothing concentrates the mind more than when you can see the consequences of any folly. I also want the goofers position to be as accessible to as many as possible. I know the last Wings didn't like an audience. I take the opposite view and the more the ship's company can get involved in flying ops the better. I also want your people, especially the officers, to spend some time with the various ships departments, particularly operations.'

'Already on it Sir,' John said. 'Terry and I have got our Senior Pilots liaising with the various Heads of Departments.'

'Excellent, so finally I want to know all about your aircrew. I don't want to pour through acres of confidential reports, they are only as good as the person who writes them. Give me a precis of each one, how well they are performing, what you think they will become in time and just to be safe, any social attributes so if we ever have the luxury of a run ashore I know who to keep an eye on.'

John and Terry exchanged a glance. 'That'll be most of them Sir,' Terry said. 'But we know what you mean.'

'Good, now while I refill those mysteriously empty glasses you can both tell me about yourselves. I've not served with either of you so we really need to get to know each other. Nothing scandalous please, I shall ask your pilots to fill me in on that in the bar in due course. I just want you to tell me about your careers so far and of course I will give you my background. We'll have individual chats in the next few days so just the bare bones please.'

Almost two hours later, two very unsteady Squadron Commanding Officers made their way back to their own cabins.

'Bloody hell,' John said. 'How much scotch did wings have in that desk?'

'Enough to get us both to loosen up,' Terry said. 'My goodness you couldn't have a different character to the last one could you?'

'Well I like him and I think the ship will too. Mind you he's no fool. His account of the attack on the Bismarck was damned impressive.'

'Yes, I think we are going to work well in the future and it's going to be what we need for this upcoming operation. Right, I might just go back to my cabin and check my eyelids for light leaks for half an hour or so.'

'My thinking too,' John said. Hoping that for once, the daytime booze would help him sleep, something he was having trouble with these days.

The next few weeks were manic. Not only were the squadrons having to fly ashore and practice flying in narrow hilly terrain but they were having to do it in company with aircraft from the other ships. Not only that but the ship was still in the process of working under the new command regime but that seemed to be going well. John threw himself into the activity, flying as much as he could and leading from the front, anything to keep his mind occupied. His pilots all seemed to be coming on well and just as importantly they were at last working harmoniously with the ship. It was starting to feel like the Invincible he remembered.

Their last exercise was a full scale rehearsal. It had been decided that the Hellcats with their massive firepower would go in first and strafe the target to try and reduce its anti-aircraft capability. The Tirpitz upper deck was littered with small calibre guns. After that, they would roam at will and attack other ships or shore based AA sites. In the near centre of Lock Eribol was a small island that represented the Tirpitz and that would be their and the Barracuda's initial aiming mark.

It didn't start well for John. As the first aircraft off, he really needed to be on the ball but even dragging himself out of bed was becoming a nightmare and he had been having plenty of those. He knew he was allowing Heather's loss to get to him and he also knew he had to put it behind him as he had a squadron and a ship who were relying on him. He also knew Heather would not want him to mope about but it was all easier said than done. So when it was time to launch just as the sun was about to rise, he found himself frozen in the cockpit. The marshaller was frantically signalling him to start his engine. He suddenly realised he had no idea just how long the poor man had been trying to attract his attention. Getting a grip, he forced himself to concentrate and made a perfect if slightly tardy take off. Wings would be having words with him when he got back of that there was no doubt. Once in the air, there was just too much to do getting the squadron formed up with both themselves and then the rest of the aerial armada and he was able to put everything out of his mind except the task in hand. Subsequently flying in loose formation at fifty feet with over a hundred other machines, once again kept him totally occupied. As soon as the call to pull up was given, they climbed up to seven thousand feet and looked ahead for the target. They were the lead squadron now and even though they had been here many times in recent days they still needed to find the loch and its little island. Luckily the weather and visibility were good and he had no trouble seeing them in good time.

Calling 'Tally Ho', over the radio, he pushed the nose of his Hellcat down in a steep dive. They would be firing live ammunition and dropping real bombs today so he made his guns switches to fire and got ready to strafe the target. Afterwards, he could give no explanation of what he did next but for some reason, he simply dived for too long. There was an urgent radio call 'pull up Boss' from someone. For a second he wondered who on earth they were talking to and then he realised it was for him and he was about to hit either the ground or the water.

'Oh bloody hell.' he shouted and pulled the stick back as hard as he could whilst cursing himself for being a complete idiot. He had seen this before from the outside, even when trying to level out and climb away an aircraft would 'mush' down and could hit the ground even with the nose well up. The world started to go grey as the G forces built up. The last thing he remembered hearing was a loud bang and then everything went black.

The next thing he knew he was coming to with the nose of the aircraft almost vertical and about to enter a stall. He frantically pushed the stick forward and regained some airspeed. He levelled off at about five thousand feet and looked around. The first thing he saw was another Hellcat on his starboard wing with the grinning face of Neville Parsons his wingman giving him the thumbs up. He realised he was sweating and feeling cold at the same time. That must have been really close and a stupid mistake that he would have had one of his pilot's guts for garters over. Then he remembered the bang he had heard. He waved a hand at Neville who go the message and dropped down and reappeared on the other side.

'Looks fine Boss, a few dents but suggest you cycle your undercart to be sure.'

John throttled back and pulled the undercarriage lever to the down position. There seemed to be a longer than normal delay before the lights went green but green they went. He also tried the flaps and hook they also seemed fine.

'All good boss,' Neville called.

'Thanks, lets go home.'

All the way to the ship, John was wondering what on earth Wings was going to say to him and what he could possibly say in response.

# Chapter 26

Jack wanted to die. Heather's idea had seemed their best option when she had explained what she was thinking but now he really didn't care. Whether they made it to England or he simply drowned he wasn't fussed. He had joined the RAF, not the damned navy. How come he wasn't sick like this when he got to England in the fishing boat the other year? The answer was simple, this bloody boat was tiny in comparison.

Over a week ago it had all seemed such a good plan. 'Look,' Heather had said. 'Those bits of wood in the ceiling must be the mast and gaff of a sailing dinghy. If they are then there is probably the boat that goes with them somewhere. Ask Marcel if it's still around.'

With Jack translating, Heather soon discovered that indeed the dinghy was around and stored in an old boat shed near the harbour. Apparently, there were probably quite a few around. Before the war, there was a strong fleet used for local racing, similar to the ones John and Heather had raced over the Channel at Lee on Solent.

However, when she suggested that they could use it to sail to England she was met with obstinate refusal from Marcel. He insisted that the distance was too great and it was far too dangerous. She pointed out that it was less than sixty miles and in ten hours of darkness they would be within ten miles of the English coast before it got light and that was if they only managed five knots. If they waited for the right wind they should be able to go much faster.

Marcel then pointed out that when the dinghies were made ready for a season they were deliberately filled with water to allow the wood to swell otherwise they would leak like a sieve and this one had been out of the water for three years not one. She countered by saying that they could wait. The debate raged for some time. In the end, Marcel gave in but only because Heather was so adamant, she even promised she would somehow pay for the boat when the war was over. Most importantly though was that they would be posing quite a risk to Marcel and his family the longer they stayed where they were. Jack kept his counsel. Heather had explained that she was an experienced sailor and that it was perfectly feasible to cross the Channel in a twelve foot long dinghy.

'What about all the German boats out there or even our own for that matter? Surely it will look odd to see a small boat like that sailing in darkness?' Jack asked later on.

'Ah but will they even see us?' Heather said. 'As you say, it's a tiny boat and as you know Marcel has said the sails are old and brown. And why would we be of any interest anyway? Anyone out there will have much more important things on their minds than attacking us.' She really wasn't sure that would be the case but what other option did they have? So, the next morning they went to see the little boat. They helped Marcel pull it down the beach and into the sea where it quickly filled with water and sank as he had removed the bung in the bottom. Once full, he replaced the bung and said it would need to stay there for at least three days letting the tide cover and uncover it. To anyone, especially the Germans who saw it, it would look like an abandoned wreck.

Jack was not impressed and turned to Heather. 'That's a tiny boat Heather is there even room for two of us? When you talked about this idea I really didn't realise how small it would be.'

'It's our one chance Jack,' she replied. 'It's that or staying here until we go mad or eventually get in contact with England and who knows how long that will be. Look, I know it's early in the year but I know quite a lot about the weather and if we pick our moment we'll be fine. Twelve hours and we'll be home. Trust me.'

So a week later, the boat was ready and all they needed was the weather window. All day it had been grey and cloudy, then late in the afternoon after some heavy rain, the sky cleared. Heather knew what that meant.

'A cold front has just gone through,' she explained. 'The wind has veered a little and we should have good wind and from the right direction. Time to go.'

Marcel agreed and so as soon as it was starting to get dark they shouldered the dinghy's mast, gaff and sails down to the boat shed. Marcel quickly rigged the mast helped by Heather. Jack just stood back and let them get on with it, he didn't have a clue what all the ropes and other things were for. Marcel then gave them some old oilskins and two very cumbersome looking cork lifejackets. He also put two large cans of fresh water in the boat. It was time to go. They all waded into the sea until the boat was floating and they could haul themselves in. Heather gave Marcel one last hug and it was time to go. They had two oars which she rigged and pulled them away from the shore. When well clear she grabbed the rope holding the mainsail gaff and hauled it and the big sail up. The wind was coming over the beam and so they immediately started to move.

'Sit on the other side Jack, our weight will counteract the pressure of the sail.'

He did as he was told and then Heather pulled up the little Jib and tied off the sheet. The dinghy quickly settled down and started sailing swiftly away from land. The darkened coast was soon lost to sight and they were in a little world of their own.

'Compass please Jack,' Heather said.

He got out his miniature compass and looked at it. It had a luminous dial and they had agreed that he would monitor it while she took the tiller.

'Come left a little,' he said. 'That's enough, right you are heading due north.'

Heather looked ahead and as it was a reasonably clear night was able to select a star near the bow and use that to keep a course. As they cleared the coast, the sea became choppier. Despite the old oilskins, bursts of spray were regularly soaking them. That was when Jack started feeling ill. He was also starting to get cold which didn't help. They chatted for a while and he kept a regular check on the compass but soon the contents of his stomach had gone over the side.

Heather told him to sit further down to keep out of the wind and spray as much as possible. She didn't seem affected at all and was even smiling as she looked ahead and kept the boat on course. Time passed but he had no idea how much. At one point, Heather relieved him of the compass and he was able to completely curl up in misery which was only interrupted when he had to lean over the side and be sick again.

Then all hell let loose. Somewhere up ahead a brilliant light lit the sky and a few seconds later the sound of weapons fire could be heard. Adrenalin settled his queasy stomach. 'That's a starshell.' He said. 'Someone's having a fight and those are high power engines I can hear as well.'

Heather eased the tiller over away from whatever was happening almost dead ahead of them. 'I'll try and avoid whatever is going on,' she said. 'But at our speed, it's probably too late.'

Get Boody Stuck In

Soon, they could actually see tracer from several weapons being fired but it was impossible to judge how far away it all was. Suddenly, there was the thud of an explosion and a gout of flame leapt into the sky. Silhouetted against the light was the outline of a boat.

'That's a British Fairmile fast patrol boat,' she said. 'I've seen them before.' Before Jack could reply the dark shape of another fast boat came into view and shot past with a roar of high powered engines. The wash from it almost capsized the dinghy but Heather quickly turned into it and minimised the effect. Suddenly, it was quiet and then quite dark as the starshell went out.

There were still flames coming from the British boat so Heather took the dinghy towards them.

'Is this a good idea? Jack asked when he realised what she was doing.

'I think so, at worst we might be able to help some survivors at best they may still be mobile and be able to take us home.'

As they got closer they could see people on the deck running around. The flames seemed to be reducing. When they were within a few yards, they started shouting as it was clear no one had seen them.

Then a voice called over. 'Who the hell are you?'

'We're British, we're trying to get across the Channel and get home, any chance of a lift?' Jack shouted back.

'Good God, in that little tub. Just hold off while we get sorted out.'

They could see that the crew seemed to have the fire under control now and within minutes they were told to come alongside. Ropes were thrown to them and a little ladder was put over the side. Heather dropped the mainsail in a heap while Jack grabbed a rope and then they clambered up onto the deck.

A young lieutenant in a reefer jacked with a white polo neck jersey underneath came to greet them. 'Think we should be able to get you chaps home. We've still got one engine. That bloody E Boat wasn't as clever as he thought he was.' Then he stopped and looked at Heather. 'Hang on, are you a girl? What on earth are you doing here?'

'Just trying to get home,' she said. 'And there's someone I need to talk to.'

119

# Chapter 27

John managed to land back on Invincible without missing the wires and ending up in the barrier. All the way back he felt like an errant schoolboy knowing he was going to have to go to the headmaster's study for a scolding.

Once on deck, he followed the marshaller, parked the aircraft and shut down the engine. He sat for a moment contemplating what on earth he was going to say to Wings when someone rapped sharply on the cockpit canopy. It was Sean. He pulled the hood back and Sean gave him a strange look.

'Flyco say they need you up there as soon as possible.' He said and reached over to help John undo his straps.

Feeling even more like it was going to be a visit to the headmaster, John went into the island and signed the aircraft in before going out into the main corridor and then trudging up the two flights of stairs up to Flyco. He told himself to stop being an idiot, everyone made mistakes why should he be any different? He answered himself because you are the CO and you are probably the most experienced pilot on the ship.

Flyco seemed unusually crowded. Little F and Wings were in their seats overlooking the deck but so was Simon Peters and even the Captain. Jesus, exactly how much trouble was he in? He decided to get his oar in first.

'Sorry Sirs that was a bad show. I don't know what happened today but it won't happen again I assure you.'

He looked up and was mystified to see everyone was smiling.

'I've absolutely no idea what you are talking about,' Wings said. 'OK you were a little late off the deck and I hear you might have overcooked it at the attack site but so what? We all make mistakes, you are only human old chap.'

'What? Oh yes, thank you Sir so what did you want to see me for?' asked a surprised John

The Captain came over and handed John a piece of paper. 'This should make it clear,' was all he said

John took the paper. It was a signal from HMS Hornet, where ever that was, to the Commanding Officer of HMS Invincible. It read 'Please inform Lieutenant Commander Hunt CO of 1854

Squadron. Mrs Heather Hunt recovered today in the Channel. She is well and travelling to ATA headquarters at Aston Down.'

He read it again and then again, trying to come to terms with the words. A massive weight lifted off his back, he found his eyes were starting to get wet with tears. He tried to pull himself together and completely failed. Suddenly, something was thrust into his hand, it was a glass of whisky. Where the hell had that come from? He didn't care, just downed it in one.

'Thank you sir,' he managed to splutter at the Captain, who smiled back

'Commander (Air) has a suggestion John and I have already approved it,' the Captain said

John turned to Wings. 'Sir?'

'John, the exercise has finished and the fleet is going to anchor in Scapa Flow. We've been given a week to re-store and ammunition. We are sending both squadrons ashore to Hatston tomorrow while we do that. Normally there wouldn't be leave with an operation so close but you can have forty eight hours and I believe Aston Down is within range of a Hellcat.'

So many emotions were surging through John's head that he didn't know what to say. Eventually, he managed to stutter a thank you to the Captain and Wings.

'Now I suggest you get down to the wardroom and tell your chaps the good news,' Simon Peters said. 'I believe Heather was an honorary member of the squadron so they ought to be told. But keep the celebrations until this evening, we still have an exercise to debrief.'


The following day, John was in a different universe. One with Heather in it. He was the first to launch the next morning despite a rather sore head. Mind you that was the same for the whole squadron. There had been particularly good celebration in the bar that evening. Although he did have to take some stick about his antics over the Loch. Apparently, he literally made quite a splash. He hadn't felt this happy and stress free for some time, so who cared about a slightly throbbing head? Leaving the squadron in the tender hands of the Senior Pilot he turned south for Aston Down. Because of the up-coming operation and the need to keep communications to a minimum the ship had not contacted Aston to tell them he was coming so he would need to do that once airborne. However, once on the way he decided not to mention who he was and why he was heading there. It would make the surprise even better.

In no time, or so it seemed, the airfield was in sight and he made a flawless approach to land. He was directed to the station flight apron and shut the Hellcat down. He climbed out and retrieved his large overnight grip and uniform cap from behind his seat. No one seemed surprised or concerned about the strange fighter that was apparently going to be there for two days. The Chief Petty Officer on the flight line simply promised John it would be ready when he needed it as long as he gave them a couple of hour's notice. Apparently, the airfield was very used to multiple comings and goings, especially as it was an ATA hub. John was offered a lift over to the ATA offices which he gratefully accepted. When he walked in, the place seemed empty. He suddenly had a dreadful thought. Had Heather already gone home or been sent somewhere else? The signal from the ship was over twenty four hours old after all. Then he heard a familiar voice from down the hall. He went to the door where he could hear the voices and pushed it open. There she was and also another man. They were peering closely at a large map on a table in front of them. Although he couldn't see the man's face, something about him seemed familiar. He didn't care.

'Heather,' was all he managed before she spun around and threw herself into his arms. Then they were laughing and kissing for what seemed to be forever until a discreet cough caught their attention.

Now John could see the man's face he immediately knew who it was. 'Peter Smithson-Wood what on earth are you doing here?'

Peter laughed. 'I could ask you the same question but actually I think that's pretty obvious. Goodness, you must have flown quickly to get here so soon.' If he didn't know better, John thought he sounded disappointed.

'Yes, well, I do have the use of one of His Majesty's finest and fastest fighters you know. My ship has just finished an exercise and there's some time to spare for a few days.'

'Fair enough, I was just debriefing your lovely wife. She has spent quite some time in enemy occupied France and had some very useful intelligence to impart.'

John turned back to Heather. 'France, what on earth were you doing there?' I knew your navigation was dodgy but getting that far off course is pretty spectacular even for you.'

The remark got John a punch on the arm. 'You try flying a clapped out old bomber with virtually no instruments or compass in cloud and see how you do.' Heather replied.

Peter tactfully went to the door. 'I'll see if I can rustle up some tea, shall I? You two can get all that pilot stuff out of your system while I do it.'

They both nodded and sat down at the table. Heather gave John an abbreviated version of events and then Peter returned with three cups of tea and offered his cigarettes all round.

'Now look you two,' he said. 'I don't want to be a party pooper but I really need some details from Heather. My job these days is to do with organising things over the Channel, you will appreciate why I can say no more. If I can have just an hour with her then I will get out of your hair.'

Heather looked at John and he nodded back. 'I tell you what,' he said. 'I've got a couple of days leave and I assume they are not sending you straight back to work are they darling?'

'No I've got two weeks leave so I'm footloose and fancy free.'

'Right, you two have your secret chat and I'll see if I can arrange some accommodation for us, somewhere close by.'

Going out into the corridor, he realised he needed to find someone with a phone who could help. There must be an admin office somewhere. As he investigated down the corridor he bumped into a tall man in ATA uniform.

The man stopped and looked at John. 'I'm guessing that you are Heather's husband?' He asked.

'That's correct, John Hunt and you are?'

'I run the place. Ray Hammond. Good to meet you at last. She speaks of you all the time and like you, we are really glad she made it back. Has she told you the story yet?'

'A little,' John replied. 'But she's closeted with an intelligence officer at the moment. I've got a couple of day's leave and was looking to try and book a hotel for us.'

'Right come with me. You can use the phone in my office and I can recommend a couple of hotels in Cirencester as well.'

Once in the office John thought of something and turned to Ray. 'Actually, before I use the phone could I ask what your plans are for Heather once she is back from her leave?'

'Good question, she's due promotion but whether she accepts it is up to her because it means the only jobs available as a Flight Captain are non-flying ones. Although she will still be able to keep current and there could be the occasional delivery if we get pressed.'

'She's been flying since the start of the war,' John said. 'I think she's done enough.'

'Frankly, I agree,' Ray said. 'But you will have to talk to her about that, it's her decision.'

That evening John and Heather had a late dinner and an early night although sleep did not have much to do with it.

As they lay back in a slightly sweaty heap of bedclothes, John lit them both a cigarette. 'I bumped into your boss this morning, he says they are offering you a promotion.'

'Ah, yes he told you then. Did he tell you it would mean no more ferry work and not a lot of flying, just sitting in an office pushing paper?'

'Yes and to be completely honest I would feel far happier if that was what you did. I don't think I could take losing you a second time.'

Heather didn't answer for some time. Then she rolled over and looked at John. 'When I was stuck in France I had plenty of time to think. The first thing I realised was how incredibly lucky I was to have got away with not killing myself. I must have made every rookie error under the sun just accepting that aircraft. I was just too eager to get home and too overconfident in my abilities. I've seen it in other people, just never thought I would fall into the same trap. And then how lucky was I to meet up with some sympathetic French people? I'm for the quiet life now. So yes I'm going to accept the promotion.'

John sighed inwardly with relief. One less thing to worry about in the weeks and months to come. 'Thank you my dear that was what I was hoping you would say.'

'There's one thing though.'

'Oh what's that?'

'You make damned sure you don't fall into the same trap.'

# Chapter 28

The briefing room was hushed. Partly because the aircrew all realised that this was it. Finally, they were going into combat but also because it was one fifteen in the morning and most hadn't managed any sleep at all.

Simon Peters stood at the front along with a large map of northern Norway. 'Gentlemen we are going in tomorrow, twenty four hours earlier than planned. Some days ago, convoy JX 58 sailed from Loch Ewe heading for Russia. It was hoped that it would attract the German's attention and they would overlook our little battlegroup to the south. It seems to have worked. Despite being attacked by a large wolf pack of U Boats over the last few days, no ships were successfully attacked and four U Boats were sunk. We also have intelligence that Tirpitz is getting ready for sea trials, she certainly did not come out after the convoy but may well be away from her normal, well protected mooring. This along with the current good weather has convinced the Admiral to bring the operation forward twenty four hours. We are now making our way to this position,' and he pointed to his map. 'One hundred and twenty miles from the coast where the first aircraft will launch at four fifteen. The Corsairs go first to give top cover, while the rest of the force launch and then will then do the same when we are over the target. There are known German fighters deployed not too far away at Bardufoss but if we come in at low level their radar should not have enough time to alert them. The Barracudas are next, there will be twenty one and seven of them will be carrying the sixteen hundred pound bombs that will hopefully ruin the whole of the morning for the Tirpitz. Our Hellcats and Wildcats from the other carriers launch last, a total of thirty in all. However, we will be into action first. Their priority is neutralising anti-aircraft fire from Tirpitz, her escorts and also shore emplacements. As we won't know exactly where she will be, the final attack decisions will have to be made when over the target.

'At half past five a second similar sized force will launch to conduct a second attack. While we are away, Seafires and Wildcats will provide force protection. So that's it. I'll let the two Squadron COs give their own detailed briefs. You've all been practicing for this for some time now and have a pretty good idea of the terrain and the layout of the fjord. All I can do now is wish you luck and I look forward to hearing all your stories in the bar tonight.'

After he had briefed his squadron John headed out to the flight deck. Sean was there.

'All ready to go?' He asked his engineer.

'As they'll ever be. How about your pilots?'

'Good question. Only three of us have been shot at before but I'm pretty confident they'll be fine. Don't forget they are all young and so they're immortal.'

Sean chuckled. 'I wonder how long they will feel that?'

'Who knows Sean, who knows.'

John usually liked to try and find a quiet spot on the flight deck to gather his thoughts before a mission, especially one as significant as this but it didn't look like he was going to be lucky today. He looked over and saw Neville Parsons walking over.

'Morning Boss. Looks like a good day for it.' He said looking up at the pitch black sky with a few stars in view.

John realised that Neville was nervous. He thought back to how he had reacted to his first operational sortie and could fully appreciate the feeling.

'You know my first trip was in daylight and on a sunny day. I got into quite a fight and when I got back, I threw up. Never stopped being scared since. You just learn to manage it, put it to one side and concentrate on the job in hand. Anyway, once we're off the deck you'll be too busy to have time to do anything but fly.'

'I know Sir, that's what everyone says. It's the hanging around now I'm not too happy with.'

Suddenly the flight deck broadcast came to life. 'Pilots man your aircraft.'

'There you are then Neville,' John said clapping him around the shoulders. 'Thinking time over, just remember to stick to me. We fight together and look after each other. You've done well so far, we've practiced this many times. Oh and I promise to pull out of my dive in good time.'

Neville gave him a grin and the two men walked between the parked aircraft on the flight deck to their own machines.

An hour later the armada of aircraft was twenty miles from the coast and there was no sign that they had been detected. The Corsairs and Barracudas pulled up heading for seven thousand feet while John led the Hellcats to only two thousand. This was high enough for them to see where they were going and what was going on in the fjord but low enough to be able to get down quickly. The dive bombers needed height to come down on the target steeply. The Hellcats needed to come in low from both sides. That way the ship would have to divide its fire.

As the fjord came into view John couldn't believe their luck. Not only were there no escorts in sight but the Tirpitz was there in all her deadly glory but right out in the middle, not tucked into a secure mooring. She seemed to be underway but not going anywhere fast. With little time to think he ordered Tom's flight to split off to take the starboard side while his five aircraft went for the port side. He pushed the nose down, glancing to one side to ensure Neville was in position and then concentrated on the massive ship rapidly approaching.

He opened fire as he dived down towards the bridge. He could even see his bullets hitting the deck and various gun emplacements along the side of the ship. There was some return fire but it was surprisingly light. It seems they had achieved almost total surprise. As soon as he was clear of her stern, he racked the Hellcat around in a tight turn. It didn't take long to line up and strafe the ship again, from stern to bow this time. He suddenly became aware of chatter on the radio, the Barracudas were starting to come in so he pulled away and flew further up the fjord at low level. There was plenty of shore fire now but it all seemed rather random. He then spotted some more coordinated fire from the top of a hill. It seemed to be directed upwards presumably towards the attacking dive bombers. He turned towards it only to see two Wildcats dive in and blow the gun emplacement to bits. There was a massive explosion, presumably where the spare ammunition was stored. Then suddenly he saw a ship ahead of him which was clearly a flak ship judging by the fire coming from it. He dropped to the deck and tore in at low level before opening fire. Neville joined in from his port side. They seemed to be doing significant damage before they had to pull up to clear its masts. As they turned round he could see they had set it on fire and her crew were jumping over the side. This seemed one of the most one sided fights he had ever been in. In fact, it was almost exactly like the practice sorties they had flown in Scotland albeit with some fairly ineffectual return fire. On top of that, there was no sign of enemy aircraft.

Realising there was little more he could do, he turned back to the Tirpitz just in time to see a massive explosion on her foredeck and a Barracuda pulling out of its dive. He was sorely tempted to have another go at her, he had some ammunition left but getting in the way of a Barracuda's bomb or the explosive results of one didn't seem like a good idea.

Just then over the radio came the message to return to base. Where had the time gone? Looking over his shoulder he saw his wing man faithfully in place so he waved and pointed out to sea. There was no need to fly back at low level. As the second wave would be inbound any time soon it would not be good to meet them head on. There had been no German fighters around when they were over the target, he just hoped the second wave was as lucky. An hour later they were back on deck. His pilots all seemed like schoolboys who had just won a major Rugby game as they chattered and noisily compared notes in the briefing room.

Once Simon Peters and one of the ship's operations officers had taken down their accounts they were told to stand down but only as far as the wardroom for some food. It was quite possible that they would be needed again, especially if the Luftwaffe finally woke up and decided to try and get some revenge.

By midday, it was all over. The second wave had also been successful. Apparently, the Germans had started to try to make smoke but all it did was hamper their own gunners. All the aircraft bar one Barracuda and two Wildcats had made it back. Initial reports said that the ship was badly damaged but still afloat and was able to make some way, which was disappointing. Consequently, everyone was told to stand by for a repeat performance the next day. However, it didn't happen, the explanation being that the defences would now be fully alert and it was felt enough damage had been done.

Once back in Scapa there was a wardroom party. A rather good one.

# **Chapter 29**

'Well if nothing else, it beats the hell out of Scapa Flow,' Tom said to John as they stood on the flight deck after the ship had come to anchor in the wide bay of Trincomalee in Ceylon.

'Yes, it's certainly warmer but just as crowded,' John replied as they looked out over the massive bay which was crammed with ships including four more carriers and several battleships including the King George V, their flagship. There were also numerous escorts and merchantmen. 'It's been a naval base since the start of the war once Singapore was lost and the RAF have a big airfield just inland.'

It was over seven months since the attack on the Tirpitz and they were late. The ship had stayed in Scapa for some time while further attacks were contemplated but they were never called upon and eventually, the RAF sank the massive ship with their new Tall Boy bombs. Shortly afterwards they were ordered to the Far East. The leave they were all granted was far too short and they were soon on their way, only to reach Gibraltar and break down. The ship was now far more crowded. In addition to John's Hellcats, the Barracudas had been replaced with two squadrons of the new American Avenger bombers and they also had a squadron of Seafires for local area defence. The naval policy of being able to get all aircraft below deck was a thing of the past and the ship now had a permanent deck park. Keeping so many aircrew and maintainers busy had not been easy whilst at anchor but finally, the ship was repaired and headed across the Mediterranean to Suez. For John the change was considerable. In nineteen forty two, the Med had been a contested sea, with the Italian fleet always a threat and the Germans occupying swathes of North Africa. Now it was quiet and reasonably safe. They stopped off in Alexandria and John had been able to introduce his colleagues into the fleshpots he remembered so well from before in forty two. Nothing seemed to have changed except for the lack of a threat from the air which had always been there before.

The transit through Suez and across the Arabian Sea had been quiet and provided an excellent opportunity to practice air operations. With such a crowded deck and hangar, the deck crews had to be absolutely on top of their game to move aircraft in incredibly confined spaces at the right times. Finally, they arrived in Ceylon and were all wondering what exactly was going to come next.

Just then Simon Peters came up to them. 'Unfortunately, the RAF field is full,' he said. 'So you are going to have to disembark to the old race course which has been jury rigged with metal sheeting for a runway and live in some temporary accommodation.'

'For how long Sir?' Tom asked.

'That depends.' Simon replied. There is a massive effort going on in Australia at the moment to set up facilities to support us and I suspect we'll be going there first before getting stuck into whatever the Admirals want us to do but for the moment we are just consolidating here and getting the ships stored and ready which is why you are going ashore.'

'So no idea how long we will be away from the ship then? John asked.

'Hopefully not too long. Being delayed in Gib didn't help so we are late as you know. But you're going to have to work pretty hard now. Apart from getting acclimatised, you will all need some jungle survival training as well as brushing up on your knowledge of the Japanese Air force. Don't worry you won't get bored. But actually I've come to say goodbye. I've been posted to Australia to help with the massive effort going on there. The whole fighter wing is going to be commanded by Major Ronnie Hay Royal Marines, I believe you know him John?'

John didn't answer for a second. 'Oh goodness and there was me attempting to make sure my pilots behave. He's not the best example in that regard. Mind you he's a bloody good pilot. He was a friend of my last CO who was also a Royal.'

'Well don't worry too much, he will be based on Formidable and so most of the time you meet him will be in the air. His job will be to command strikes from above, coordinating the attack as things develop. It's a new idea but seems to make a great deal of sense to many of us including Admiral Vian who will be commanding the First Carrier Squadron which you will be part of. And on that note, the Admiral is a force of nature himself but hopefully one for good. Now will you excuse us Tom but I need a word in private with John.'

The two men left the flight deck and went below to Simon's cabin. 'Another development John.' Simon said as they sat down. 'As we now have four squadrons on board and we've got rid of the Barracudas and have the American Avengers instead we need to nominate someone to be the senior aviator. That's going to be you.'

'But I'm pretty sure one of the Avenger COs is senior to me Sir,' John said.

'Maybe in years in the rank but nowhere near in terms of aviation experience. We can't afford to be pedantic about military protocol here. The job will primarily to be the Captain's aviation advisor along with Wings. And then, if the ship conducts a solo operation you will have a similar role to Major Hay and coordinate the mission from the air. And just so you know as of tomorrow the twenty second of November, the British Fleet formally comes into existence so best of luck.'

Two weeks later and John wasn't worried about luck. There were too many other things to worry about like lousy food, inadequate shelter and an incredible number of bugs, mosquitoes and other local wildlife that all seemed hell bent on biting or stinging them. If you didn't check your flying kit in the morning there was a very good chance you would be flying with an uninvited guest or sometimes even more. They had been operating a tropical routine since coming ashore which meant an early rise and a secure from flying by eleven to avoid the worst of the tropical sun. This left the afternoon available to hide away from the sun and then get ready for an evening in Colombo.

John and Tom were sitting in his so-called office, just another palm roofed shack like the accommodation but it at least allowed them some privacy.

'Who was the clot who landed with his hook down this morning' John asked. 'It made enough noise to wake the dead. Sean says the runway will be unusable for a least a day while they put all the metal sheets back.'

'Not one of ours thankfully,' Tom replied. 'But I believe the miscreant will be helping the sappers rebuild it rather than going into town tonight. And talking of which, I believe it's Hamish's Birthday party tonight at the Galle Face Hotel. I take it you're coming?'

'Wouldn't miss it for the world,' John replied. 'He can throw his midshipman's patches away now and put up his first stripe as well.'

'Yes, he has the uniform all ready.'

'Good, well I'm going to attempt some shut eye despite this heat. Some bloody awful insect kept banging into my mosquito net all night.'

That evening, all the pilots met up at their regular haunt, the hotel in the town and toasted Hamish before sitting down to dinner. Afterwards, it was suggested they all head out to the Silver Fawn nightclub or as it was more normally called, the 'Silver Prawn'. Not surprisingly many of his chaps had already made attachments with some of the girls from the naval base and by midnight the party was in full swing. At one point between formal acts, Neville had been coerced to play the piano. He sang a wonderful song about Little Angeline which actually started off quite innocuous and by the time it got to the end was extremely rude and extremely funny.

'How the hell does he get away with it?' Sean asked John as they sat at a table.

'No idea,' John replied. 'It must be the look of innocence on his face and then when you've digested exactly what he's just said it's too late and he's moved on to something even more disgusting.'

Just then the twins came up with two very pretty girls on their arms. 'Can we join you Sir? This is Mabel and this is Lucy.'

John moved over and the four of them sat down. The girls were very chatty and affectionate to everyone but the twins didn't seem to mind at all. At one point both girls dragged John onto the dance floor. Despite the amount he had had to drink and the lithe frame of the ladies who seemed more than happy to mould themselves to him, he really wasn't in that frame of mind. The girls soon got the message. He suspected that as a Squadron CO, he was a target and some sort of challenge was in the air as they both looked a little put out. Not that he wasn't tempted and when at the end of the evening there was a suggestion to go skinny dipping he was sorely tempted. All he could hope for was that they got back on board and on their way soon before he succumbed to the wildlife, both the insect and female variety.

# Chapter 30

John's wish was granted soon after Christmas. They and all the other squadrons were ordered to re-embark and on the sixteenth of January, Task Force 63, the largest force ever assembled by the Royal Navy sailed out of Trincomalee for Australia. What they didn't know at the time was that there was going to be a diversion on the way. As soon as they were at sea they were all called to a major briefing.

As the aircrew crammed themselves into the operations room they could see a map of a large island. 'Sumatra,' someone muttered. 'What the hell are we going to do there?'

He didn't get an answer as the Captain appeared along with Wings and they all stood to attention until he waved them to be seated.

'Gentlemen, Admiral Nimitz has kindly requested that, as we have to sail past Sumatra to get to Australia, would we kindly pop over to the eastern side and do some damage to two rather large oil refineries just south of the town of Palembang,' he pointed to an area on the map, near the bottom of the long island. 'These two refineries are reported to produce seventy five per cent of the aviation fuel used by the Japanese in this part of the world. The Americans tried a high level bomber raid last year but with little success. We have agreed to do this for several reasons, not the least because it will show the Americans what we can do and that we are a force to be reckoned with. It won't be easy, these refineries are well protected with anti-aircraft guns and there are at least three airfields close by with fighters ready to repel any attack. Now I know some of you were on Operation Tungsten last year when we attacked the Tirpitz. We were incredibly lucky that time. There was no air opposition and we caught them with their trousers down. Don't expect to be that lucky this time. I'm going to hand over to Commander (Air) now who will give you some more detail. Good luck.'

So saying he left the room and they all stood again.

Wings took the stage. 'So that's the outline chaps. To give you some more details, we have been working up plans of attack for some time now. The first attack will be on the biggest refinery and called Operation Meridian One. Before the main force goes in, the three airfields will be attacked by the Corsairs from the other ships. Low level ground attack raids and will be known as Ramrods. Then our and the other ship's Avengers will go in using five hundred pound bombs to selected targets. Our Hellcats and those from other ships will escort and protect them. There will also be a squadron of Fireflies that have the job of attacking specific targets around the refineries. Seafires and some Hellcats will remain over the fleet for our protection. We understand that the Palembang airfields are used as training centres so we can expect at least some of their pilots to be experienced. So it's important that the Ramrods are successful. I won't go into detail now, that will follow on but we will have picket ships and submarines stationed off the coast ready to help aircraft in trouble on the way back. Your routing in and out will be carefully planned to ensure that we know it's you returning and not the enemy. We have five days to get up to speed and much to learn so let's get to it.'

Five days later you could cut the tension in the ship with a knife. They had all attended briefings on the targets, on the likely enemy aircraft they would encounter and more lectures on jungle survival. There was no doubt in anyone's mind that this was going to be a difficult and dangerous operation.

They had all been called early and then almost immediately stood down. The weather was foul with mist and low cloud. They would need to transit most of the island from the west coast where they were to the target on the eastern side. There was a low ridge of mountains just inland which they would have to fly over but not in this weather.

John was sitting the wardroom chatting to some of his pilots.

'This sitting around is not good Boss,' Hamish said. 'The Met man reckons it's going to take two days to clear.'

Just then, Sean came over and plonked himself down. 'There's talk of a deck hockey tournament this afternoon chaps. I think we should put in a squadron team.'

'That's fine,' John said. 'But any pilot who damages himself will earn my wrath. I've seen how vicious they can become, especially if you end up playing the stoker's mess.'

'Wardroom movie this afternoon as well,' Tom said. 'And no doubt that illegal poker school I know nothing about will be up and running.'

'I didn't hear that Senior Pilot,' John said. 'But count me in.'

The day passed in a sort of tense limbo for all of them and the same happened the next day but towards dusk, the weather was seen to be clearing as predicted. So early the next morning at two o'clock they were all called for a final briefing ready for a dawn launch.

John stood at the front of his ready room and looked at his pilots. 'Jesus Christ you lot. What sort of war do you think you are in?'

Nearly all of the pilots were sporting knives and in one case a massive machete, as well as pistols. John knew that most also had large quantities of gold coins sewn into various parts of their clothing as well as paper chits written in the local language promising rewards if they returned the person safely. He knew that because he had exactly the same things in his overalls. The stories of what the Japanese would do to you if you were caught had clearly been well understood. In reality, none of these preparations were likely to be of much use but it was clearly good for morale if nothing else. He also noted several pilots with odd looking trinkets, lucky charms that some of them always flew with. He knew that one of his pilot's aircraft was permanently occupied by a rather scruffy Teddy Bear. Apparently, the engineers took as much care of him as his owner. Silly it might seem but none of this mattered if it kept them focused.

'Don't answer that question,' he said with a smile. 'I think we do know what sort of war is coming. Now you've heard the Met man's lies, you've been briefed to death. All I want to say is remember the brief, stick in your flights and do the job we are there to do. Good Luck everyone.'

The pilots dispersed to get their Mae West life jackets and flying helmets as well as a final visit to the heads, something John was keen to do. As he stood at the urinal, Tom came and stood alongside doing the same thing.

'Here we go again Boss and the real thing this time,' he said.

'At least we are not doing the bombing Tom,' John said. 'The chaps in the Avengers are going to have the worst of it.'

'Not sure the Ramrods will be that much fun either,' Tom replied. 'It will depend on how well defended the airfields are and this delay due to weather hasn't helped. I'm pretty sure they'll be expecting something.'

Tom's words echoed in John's head as he climbed into his Hellcat and did up his straps. This raid was going to be an order of magnitude more testing than anything they had done before. The Swordfish raid on Taranto had been a great success but that was at night. And achieved complete surprise. This was going to be nothing like that. Then it was time to start up and put his doubts to one side, there was a job to do.

# Chapter 31

The drone of his engine was quite soporific and despite the tension he felt, John was having to fight to keep his eyelids open. Sleep had been hard to come by in recent days and when it did he nearly always had dreams that left him sweaty and with a weird sense of doom and anger. He couldn't remember them when he woke up. There was just the aftertaste of something not right. He was also missing Heather. They had been writing regularly and at least he knew she was relatively safe but she was now thousands of miles away. He was even having trouble remembering her face and had to go through the photos he had brought with him to keep her properly in mind.

'Corsairs low,' someone called on the radio. John looked down. Below were the flight of Avengers they were escorting and under them, he could see a large flight of Corsairs going much faster and overtaking them all. It must be the Ramrod team, something must have delayed their departure. He just hoped they got to their targets on time.

The weather was as good as the Met man had promised and they had no trouble clearing the hills and then it was the long flog across the low lands towards their target. The terrain looked really unhospitable, just miles of rain forest, definitely not the place to try and crash land or walk out of, for that matter. Keeping well above the bombers, the Hellcats were weaving, partly to keep their speed down as the Avengers could only manage one hundred and eighty but also to keep an eye out for fighters. The Japs had two land based machines they might expect to encounter, the lightly armed and fragile Oscar or the more rugged and better armed Tojo. On paper neither should cause much of a problem to the modern fighters they were flying but the Japs would not be trying to mix it with them, they would be going for the bombers.

As seemed common in aerial fighting, one moment nothing was happening the next all hell broke loose. For some time John had seen the refinery they were heading for. It was situated next to a river and easily identifiable. Then the sky above it seemed to turn white as anti-aircraft fire suddenly started. That must be for the wave of bombers ahead of them he realised. Chatter on the radio started and it was hard to make out much of what was being said but one word he heard clearly was 'balloons' and indeed there they were rising like bubbles from the ground all around the refinery. They had not been mentioned in the intelligence briefs and were going to cause the Avengers real trouble. They would either have to bomb from above and lose accuracy or dive down through the cables.

He saw bombs start to explode at the refinery and soon tall flames were licking up from various buildings. Suddenly, someone yelled 'Bandits ten o'clock' on the radio. John immediately saw them and that they were still quite far away but heading towards the Avengers pulling up from their dives as the ones he was escorting started their attack. Then the radio went mad with all sorts of calls and shouts. Ronnie Hay was not going to be directing anything with all this noise. It seemed as if everyone had forgotten their training at once. It got worse. Suddenly, Hellcats were engaging the Japanese fighters and a massive dog fight started. The problem was that no one except perhaps himself was watching out for their bombers. Sure enough, several more Jap fighters appeared from cloud on the right hand side and were much more of a danger. John desperately tried to get a word in edgewise on the radio but to no avail. He looked over and saw that at least Neville had stayed with him. He pointed to the other Jap aircraft and slammed the throttle fully open. There were only five of the machines which John recognised as Oscars. It should have been a turkey shoot if there had been more of his squadron with him. Whoever was flying the one he latched on to was a rooky. He easily closed into a few hundred yards and gave Jap a few seconds of fire. The Oscar simply exploded in a ball of flame. Out of the corner of his eye, he saw Neville despatch another in a similar fashion. Unfortunately, the other three pressed on and by the time they caught them up one Avenger was already going down in flames. In desperation, he opened fire from what felt like too far away and was amazed to see the Oscar blow up like its predecessor. The final two turned away and used their superior manoeuvrability to escape. It would have been easy to bag them but that was not his job. He let them go, to give the Avengers who were now streaming home some cover. The Avenger formations were all well split up now but he found a group of six and stuck with them. Once was trailing smoke but seemed to be able to keep flying. Nearly all of them had signs of damage of one sort or another.

Suddenly, he recognised Ronnie Hay's voice on the radio. 'All fighters break off and escort the bombers back. Do your bloody job.'

It didn't make any difference, the Hellcats and Corsairs were now spread out far too much to be able to produce a cohesive defence for the transit home. Looking around John could see aircraft straggling back all over the place. It seemed to take forever to reach the mountains and then the coast. Just as they crossed the coastline the Avenger that was smoking gave up the fight and glided down to the sea with its propeller stopped. He saw it hit with a splash but stay afloat. Hopefully one of the rescue submarines would be able to get to them. Then the fleet came into sight. He stayed clear of Invincible while the Avengers landed on. At least two of them took the barrier. Most of his squadron had appeared now and he let them go ahead and land before him. Then it was his turn. After landing as he taxied forward he could see the state of some of the aircraft. The engineers were going to be busy tonight. Keeping his feelings to himself, he went down to the ready room where his pilots had gathered. The room was full of excited chatter as they exchanged stories. All of them were on the adrenalin high of a successful operation and happy to be alive. He was going to make them wish they weren't.

He stalked to the front of the room and rapped on the wall to gain their attention. Smiling faces turned towards him.

'What was the mission brief?' He asked the room.

Puzzled expressions met his words.

'What was the job we were sent to do?'

'Attack the enemy Boss,' someone said.

'No, it bloody well wasn't. That was the job of the bombers. What were we there to do?'

'Escort the bombers,' another voice said.

'Exactly so what the hell were you lot doing chasing enemy fighters that were nowhere near the bombers? What the hell were you doing shouting at each other over the radio so no one could actually use it? Where the hell were you when other fighters attacked from the other side, much closer and shot down at least one of our comrades? Only Neville and I were there because you lot had buggered off glory hunting. You should all be bloody ashamed of yourselves. All the training you've had all the times we've practiced this and at the first encounter with the enemy you forget it all and act like fucking idiots.'

John could see his words strike home. He had never used profanity like that before and everyone clearly realised just how angry he was.

Silence greeted his words. 'Right I'm so bloody upset with you fools that I'm not going to say anything more. Get to the operations room and make your reports. We will reconvene here this afternoon and we are going to go through the whole operation and you are going to learn how to do your job properly. Any questions?'

Strangely there were none.

# Chapter 32

As soon as John had given his own operations report he went down to the hangar, he had an idea in mind. Ops had told him that his squadron was not on standby for the moment as the Seafires were being used for fleet defence. As he went through the airlock doors it was like entering Dante's inferno. The lifts were up sealing the hangar against any enemy attack which was quite possible. The temperature had him sweating immediately. Even so, he was keen to know the state of his aircraft.

He found Sean in his office to one side of the hangar. 'How are they Sean?' he asked.

'Your pilots or the aircraft?' Sean answered with a smile. 'I hear you gave them a right chewing out.'

'Good God, the grapevine works fast but no, the aircraft. Any significant damage?'

One machine has some bullet holes in the tail and a few flak splinters but that's about it. The Hellcat is built like a brick shithouse thank goodness. I'm not so sure about the Avengers though. I've got half my chaps working with them, they've got a lot of repairs to do.'

'So our machines are just about ready to go then?'

'Apart from one having an engine change but you already knew about that. You know I will give you a serviceability report as soon as I have it. I have a suspicion you have something else in mind.'

'Yes' John said. 'I did notice that some of them are looking a bit shabby and could do with a good clean. You know a good scrubbing, get the paintwork nice and shiny again. I'm sure the Japs would appreciate being shot down by well presented aircraft.'

'I haven't got the manpower for that Sir,' Sean said and then stopped as the penny dropped. 'How long can I have them for?'

'We've got a full mission debrief after lunch and then you can have them from about three o'clock, say for about three hours. Make sure they do a good job.'

Sean gave an evil grin. 'Leave it to me Sir.'

'Was I too hard on them?' John asked Tom that evening in the bar. 'It was their first real operation after all.'

'Frankly no and I think the same conversation was had in the other carriers.' Tom replied. 'I expect Ronnie Hay has been having words as well. You heard him on the radio towards the end. And look I'm sorry I went with them, I was trying to get them to turn around but then got bounced myself and you know what combat is like. One moment it's mayhem and the next everyone has disappeared. Got the bastard though, they do seem very vulnerable.'

'And not flown by anyone with any skill either,' John replied. 'And did they enjoy their time in the hangar?'

'You know, strangely, I actually think they did and the engineers seemed to appreciate it as well. We should do it more often if time permits and as a bonus have the shiniest aircraft in the fleet.'

'Right then, time to mend some fences I think.' So saying he went over to his huddle of pilots who for some reason were avoiding him.

Before he could speak, Hamish stood up. 'Sorry Boss, it won't happen again.' The other pilots all nodded.

'Good, then it's now officially water under the bridge, lesson learnt and all that. So who's shout is it?'

Five days later they were told they were going to have to do it all again against the second refinery, Operation Meridian Two. The air of trepidation in the ship was palpable, especially amongst the Avenger crews. But John knew his pilots had been extremely lucky last time, they were one of the few squadrons not to lose anyone. He knew the odds against that happening a second time were slim. He didn't say anything to his chaps, he didn't need to, they knew how many hadn't returned last time. And of course, this time, the Japs would be well warned, especially if any of the downed aircrew had been captured and revealed their intentions.

So once again they got airborne as the sun was rising. The plan hadn't changed, they would escort the bombers and the Corsairs would go in to try and take out the enemy on the ground. They knew now that the Japs would have a massive balloon barrage again but it had been decided on high not to spare any aircraft to try and go in ahead and shoot down as many as possible. There weren't enough fighters for the job if they wanted to provide air cover as well. The

Avenger crews were far from happy but as usual hard decisions had to be made and the balloons hadn't been that effective last time.

It was all so similar to the previous operation. The sky above the refinery became full of flak as the balloons rose and the waves of Avengers dived down. The air filled with chatter although it was clearly more disciplined. Enemy aircraft were soon seen but none of John's squadron jumped the leash. He was watching a flight of at least eight enemy who probably thought they hadn't been seen as they were coming directly down sun towards them. They were well above as well but John wasn't too worried. His job was to keep them away from the bombers that was all. Once again he was proved wrong. As the enemy started to dive down towards the bombers he realised that these were Tojos, potentially far more dangerous than the Oscars and at least one pilot knew what he was doing.

Warning his crew of the danger, they held formation until they were in a position to intercept and then it was the usual chaos of combat. John picked the lead aircraft and managed a long range deflection shot which didn't cause any damage but certainly caught the pilot's attention who now had a decision to make. Should he carry on towards the attacking British bombers or turn to face his attacker? He turned and tried to carry out a head on attack. John wasn't playing that game and pulled up hard and rolled over expecting to be on the Tojo's tail. He wasn't there. The Tojo had immediately turned away and was heading towards the bombers again. John realised that this chap knew what he was doing.

Slamming the throttle to its stop John dived down towards the enemy who had already started to engage an Avenger. He was about to open fire when he felt the Hellcat shudder. Shit, there was someone on his tail. However, he had his priorities and opened fire on the Tojo ahead of him. Once again the Japanese aircraft stayed true to form and blew up in spectacular fashion. It seemed the Tojo was no better protected than any Japanese fighter. Immediately he threw the Hellcat into a tight climbing turn looking desperately behind him to see who was attacking. He caught sight of the nose of another Tojo but it was falling behind as his superior speed left it standing. He quickly glanced at his gauges, they all seemed fine and the aircraft felt normal.

Where was Neville?  Unsurprisingly, they had become separated, he looked around trying to see any fighters and like many combats, the sky that one moment had been full of whirling machines now seemed empty.  Glancing over at the target it was clear that the raid was over and he could just see Avengers straggling back so he headed their way to give what cover he could.  He didn't get that far.  With a sudden bang, his engine started to run roughly.  He quickly scanned the gauges and all seemed nominal.  He peered along the nose of the aircraft and immediately saw something.  The engine cowling looked distorted and a trickle of oil was starting to stream back towards him.  It would seem that he hadn't escaped unscathed from the earlier attack after all.  Looking forwards the coastal hills seemed a long way away.  Below was just endless rainforest, he would just have to hope that the Hellcat's legendary robustness was true.  He adjusted the engine controls and throttled back but also tried to get the aircraft to climb, height was now his friend.  For what seemed like an endless period the shuddering fighter flew on and then he was clear of the hills and could see the sea.  At least now he had a chance to ditch and be picked up.  Then another Hellcat appeared on his wing.  Somehow Neville had found him'

'Looking rough Boss,' Neville called on the radio. 'I'll follow you.'

'Thanks, old chap,' John said knowing that if he had to ditch at least someone would report his position.'

'But I'm very low on fuel,' Neville said. 'So I can't hang around.'

'Understood.'  And then John looked at his fuel gauges carefully and realised he was going to find it tight as well.  He realised that many of the returning aircraft were going to have the same problem.  Getting onto a deck, any deck would be interesting if everyone needed them at the same time.

Soon, the fleet came into sight.  John called his ship but it was clear he wasn't the only one in trouble.  Then his decision was made for him.  With another almighty bang, the engine simply stopped.  He was now in a very heavy glider.  Looking around he could see a destroyer not too far away and turned towards it.  The Hellcat was meant to be a good ditching aircraft now he was going to find out.  He had enough hydraulics left to lower the flaps and then he was levelling off a few feet above the sea which was suddenly rushing past his wings. He kept slowly pulling up the nose and the speed washed off until with the stick almost back in his stomach the Hellcat stopped being a creature of the air and dropped the last few feet into the water with an almighty splash and shudder. The windscreen was covered in spray and he was thrown violently forward in his straps. Then suddenly it was quiet. The aircraft was stationary and didn't even seem to be sinking. Quickly undoing his straps, he slid the hood open and clambered out onto the wing. He couldn't help but remember the last time he had to get out of a ditched aircraft, this time it seemed almost laughingly easy. He didn't even get wet.

Then a voice called out to him. He saw a ship's boat approaching with an officer at the stern. 'I say old chap do you need a lift?'

# Chapter 33

The Captain of the destroyer HMS Fawn welcomed John onto the bridge. 'Busy morning it seems, are you alright? Did the doc check you over?'

'Yes Sir, I'm fine. I'm John Hunt CO of my squadron and yes the Hellcat seems to like the water.'

The captain laughed. He was a tall fair haired naval commander. 'Well welcome on board. You chaps seem to have been having a busy time. You're not the only one who's taken to the drink I'm afraid.'

'I'm not surprised Sir, we had a long way to go and many are very low on fuel. Any idea how long before I can get over to my ship, as the squadron CO I really need to find out how my chaps got on.'

Before the captain could answer a voice called up from below. 'Bridge radar room we have a raid coming in, seems the Japs have found us at last.'

John decided it would be a good time to make himself scarce. However, the captain saw him moving towards the bridge ladder and called him back.

'Please stay, I would value your airman's thoughts,' he said.

Just then another voice called over a set of orders from somewhere and the captain ordered a change of course and an increase in speed. Soon the whole fleet had turned west away from the coast and the incoming raid. It was quite a sight with the battleship KGV and the carriers starting to throw up massive bow waves along with the escorts. John found it immensely exhilarating.

'Radar reports the raid is splitting up Sir. It's not a coordinated attack they all seem to be heading towards different ships.'

The captain turned to John and raised an eyebrow.

'Looks like we are going to encounter Kamikazes Sir,' John said.

'I agree,' the captain said. 'This is going to be interesting.'

That was a massive understatement. The enemy aircraft were soon seen.

'They're Helens and Sally's sir. Heavy bombers.'

He wasn't answered because the fleet opened fire. Even with the ships spread out, the effect was awesome. Fast firing anti-aircraft guns, medium calibre guns from the escorts and carriers themselves. The twin turrets on the front of the ship opened up as well as the smaller Oerlikons on either side of the bridge. John could barely hear himself think. The sky was full of tracers and bursting shells. They could see aircraft. Seafires were chasing some of the bombers and then some Hellcats joined in. John admired their bravery as flying into a maelstrom of fire was really dangerous, the chances of being taken out by friendly fire were very high. Two of the Sally bombers were shot down immediately but John saw another one making for the stern of Illustrious and then at the last moment it dived into the sea with an enormous splash.

Someone started shouting and pointing to starboard. A bomber was approaching but clearly intent on the Invincible on the other side of them. As it approached, they saw a Hellcat on its tail who fired from close range and the Helen reared up and then crashed into the sea only yards behind them. John suddenly realised that one of the Oerlikons was still firing and targeting the Hellcat. The gunner must have been completely carried away.

'Sir, can you stop that gunner,' he yelled into the captain's ear. 'He's firing on one of ours.'

The captain didn't hesitate and leant over the edge of the bridge and cuffed the back of the steel helmet of the gunner who looked back in surprise. 'Stop firing at our aircraft you blithering idiot,' he yelled.

The sailor looked confused for a second and then clearly the penny dropped and he swung his gun away and started searching the sky elsewhere. A few seconds later, the Hellcat roared overhead before pulling up into a climb. John wondered just how many of the defending aircraft had been hit. There was clearly a need for better training for the fleet's gunners in aircraft recognition and discipline.

And then it was over. The guns fell silent and there were no more enemy machines in sight. 'Radar reports clear Sir,' a voice said.

'Well, I said that would be interesting and I wasn't wrong,' the captain said with a boyish grin. 'Why do I think we're going to be doing that quite often in the future?'

'I agree sir, we just need to make sure the chaps on the end of the guns can tell friend from foe.'

'Oh don't worry about that John, Able Seaman Jenks and all my gunners are going to have some serious training over the next few days. Now, why don't you go and stand down in the wardroom until I can arrange a transfer for you. It might not be for a while I'm afraid but I'm sure my officers will know how to look after you.'

It wasn't until the evening that John was taken over to the Invincible in a sea boat and then had the fun of a hazardous climb up the towering ship's side using a rope ladder. The amount of scotch he had been given in the destroyer's wardroom didn't help but somehow he made it up and was immediately pounced upon by the ship's doctor. It didn't take much to convince the doc that he was absolutely fine if rather tipsy and he was allowed on his way.

The atmosphere in the wardroom was very strange. The place was crowded as it often was at night and everyone seemed to be drinking but in almost total silence this time. Wings must have seen him as he came in and made his way over.

'Welcome back John, we had a signal to say you had been picked up,' he said but John could see there was far more he wanted to say.

'How many and who Sir?'

'Three Avenger crews and two of yours I'm afraid.'

John didn't answer.

'It was Johny Preston and Brian Steel. We don't actually know what happened to Johny he just disappeared. No one saw him crash or get shot down so he may be alive but if so he's almost certainly on the ground.'

They both knew what that meant. 'And Brian Sir?'

'Pranged on the refinery site, your Senior Pilot saw it. No chance I'm afraid.'

'Thank you Sir I'd better go and see my chaps.'

John went over to one corner of the wardroom where all his pilots were sitting, drinking and like everyone else, almost completely silent.

'Welcome back Boss,' Tom said as he came over. 'We heard you went for a swim.'

'I hardly even got my feet wet, the Hellcat is a good floater. Chins up chaps, next stop Sydney.'

Neville looked up at John. 'Forty one aircraft and over thirty of us killed or missing that's just over ten per cent of the whole force and in only two strikes. What the hell was it for Sir?'

John needed to nip this in the bud and quickly. 'Look everyone, I'm as gutted about Johny and Brian as much as you but this is war and it's not going to get any easier. I can't tell you that this sort of thing won't happen again because it will. I can't tell you that you will get used to it because you won't. What I can tell you is that it's necessary and it's what you signed up for.'

He could see that Neville was about to speak again and cut him off.

'What was this all about? It was to attack the enemy and deny him his refineries and it seems we did a damn good job if the destruction I saw was anything to go by. But it was also more than that. This is a new type of warfare for all of us and we're doing it with new machines against a new enemy. One way or another we will have to learn how to fight out here and these raids have taught us an immeasurable amount and I don't just mean us pilots. Everyone from the Admiral downwards right down to the chaps firing the guns is better for what we've done. Now I suggest we all get royally tight and remember our fallen friends and tomorrow we wake up and get on with it.'

John suddenly realised that the whole wardroom had gone quiet. They all must have heard what he had said. Wings came over with a large scotch and handed it to John. 'Well said old chap.'

# Chapter 34

'Good God, has the whole of Sydney come out to meet us?' John exclaimed as he looked at the thousands of people lining the shore. Most of them were waving Union flags and cheering as the fleet entered the harbour to drop anchor.

'Seems we are more popular with the people than their government,' Tom said. 'I've heard that they put up some resistance to us using their little island as a base.'

'Yes but they've come round now I believe. This is just what we all need now, a bit of a break and a chance to unwind. Who knows when we will be heading north again.'

'It won't be long I'm sure,' Tom said. 'The Yanks seem to be making good progress and I know our political masters will want us involved well before the end.'

'So let's make the most of it while we can.'

They were going to stay on board for the first week and then fly ashore to one of the new airfields that were being rapidly constructed around the area. As they made their way back to the wardroom after the ship was secured at anchor they met Neville heading the same way.

'Are you going to the briefing this evening Sirs? He asked in an enthusiastic tone.

'Don't think so Neville what's it all about?' John asked.

'Apparently, the First Lieutenant has been here before. He's going to give us a talk about Australian social etiquette and how to be attractive to their women.'

John and Tom exchange amused glances. 'I'll leave that sort of thing to you and the rest of the chaps. Married man remember?' John said.

When Neville had bounced away Tom turned to John. 'It's amazing what the prospect of a run ashore and a bit of misbehaviour is doing to morale, don't you think?'

'Yes it's nice to see them bouncing back. Mind you it would be interesting to see how many of them fall for that old trick.'

Tom chuckled. 'It's one the navy seems good at, we've all fallen for a wind up at some time.'

Three days later and John was sitting in a deck chair, on a beach, in the sunshine and sipping a cold beer. The contrast to the last few weeks and months couldn't have been more stark. The ship had hosted a cocktail party the second day in harbour and John had been invited to spend the weekend with a lovely Australian couple, Dick and Joanna Anderson at their home on the beach. They had come to Australia in the twenties from Britain and like many John had met already, never quite seemed to have left it completely behind. Dick ran an engineering firm and seemed to be doing very well out of the massive investment being made in the country to set up the supply bases for the fleet. He had been made incredibly welcome, his hosts clearly felt they had to try and support the effort against the Japanese and the story of the oil refinery raids had somehow reached Australia before the fleet. However, John was glad that apart from a brief mention of the operation nothing more was said. He wasn't sure there was any way he could adequately explain how he felt about it or what it had been really like.

The previous night, they had had a wonderful dinner and John had managed to stay reasonably sober. Today, his hosts had told him they realised he needed some quiet time and suggested that he spend the day unwinding on the beach although they did warn him about going swimming on his own. Apparently, sharks were well known along this shore. The warning was enough to keep him in the shallows, purely to cool off when it got too hot.

Suddenly the view got immeasurably better. Tracy, the Anderson's twenty year old daughter, came into view. To say she was stunning was a gross understatement. She was wearing shorts that more than adequately highlighted her long slim legs and a halter top that would have probably got her arrested if she had worn it on an English beach. Long blonde hair framed a pert nose, large blue eyes and a slightly freckled face. John had been introduced the previous night but at least that time she had been fully dressed.

Completely oblivious to the effect she was having on him, she sat down on the sand and reached over to take one of his beers.

'Do you mind?' She asked. 'Dad gets funny about me drinking beer from a can, apparently it's not lady like.'

'Please help yourself,' John said smiling. 'Where are they by the way?'

'Oh, Dad asked me to come and tell you they've had to go out. Some crisis at the works and mum has gone with him. So it's just you and me.' The last remark was accompanied by a mischievous grin. 'I'm to make you lunch in a minute and look after you until they get back.'

'I can think of worse ways to spend the day,' John said grinning back and finding it very hard not to be totally entranced by this lovely young girl.

She took a swig of her beer. 'Has it been horrible? The war I mean.'

'That's a very difficult question to answer,' he said. 'Of course it's horrible but we didn't start it and we had to defend ourselves just as you lot would have done if the Japanese had landed in Australia. But I've lost more friends than I care to count and as you might just have noticed I even managed to lose my foot.' John had taken his prosthetic off to give the stump some air.

'So tell me how did that happen?' Tracy asked.

John gave her the abbreviated version but that led to her asking about his other experiences and he found that talking to someone with no concept of what the last few years had been like was almost cathartic. She listened to every word in rapt attention and whenever he started to dry up asked a clever question that got him going again.

After a while, he stopped. 'Goodness Tracy you now know more about my career than my wife.'

Her expression wavered for a moment. 'Yes but she's eight thousand miles away. Do you miss her?'

'Every moment. It's not that she isn't as good looking as you because she is.' That raised another smile. 'But we've known each other since we were kids and what's worse I have a sneaking suspicion she's a better pilot than me.'

'What? She flies? Tell me how she can do that.'

Half an hour later and Tracy knew all about Heather. 'I am so jealous John,' she said. 'Girls aren't allowed to do anything like that here. Maybe I should come and visit when the war is over.'

'I strongly suspect that once it is all over so will the opportunity for girls to fly professionally. The same happened after the last war you know. Not pilots but many men's jobs were filled by women but as soon as it was over they were back to being house wives and mothers. But who knows, I suspect many things are going to change this time. I suppose time will tell. Now, what about that lunch you promised?'

They both went inside and Tracy made some sandwiches. 'What do you want to do this afternoon John?' Tracy asked.

'Well I think I've had enough sun, I'm starting to look rather pink in places. What do you suggest?'

'Well Dad has his old sports car in the garage, how about we go for a drive and I show you the sights?'

'Now that sounds like a great idea. You can show me some Kangaroos and Koalas.'

She laughed but agreed that they might be able to find some. It was a wonderful afternoon and about as far away from the war as John could get. Tracy drove like the wind but the roads were quiet and John only had to grab onto his seat and try for the imaginary brake pedal a couple of times. They went along the coast for a while and then back into the city so she could show him the famous bridge and he could see the fleet anchored in the bay outside. Seeing all the grey and worn ships from the vantage of the bridge made such a contrast. He wondered if they would ever really escape the war, it had been going on for so long. He didn't say anything to Tracy.

When they got back, so were Dick and Joanna and more beer was offered followed by a leisurely meal outside. Dick had made an outside grill which he said they used nearly all year round. It certainly gave the food a unique taste.

'So what did you two get up today?' Joanna asked.

'I got sunburn on the beach and then your daughter tried to scare me to death in that old Riley,' John said before Tracy could say anything. 'And it was one of the most lovely days I've had for months as has the whole time you've all looked after me. I can't thank you enough.'

'It's the least we can do. I know you have to go back to your ship tomorrow but you are welcome here any time,' Dick said. 'Tracy told me a little about what you've done since the war started. I can't imagine what you've been through but thank you all the same. Now I happen to have a rather nice bottle of scotch hidden away somewhere. I think we should give it a serious seeing to. What do you say?'

Much later, John made his way to his bedroom with just a little weaving in his step. He managed to put his clothes tidily on the chair before turning off the light, lying back in bed and staring at the ceiling. It was still very hot so he didn't bother with any bedclothes and as he hadn't packed any pyjamas he just let the night air cool his skin.

He was just letting his eyelids droop when he heard a noise. It was pretty dark so he couldn't actually see anything. Then there was the sensation of someone sliding onto the bed next to him. He turned to the side put out his hand to find out who it was and felt what was definitely a breast and nipple.

Tracy's voice whispered in his ear. 'She's eight thousand miles away but would I be an acceptable substitute for one night?'

# Chapter 35

John looked at the building in surprise. Dick had told him that the Kings Cross area of Sydney was looked upon as slightly disreputable, rather like Soho in London and this was clearly a car showroom. However, it was the place he had been told to report to and so he thanked Dick for everything and promised to keep in touch. Wearing uniform again felt slightly strange even after only three days in civvies. He went to the doors on one side of the showroom and there indeed was a sign on the door declaring that this was the headquarters of the British Fleet. Inside the stairs were quite wide and he could hear conversation and the clatter of typewriters floating down.

When he arrived at the top there was the obligatory third officer WRNS sitting behind a desk. She looked rather harried as she saw him approaching.

'Lieutenant Commander Hunt to see Commander Peters,' he said forestalling any questions.

'Down the hall there Sir.' She said pointing to the left. 'Third door on the right.'

Thanking the girl, he set off and knocked on the requisite door.

'Come,' he heard from inside so opened the door and went in. Simon Peters was sitting behind a very cluttered desk. John thought he looked tired but he smiled when he saw John.

'Come and sit down old chap, grab a seat,' he said and then went and put his head around the door and shouted something down the corridor.

When he came back he also sat down. 'So how are you John?' he asked. 'It seems that Sumatra raid was pretty rough.'

'Yes Sir, it was. I lost two of my men and had to ditch myself so that's another of His Majesty's fighters I've had to swim away from.'

Just then the door opened and a young Wren came in with a tray with two cups of tea and some biscuits. She put them down and left silently.

'Thank you Angela,' Simon said to her retreating back and then turned to John. 'It may have been a bit bloody but the Yanks were seriously impressed. It seems some of the American hierarchy want us here and some don't. Admiral King, the US Navy boss is no Anglophile but Nimitz who has his feet on the ground over here is the opposite. Sumatra has shown all of them that we mean business. The problem we are all facing now is getting everything set up here to support you lot thousands of miles away. You would not believe the effort and the cost. In some ways, I envy you as your job is straightforward. Anyway, I asked you to talk to me because one of the many hats they've given me to wear is that of officer's appointments. And I want to discuss your future career.'

Completely taken aback, John didn't know what to say.

'Look John, you've effectively been operational since nineteen forty with very little in the way of a break. You've got a DSC and a Bar after Operation Torch and also lost one of your feet into the bargain. I think it's time you stood back from ops and went home. People with your experience are getting very hard to come by and I feel you would be of far more use passing that on than just being another bum on a seat.'

'I rather think I'm a little more than that,' John said with a note of asperity.

'Sorry, you know I didn't mean it disparagingly,' Simon said. 'But there are others who could do your job now but very few who know what you do and we are going to need people like you when this war ends.'

'So you're relieving me of my command?' John asked. Inside he was at war with himself. The thought of going home, seeing Heather and finally standing back from the peril to come was incredibly tempting.

'No I'm not doing that, it's your choice but I would strongly urge you to consider the idea,' Simon said.

'There's nothing to consider Sir,' John said. 'I stood up my squadron from scratch, all my men, both pilots and engineers trust me and I trust them. We are about to go into a major operation. There's no way I would abandon them now. I'm not arrogant enough to think that I'm irreplaceable but in my experienced opinion,' he stressed the word 'experienced'. 'We have a better chance of being effective if we keep the team together at a critical time. Sorry Sir no way.'

Simon sighed. 'I had a bet with myself that you would say that John but I had to ask. Alright but you take care. It may not seem like it but this will all be over soon and the navy will need officers with your knowledge and experience in the years to come. Anyway, think it over, the offer will be good for a couple of weeks. You know where to find me.'

Realising it was time to go, John left but despite his firm response to Simon he was still in turmoil inside. The temptation was enormous but he knew deep inside that he was right. It wasn't too long a walk to the harbour where he could get a boat back to the ship. They were flying ashore that afternoon and he could lose himself in the routine of the squadron.

Four days later and they had settled in at the air station about thirty miles inland from the city. John and Tom had drawn up a programme of training flights. Two new pilots had also joined as replacements and John wanted to get them up to speed as soon as possible. Mike Turner a rather quiet sandy haired Irishman had flown Wildcats previously but had never experienced combat. Mark Simmons, a tall, red haired, Scot was straight from training but had very good reports. John had just finished a single combat sortie against Mark and had sent him back to the airfield. He was about to indulge in a few minutes of aerobatics when a Corsair appeared from nowhere and drew up alongside. There were several squadrons operating from the field but initially he didn't recognise the machine because it was painted dark blue with a white stripe and roundel. He knew that all the aircraft were going to be painted like that soon to make them look similar to the Americans. It was hoped it would reduce the chance of American pilots mistaking the British ones for the enemy. John wasn't convinced but it wouldn't hurt.

John looked over closely and suddenly realised he knew the pilot. Without warning, he pulled up sharply rolled hard and pulled the turn as tight as he could to try to get on the tail of the Corsair. However, the other pilot was having none of it. For fifteen minutes, the two aircraft tried to get on each other's tail but neither succeeded, then the Corsair did its party piece and used its superior speed to pull away. It only worked for a minute or so as they both had to descend from the fifteen thousand feet they had been at, to get back to the airfield. In a dive, the Hellcat could easily keep up with the Corsair. And so five minutes later the two machines joined up in formation and called to rejoin the airfield. Once given permission, they flew along the main runway flat out and quite low then broke hard left to slow down on the downwind leg before turning to land.

They taxied back to John's squadron and shut down. Both pilots jumped out and went to greet each other.

'Mister St John-Stevens,' John said with a wide grin. 'So you've finally decided to come and join us. Where's the rest of your outfit? Please don't tell me you've lost them?'

'And up yours too,' Freddie said affably. 'No, the aircraft are being unloaded as we speak but they're in crates and are having to be reassembled. We all came over in a merchant ship. This is the first Corsair so I pulled rank to do the test flight and pop over here to check out the facilities as we will be working from here as well. Then I heard your dulcet tones on the radio and came over to play.'

'Well, it's really good to see you. We've got a lot of catching up to do. Which ship are you going to?'

'Indom, so we won't be cluttering up your deck. And I hear you had a rather tough time at Sumatra?'

'I'll tell you all about it but come on in and meet my lot. Then we can have a cuppa and proper chinwag.'

John introduced Freddie to his pilots and then the two men retired to his office. John brought him up to date, firstly about the Tirpitz attack and then the raid on Sumatra.

'Well you really have been having all the fun,' Freddie said when John finished. 'We worked up in Florida and then sailed to the UK but our aircraft were on a freighter that got torpedoed so suddenly we had no aircraft, which was rather awkward. I think at that point there was a possibility that we would be disbanded and split up to other squadrons. However, I did some lobbying with the Admiral's staff and we stayed together. They decided to send us here and wait for a new shipment of Corsairs which is why we are a little late.'

'Goodness and a little rusty too I would expect. Have you done much flying in recent months?'

'Nothing like as much as I want so we're going to be pretty busy for the next few weeks.'

'Well, I can probably help. If we work together we can help get your chaps up to speed and it will give my boys something different to do.'

'Thanks John, I was rather hoping you would say that. Now I'd better get back and keep my crowd of reprobates in order.'

The two squadrons kept themselves busy for several weeks but soon orders came for all the disembarked units to get back on board. They would be sailing in a few days. Word had clearly gone around the local community and invitations to parties ashore flooded the ships. Two nights before they were due to depart, John accepted an invitation to a party at a large local hotel, hosted by several local companies. It was a busy affair with many ships' officers present including Freddie who John spotted chatting to some young ladies which wasn't to his surprise at all. As he was walking over he suddenly recognised one of the girls. It was Tracy. She saw him coming and gave him an enormous smile.

'John, I thought you might be here,' and she leant over and gave him a peck on the cheek.

'Oh, so you two know each other I take it,' Freddie said.

'Yes,' John said. 'I stayed at Tracy's parent's house a few weekends ago when we first arrived. They were very hospitable.'

'Yes my father is one of the sponsors of the evening,' Tracy said.

They all chatted for a few minutes and John noticed something he had never seen in Freddie before. He couldn't seem to take his eyes off the girl. He had to admit she was dressed to kill with a light summer frock that showed off her curves to perfection. Her hair was up in some sort of complicated plait, she did look stunning. But John had seen Freddie in action with girls many times in the past but for some reason, this seemed different. Tracy seemed just as fascinated as Freddie and the two of them were almost oblivious to what else was going on around them. John announced he was off to talk to some of his squadron who were propping up the bar.

Freddie didn't even seem to notice. Tracy turned to him. 'Thanks John, I get the feeling that your friend might be more susceptible to my charms than you were.'

# Chapter 36

'How long have we been here? I seem to have completely lost count of the days,' Sean asked John as they stood on the flight deck, along with most of the ship's company in the vain attempt to get some breeze.

'Seems like forever but only six days,' John said. 'But be thankful you're not one of those poor Yanks ashore.

They looked over at the shore of the island of Manus in the Admiralty Islands which had just been liberated from the Japanese and was now being turned into a major logistical base, including warehouses and an airfield. Apparently, there would soon be over a hundred and fifty thousand men there.

'Anyway, we will hopefully be on our way soon. I've heard that the Admirals have finally reached some agreement on where we are to be employed.'

Just then the ship's Tannoy broke into life. 'Do you hear there, the ship is now under sailing orders. The fleet will sail at oh eight hundred tomorrow, all squadron commanding officers are requested to go to the operations room that is all.'

'Well that's a relief,' Sean said. 'These ships were just not designed for his heat and humidity.'

'Well we are just about on the equator here,' John said. 'So going north will be an improvement but as we will be in the northern hemisphere and it's now March, things will be warming up wherever we go. Anyway, I'd better go, maybe our fate has been decided.'

The captain was in the operations room along with Wings, the Commander and the operations officer.

When they were assembled, the Captain spoke. 'Well gentlemen our fate has been decided. Admiral King has relented and we are to be employed with the US navy in direct operations against Japan. They have reserved the right to redirect us to support the Philippines operation under McArthur at seven days' notice but frankly once we are committed to northern operations that won't be practical. So we are now task Force 57 under the overall command of Admiral Nimitz. Admiral Vian will be in command when undertaking air operations and Admiral Rawlins will retain fleet command. So tomorrow, we head north for Ulithi in the Caroline Islands to refuel

160

and get our specific tasking. And before anyone asks I don't know any details yet. Once we've sailed I will make a broadcast to this effect to the ship's company but I felt it proper that you should know straight away.

As he went down to the wardroom John felt a strange sort of relief. Until then no one had really known what the future held. At least now they had a pretty good idea and in a few more days would hopefully have the full picture.

Ten days later, there was another briefing but this time for all the squadron COs and senior officers from all the carriers. John was sitting in Indomitable's wardroom next to Freddie.

'So what's this Admiral Vian like?' He asked. 'As a newcomer, I've never met him although I've heard some stories. Some say he's just a jumped up fishead with no aviation experience and others that he's pretty good at looking out for his aircrew.'

'Hmm, he was pretty committed at Palembang so I could see why people thought he wasn't an expert on air operations but he listens to advice. I believe Ronnie Hay has been instrumental there. But in my opinion, he's a tough cookie, as our American friends would say. Or a fighting Admiral, as we would say.'

He didn't get to say anything more as the room was called to attention and the subject of their conversation strode in.

Short, stocky, with piercing eyes, Admiral Vian surveyed the room with a grim expression.

'Sit down Gentlemen except for the flying boys. I've got a short message. Don't bother taking notes, you'll get the detail in a minute because it's only four words for you to take back to your aircrews. GET BLOODY STUCK IN! Any more questions? Right and the best of luck to you.' He strode back out.

There was silence in the room for several seconds and then a commander stood up. 'Well that sums it up rather well I think. I'm Commander Jones and I work for the Admiral. You will have gathered what he wants you to do. I will now give you the detail he mentioned.'

A map of the East China Sea was uncovered on an easel. He pointed to a chain of islands south of Japan.

'This is the Ryukyu Archipelago which, as you can see, leads directly to Japan. The biggest island is Okinawa. The Americans desperately want to take it for one major strategic reason. If they can, then they can quickly build an airstrip capable of operating their new B29 bombers which have the range to reach the Japanese mainland. It will be a major step towards stopping this bloody war. Of course, the Japs know this just as well and the place is heavily defended. There are estimates of one hundred thousand troops dug in and waiting. It's called Operation Iceberg and it's going to be hard work, believe me. But this is not what we are going to be doing. If you look further south and east you will see the Sakishima chain of islands which are a little like stepping stones between Formosa and Okinawa. The Jap Air Force is just about a spent fighting force but as you all know they have resorted to Kamikaze attacks which can be horribly effective even with poorly trained pilots, especially to American carriers with wooden flight decks. We know that many of the Kamikazes are being trained on Formosa and then operating from airfields in the Sakishimas. The islands also act as a supply route for Okinawa for general supplies. So, we are effectively a separate and independent force and our job is to stop the threat to Iceberg by neutralising the Sakishima airfields and taking out the Kamikazes in the air or on the ground.'

'How sir?' A question came from the audience.

'The fleet will stand off and we will launch regular, small, low level Ramrods, but lots of them followed up by bombing by the Avengers. It won't be like Palembang as we have at least six airfields to account for on these two islands, Ishigaki and Miyako. They operate both navy and Air force aircraft. We believe they will be heavily defended with anti-aircraft guns but hopefully not balloons.'

Cynical laughter greeted the remark.

'To start with we are working on four raids a day. You are going to be very busy and this is going to be hard work.'

More questions were asked but to John, it seemed straightforward and afterwards he discussed it with Freddie. He warned him about the lessons learned from Palembang particularly radio discipline. 'Oh and never ever go back and attack from the same direction. The chances of the gunners getting you go up enormously. If you really have to go back come in from a different direction.'

Later that evening, back in his cabin in Invincible, he reread all his letters from Heather. They always comforted him although he would have to be careful as the humid environment below decks was slowly ruining them. He lay back on his bunk and looked at the deckhead above him. There were all sorts of pipes and wire trunkings, he had no idea what they did but could tell you intimately what sort of noises they made. What a contrast, three weeks ago he was in sunny Australia fending off the advances of a beautiful, oversexed Australian girl. Now he was back in his sweaty steel box with God knows what to expect and he had even been given the chance to go home. Well that didn't matter now all he had to worry about was what was to come and he now knew it was going to be hard.

# Chapter 37

'This has just got to be one of the most beautiful places I've ever seen.' Sean said to John. They, along with most of the ship's company were lounging on the flight deck which was temporarily a sun deck. There had been no flying for the day as final preparations were being made for the first attacks in the morning. The engineers had been working on the aircraft and the pilots had their final briefings. Mid-afternoon, all was as ready as it could be and so the Captain ordered a stand down for all those who could be spared. It was the last time it would happen for some unforeseeable time. The deck had been cleared as much as possible and given over to recreation. The sun was due to set soon and the tropical heat was fading. On the far horizon, massive towering clouds were slowly turning a golden pink by the setting sun but the sea was still a deep blue.

'Look,' John cried as he pointed over the side. A shoal of flying fish were skimming the surface of the sea. 'They do that to escape predators you know. There's probably something big and nasty not far away.'

'You talking about the Japs again Boss?' Tom asked as he sat down next to the other two men.

'I could be I suppose but no, just flying fish,' John replied. 'You know what gets me is just how enormous this part of the world is. If you get a world globe and centre it on the Pacific then you can only see the sea and a few islands. No real land at all. I'm used to the Med and Atlantic. When we get to these islands we're going to be attacking it's still over a thousand miles to Japan.'

'Big and beautiful it may be sometimes,' Tom said. 'But the weather can pretty damned awful too. That squall that hit us early morning was pretty rough and the Met man was saying that this time of year we can expect very variable weather.'

'Well if we can't fly, nor can the enemy so we can all hit the bar instead,' John replied. 'Now that I've got you two together let's talk about the squadron; how are the pilots and how are the machines?'

'The machines are all ready to go,' Sean said. 'We had to change the engine on Brian's aircraft. It's been test run and all looks good but he'll need to keep an eye on it when he gets airborne.'

'I'll make sure he's the last to launch,' Tom said. 'That way if he has any problems he won't hold the rest of us up.'

'Good thinking,' John said. 'And the reprobates? I know we've all been at briefings and they seem in good order but as the CO, I can never get as close to them as you can Tom.'

'It's strange, it's almost like Palembang never happened or maybe it's because they came out of it in one piece,' then he laughed. 'Or maybe it's just that they are young, have short memories and deep inside know it won't happen to them. Mind you I don't expect any of them will be hitting the bar tonight.'

'Good,' John said. 'I haven't said anything but I want them all sharp tomorrow it's an early start. And on that note, I've got some admin to do as well. So I'll see you at some horrible time tomorrow morning.'

He went down to his cabin, sat at his desk and started to write to Heather. Or at least he tried to write but for some reason, he couldn't find any words. His pilots might be taking things in their stride but he had been here too often before. He knew he was a good pilot and probably had more combat experience than anybody else in the ship but experience and skill didn't stop stray bullets. In the end, he broke his own rules and fished out his illegal whisky bottle. He wasn't hungry and couldn't be bothered to go up to the wardroom and slowly drifted off to sleep.

The bugle sounded loudly over the ship's Tannoy followed by the call 'Hands to flying stations.'

John and his squadron were already getting kitted out with their Mae Wests and survival gear when the bugle sounded. 'Right you lot,' he called over the pilot's chatter. 'Keep it tight, keep the noise down and what else?'

'Never go back for a second run,' the voices all chorused back.

'That's it and good luck to you all.'

'Aircrew man your aircraft,' came over the Tannoy. They all trooped out along the corridor and up the ladder to the island and onto the flight deck. It was something they had all done so many times before it was almost automatic.

The rear half of the flight deck was a mass of aircraft, with John's squadron at the front. They would be first off. Behind were the Avengers who would follow on escorted by the second Hellcat squadron who would launch after them and use their superior speed to catch them up. Finally right at the rear were the Seafires. Their limited range meant they could not get to the islands and back. Their job was to protect the fleet from attack especially by the dreaded Kamikazes. Some of the Corsairs and Hellcats would also take on this role on a rotation basis or after they had conducted a strike. It was going to be a long day with many more to come.

As soon as he was strapped in, John's nerves calmed. This was his place and he was sitting inside one of the best fighters of the war. He suddenly felt confident. The call for the aircraft to start up came and he automatically went through the procedure. As soon as the marshaller indicated and the light on the island went green, he opened the throttle fully while standing on the brakes. As soon as he felt the brakes struggling, he let them off and the Hellcat leapt forward. Despite the shortness of his take off run as he was ahead of all the other aircraft, there was plenty of wind over the deck and he was airborne before crossing the bow. Climbing up into the holding pattern he waited for the rest of the squadron to join him before setting off over the deep blue sea towards the island of Ishikagi.

Three hours later they all returned. Two days later Task Force 57 withdrew three hundred miles as there was the possibility of a Typhoon and they needed to refuel.

The next day, John was sitting in the ready room when Neville found him. 'SPLOT says you have the latest reconnaissance photos Sir?'

'Yes, just looking at them now, here have a look yourself. What do you think?'

Neville looked for a few minutes at the large black and white photographs taken by a Hellcat first thing in the morning at the start of the day's raids and then just before they had left the area. There were twelve of them all together, two for each airfield.

'Well we pasted all of them on the first day,' Neville said frowning. 'But the morning photos seem to show all the runways in use again and the evening ones show the same sort of damage as the end of day one.'

'Don't be surprised Neville,' John said. 'During the Battle of Britain, the Jerries bombed the hell out of our southern airfields and with the help of a few bulldozers most were useable again in a

166

matter of hours. The Japs are doing the same thing. A crater in a runway is actually quite easy to fill in.'

'So that's what we are going to be doing for weeks ahead Sir? Seems a pretty pointless exercise. I know our losses were relatively light so far but if we are going to be doing this for weeks it's going to take its toll.'

'Very perceptive of you old chap but we have to do it to keep the American flank protected. Look at it this way if we stop them using the airfields by day and it takes them half the night to repair them, they are not going to be in much of a position to launch an attack on the Yanks.'

I suppose so Sir and at least they don't seem to have any real numbers of fighters they can use to get at us.'

'Ah, now there you might be wrong. Not from these islands maybe but remember Formosa is not too far away.'

'But surely its' too far to strike us and get back and we will have denied them the use of the closer islands.'

'Who said anything about them going back?' John said grim faced.

# Chapter 38

John's fears were soon realised. Easter Sunday the First of April 1945 saw task Force 57 ready to go again. At six fifteen, strikes of Corsairs and Hellcats launched to attack Miyako and Ishikagi. However this time John's squadron was in reserve and scheduled for a second midday Ramrod. With the ship at action stations, all the aircrew were required to be on standby in the ready room or up in the goofers just in case they were needed in a hurry. The Seafires were already airborne and patrolling above the fleet and a picket of a cruiser and destroyer were out to the west. Any aircraft not identifying itself to the picket on return from an attack would be considered an enemy and that was despite all the fleets' aircraft now being fitted with IFF transponders that should identify them to all ship's radars. The command were starting to take things very seriously. This was the day the Americans were going to start the attack on Okinawa.

Just before seven, the Tannoy burst into life. 'Alarm aircraft, to the west. Twenty plus bandits. Launch the standby squadron.'

The ready room emptied in a heartbeat as the pilots ran to their aircraft. Within what seemed, seconds John was climbing in and starting up even as the ship heeled onto a flying course. As soon as the green light came on he was on his way with the rest of the squadron streaming behind. There was no time to get organised just climb and head for the danger.

'Cormorant Squadron,' came the cool voice of the ship's direction officer. 'Vector two six zero, twenty bandits at angels eight.'

John acknowledged the call and looked ahead. As expected, the puffs of anti-aircraft fire were starting to show him where the enemy probably were. At the moment it would be the large calibre guns of the big ships and carriers but soon the sky would be a hell of fire from all the smaller but much faster firing Oerlikons and poms poms. He was torn between getting to the enemy or getting out of the range of their own weapons or both.

Then the direction officer came back on the radio. 'Bandits are splitting, ten are staying on heading but the others are splitting off and look like they are going to attack from the south. Cormorant squadron vector south to intercept.'

It was a good tactic John acknowledged, causing them to split their own defences. This wasn't going to be like fighting the Germans and Italians in the Mediterranean. Those pilots had at least some expectation of getting home and a determined enough defence could break up their formations and send them packing. If these really were Kamikazes they would have no such inhibitions. He glanced to one side and saw that Neville had joined him and there were several other aircraft trailing behind. He then concentrated on looking ahead for the enemy. Once again, the anti-aircraft fire gave him the clues he needed and he spotted a gaggle of dark shapes ahead and below him.

'Tally Ho,' he called and pushed his nose down. They looked like Zekes more often called Zeros and the aircraft that had caused so much damage at the start of the war. Not now he knew, they had no armour and though very manoeuvrable were intent on the ships of the fleet and not getting into dog fights. Sure enough, he was able to latch onto the tail of one and opened fire from about a hundred yards. Just like Palembang, the Zero simple blew apart and he had to take drastic avoiding action to avoid flying through the debris. Off to one side, he saw another Zero simply dive into the sea, presumably Neville's kill but then they were flying into the curtain of bursting shells and flak. It was getting hard to even see the enemy aircraft because of the amount of anti-aircraft fire and he felt the shudder of near misses. Despite having already been shot down by his own side in similar circumstances some years ago he kept going. The suicide aircraft had to be stopped. And then off to his right, he saw one of the carriers disappear in a massive ball of flame and smoke. Surely no ship could survive that. Then the radio came back to life. 'All aircraft break off and return to your units, all bogeys have been splashed. Aircraft from Indefatigable are to declare their fuel state and will be allocated a diversion deck.'

So that was who had been hit John realised. He looked around again and to his surprise, there was Indefatigable steaming clear of the smoke. Her deck looked a mess but she was upright and clearly still well under command. Then it was time to get back to his own deck and mix in with all the other machines trying to do the same thing.

It was organised chaos for some time, not only were the other ships having to find room for the stricken carrier's aircraft but the inbound Ramrods had been recalled the moment the attack on the fleet had been detected. They didn't have the fuel to turn around and continue now. All the carriers were striking down as many aircraft as they could to make room on the decks. As a result, his squadron was instructed to climb above the fleet and act as Combat Air Patrol. The Seafires were also running short of fuel by now just to add to the complicated situation.

From ten thousand feet he could see the whole massive fleet; the two battlewagons the carriers and the massive number of escorts. The initial smoke and flames from the Indefatigable had been distinguished and he could see frantic activity on her deck. He wondered just how many had died. And then, amazingly, only forty five minutes after the attack she started launching Seafires and then called all her aircraft back. How on earth had she come through that massive explosion and been able to recover so quickly?

Later on that day he found out. It was the talk all around the fleet. The Zero had impacted the deck in an almost vertical dive near the island. Several sailors had been killed outright and some more inside, including a doctor who manned a temporary sick bay there. The damage to the flight deck consisted of a large dent which had been filled with quick drying cement.

John had got the pilots and senior engineers together to tell them all as there were going to be a great deal of lessons to learn from this attack.

'So it's not just the Japs that can fill in holes in runways,' Neville said.

'No and you can thank your stars you are in a British carrier with an armoured deck,' John said. 'In a Yank carrier, it would have gone straight through their wooden deck into the hangar. Can you just imagine the result?'

Silence greeted his remark as everyone contemplated the scenario.

Then Sean spoke. 'That may be Sir but it's made us all realise that this is now a whole ship war. Up until now, you chaps have been the ones taking the risks and all we had to do was wait for you to come home, fix you up and send you off again. I think everyone in the ship's company now realises that they are in the firing line as well.'

'I understand Sean,' John replied. 'To that end there are going to be some new procedures on the flight deck in particular, to get everyone under cover if we are attacked again and let's face it, it will happen.'

Grim faces greeted his remark. Next time it might be their turn.

# Chapter 39

The next fortnight was tough for everyone. Ramrods continued several times a day. They would attack for two days and then retreat for two days to replenish and then back into the fray. They were flying up to six hours a day either attacking the islands or flying patrol over the fleet and sometimes both. It was clear that the strain was beginning to tell. There were several more Kamikaze attacks. Most were beaten off but on one occasion a Zeke hit the masts of Illustrious before crashing over the side and exploding in the sea.

And then they got a change of scenery. The fleet left the Sakishimas and headed for Formosa. Apparently, the Americans had asked if the British could have a go at the source of all the trouble coming up from there.

The first day was almost a washout. The target airfield that John had been given was totally obscured by cloud. All they could do was shoot up some industrial buildings and a railway depot. The second day saw better weather and the Japanese managed to get a number of fighters airborne but it had been a turkey shoot. Their machines were out outmatched and their pilots inexperienced. For the Corsair and Hellcat pilots, they finally got to do what they signed up to do and fly like fighter pilots. However, John's squadron was confined to fleet defence and no enemy aircraft made it that far. His pilots were frustrated, he was not.

Then it was back to Leyte for another regroup.

That evening there was quite a party in the mess as everyone celebrated a successful mission for once. Sixteen enemy aircraft had been shot down for only three British and none from their squadron. Also, significant damage had been done ashore. There was also some hope that maybe they might be employed doing something new once they had replenished.

Later that evening, John was sitting at the rear of the quarterdeck that looked out over the stern of the ship. He like many others had taken to sleeping there to escape the stifling heat in their cabins. The front of the deck space was full of mattresses. However, John was at the rear guardrail watching the sea and the wake of the ship being churned up by the ship's massive propellers.

It was a dark clear night with no moon. The wake was alive with light as it was lit with bioluminescence, beautiful and hypnotising.

'Mind if I join you, Boss?'

John turned to see Tom standing next to him. 'No of course not, although I may not be good company tonight old chap.'

'What's up?'

'You know, I think the novelty's worn off a little bit.'

'Hah, tell me about it,' Tom said with feeling. 'We've been at sea for weeks, the food's bloody awful, and the heat is really getting to everyone. I've got prickly heat on my arms and it's driving me mad. But look on the bright side we are the only squadron that hasn't lost a pilot.'

'Yet,' John said in a grim tone, then he sighed. 'Actually, I was talking about flying in general. Before the war, I already had a licence but all I wanted to do was fly a fighter. I did that and flew Hurricanes and moved on to Wildcats. Even though I had a few scrapes it was still exciting. I even did some test flying for that boffin, Barnes Wallace and then they gave me 1854 and that was yet another challenge. Look Tom, I shouldn't be saying this and it's probably because I've had far too much to drink but I just want it all to end. I've had enough.'

Tom didn't say anything for a while. 'Yes I'm sure that's the booze talking to a degree and you are very definitely not the only person feeling like that. But you need to know something. You are incredibly well respected in this ship. We all know about your past, dammit, the Battle of Britain, two DSC's, Operation Torch and only one foot but you've kept on. You've shot down more aircraft than just about everyone else on the ship combined but you don't shoot a line about it. Not only that but you're a damned good Commanding Officer. You make the guys work hard but know when to let your hair down. Sorry old chap but we can't afford to lose you. Look, if the Yanks take Okinawa it's all going to be over soon after that at least for us. Maybe not the war itself but with Japan in range of bombers how long do you think they will really hold out?'

'Well if they fight on the mainland like they are in Okinawa who knows.'

'Yes but we won't have a role and we will be the ship that's been out here the longest by then so it will be our turn to go home anyway.'

'I take your point Tom. Let's all hope you're right and we are around to see the end.'

The two men stood staring at the wake and then John excused himself and went to his mattress. Tom's words had ignited a spark, he had almost forgotten was there, he just hoped he wasn't so drunk that he could remember it in the morning.

A few days later and they sailed from Leyte. John was sitting in the wardroom when the Captain came on the Main Broadcast. John already knew what he was going to say as he had attended a briefing only a few hours previously.

'D'you hear there, this is the Captain speaking. As usual, now we have sailed I can tell you all about our future plans. The Americans are having a tough time at Okinawa and have experienced some serious Kamikaze raids in recent days.'

'Oh shit I know where this is going,' someone muttered.

'So we are going back to the Sakishimas to carry on as before, our role is seen to be both important and effective....'

The Captain's voice was drowned out by jeers and catcalls from many of the aircrew.

John turned to Tom who was sitting next to him. 'The lads don't seem happy.'

'Well nor am I but I suppose it has to be done,' Tom said. 'At least it appears to be worthwhile. As soon as we left Formosa the attacks on the Yanks ramped up from what I've heard.'

'Yes, that's exactly what the Captain told us earlier.'

So the grind started again but not the squadron's run of good luck. On the first day back John led a Ramrod to Miyako to attack an airfield to the north of the island. It was the second raid of the day and the Japanese defences were waiting for them. They had split into two flights to come in from different directions. As they thundered at low level towards the first site, John was amazed to see a line of aircraft parked up beside one of the makeshift hangars. They were off to one side but perfect targets for the other flight. Something didn't look right but with this sort of attack split seconds were all you had. He concentrated on his target which was going to be the hangar. He had just time to register his hits and the almost complete lack of anti-aircraft fire, when he caught the dreadful sight of a Hellcat rolling and exploding down the cratered runway. Then as he pulled clear and turned he saw another aircraft bracketed by concentrated enemy fire turn slowly upside down and dive into the ground.

'Abort abort,' he called over the radio feeling sick inside. It had clearly been a trap. The line of aircraft were almost certainly dummies and the enemy had used them to lure the attackers into an approach along which they had concentrated their fire. It also explained why his flight had been effectively left alone. It was a new and deadly tactic and he needed to get back to the ship and get a warning out to everyone.

As soon as they were back on deck he found out who they had lost. Malcolm Patterson and Peter Robinson. That was now four out of the original ten pilots that had got together in Northern Ireland last year, almost half the squadron.

That evening John got to the bar late. He had been in his cabin writing letters to the parents of his two lost airmen. Of all the tasks the war had thrust upon him, this was the one he hated the most but it had to be done. Strangely, he found it easier than writing to Heather at least he knew what he had to say. With Heather he had to be careful what he wrote and not just because of military secrecy but because he didn't want her worrying.

The mood in the bar was sombre and the beer was flowing. John joined his chaps and deliberately didn't mention the events of the day except to get them all to raise a glass to lost comrades. Then they all proceeded to get very drunk. Again.

The next day they went and did it all again.

# Chapter 40

'They're going to do what?' John exploded. 'What the hell have we been doing over the last weeks and now the command have got a better idea. I don't bloody well believe it.'

'Calm down John,' Wings said. 'I understand your point but the Admiral wants to give it a go, if for no other reason than to give his crews something to achieve, apparently morale in the heavies is not good.'

'What the hell have we been achieving then Sir? What about our morale? We're losing aircraft almost daily.'

'Actually, I agree John,' Wings sighed. 'But we have to do as we're told, I just pray this doesn't all end badly.'

Wings and the Squadron COs were in their daily evening briefing after the day's flying had finished. 'So as I said, tomorrow no Ramrods and no bombing, instead the KGV and Howe along with her escorts will close Miyako and bombard the island with their guns.'

'And we will be thirty miles south with reduced radar coverage and over half our anti-aircraft capability missing,' someone said.

'That's true,' Wings replied. 'But with no shore attacks to conduct, we can put a very strong CAP much more than we normally have. Now look I'm not happy with this either but it's not our decision. The Captain will do his normal evening briefing later on but you chaps need to look at tomorrow's flying programme carefully as it's very different from what we normally do. All the Avengers will be struck down as they won't be used and the fighters will be ranged and either airborne or ready to go at short notice. Thank you gentlemen, that is all.'

When the change of plan was announced by the Captain to the ship's company that evening there was stunned silence in the bar.

'If the big guns can do the job then why haven't they done it already? What the hell have we been bleeding to death for, over the last weeks,' Tom said angrily.

It was clear that that was a universal feeling amongst the pilots but in the end, as Wings had pointed out there was nothing they could do about it.

So the next morning the two massive battleships and ten cruisers broke formation and steamed majestically north, leaving the carriers and destroyers to fend for themselves. John watched it all from the goofers and then as the first CAP aircraft left the deck. He wasn't programmed to fly until later so decided to stay in the sunshine while he could. It was a beautiful day.

It didn't take long for the peace to be shattered.

'*Alarm aircraft, green nine zero. Raid inbound twenty plus bandits to the north.*'

John didn't even think. His reaction was purely automatic. He ran into the island down two ladders and onto the flight deck, except there was nothing he could do. His aircraft was at the back of the deck hemmed in by many others. That said, other pilots were rushing to their machines as well. He stopped, hesitating, wondering what on earth to do when all the ship's armament started firing. The noise was immense, from the savage thud of the four point fives to the rapid chatter of the quick firing guns. He looked up to see where they were firing and saw several specks in the sky one of which was coming straight at them. All too fast, he saw it was a Zeke and nothing was stopping it. He dived for cover just as there was an almighty explosion. The concussion hurt his ears and suddenly he was blind. Disorientated he clambered back up to his feet scrabbling at his eyes, something was obscuring his sight. He pulled it off and looked at it. He couldn't work out what he was seeing, it looked like a steak, the sort you buy from a butcher's shop and then it dawned on him what it was. It was a piece of a human being. His stomach clenched and he was violently sick all down his front as he flung the offending piece of meat away.

Sean wandered up to him with a strange look on his face. He was clearly in shock but he had seen what John had done.

'It's alright boss, no need to worry,' he shouted over the noise. 'It wasn't one of ours, it was the pilot of that.' And he pointed forward.

Parts of a Japanese aircraft were strewn over the forward part of the deck and John could see the rest sinking in the water just off to one side.

'Oh well that's alright then,' he said in a slightly hysterical voice and promptly sat down. A few minutes later a medical party found him and gently took him to sick bay.

'Drink this,' the doctor said handing John a full glass of scotch.

'Is that you medics remedy for everything? John asked as he downed the lot in one.

'Fraid so old chap. Now you're fine, nothing broken just a bit deaf from all the banging going on. Go and lie down for a while, you'll be right as rain. Oh and I'm grounding you for two days.'

John opened his mouth to start to argue then shut it again, they would be heading south for resupply and Tom was more than capable of managing any flying they did on the way or in Leyte and he could really do with some sleep. So he just nodded and wandered back to his hot, sweaty, noisy but private cabin but in the end, he was too wound up to sleep. He sat at his desk and tried to write to Heather but what could he say? He had narrowly missed been blown up and ended up with a bit of Japanese pilot over his eyes? Even as he had the thought he started feeling queasy again. No this wouldn't do. The guns had stopped firing some time ago but that didn't mean that there wouldn't be more attacks. He decided to go and see what was happening so made his way up to Flyco.

'You alright John?' Wings asked when he saw John standing at the back looking out of the window over the flight deck. 'The Doc told me you were caught up in the little drama.'

'Something like that Sir, I'm grounded for a couple of days but I'm fine really. Any damage to the ship?'

'Not much, all the aircraft were ranged aft so all the Jap did was scrape the paint.'

'And get himself blown to bits,' John said. 'A bit of him hit me in the face.'

Wings clearly didn't know what to say to that so changed the subject. 'Look over there John. It doesn't look too bad now but Formidable took a big hit, right by the island.'

John looked where Wings was pointing and could see the ship with some wisps of smoke and frantic activity on her deck but nothing else.

'She says she will be able to recommence flying in half an hour which frankly, is quite amazing but she's had some serious casualties.'

'Do I get a chance to say I told you so to the Admiral Sir,' John asked in a weary tone.

'Sorry John, you are at the end of a very long queue.'

# Chapter 41

They refuelled, re-armed and made their weary way back north to start all over again. John received two new pilots and two new aircraft and then it was back to Ramrods and the occasional task of CAP. The Kamikazes seemed to be leaving them alone and the fleet had not been attacked again.

A few days later, the wardroom was its usual busy late evening self when the Captain came on the intercom.

'D'you here there, this is the Captain. I have just received a signal from the Admiralty, I shall read it out. Today the German High command unconditionally surrendered to the Allied forces of Great Britain, the United States of America and Russia. The war in Europe is over. The Prime Minister has just announced this to the nation. His exact words were, *we may allow ourselves a brief period of rejoicing but let us not forget for a moment the toil and efforts that lie ahead, Japan with all her treachery and greed, remains unsubdued. The injury she has inflicted on Great Britain, the United States and other countries and her detestable cruelties, call for justice and retribution. We must now devote all our strength and resources to the completion of our task, both at home and abroad.*

So gentlemen, our loved ones are now safe but as the Prime Minister said we still have a job to do. That is all.'

Muted cheers met the Captain's words.

'Well I expected a better response than that,' John said to Neville and Tom who were propping up the bar with him.

'Really Boss?' Tom asked. 'Did you see that newspaper that was doing the rounds? You know the one where the Kamikaze attack on Indefatigable was on page three?'

'I know, I know but does that really matter? The simple fact is that the Japanese are still there and we might as well do the best job we can.'

Later that evening, John was having a shave. It was a habit he had long been into. It was one less thing to have to do when getting up early in the morning. Many of the chaps have started to grow beards, those that could, some were still far too young. The thought of yet more sweaty growth on his face in this climate was something he simply didn't need.

He looked at himself in the mirror. God he looked old and tired, there were bags under his eyes. It wasn't the face of a man in his mid twenties. He started thinking about Heather and what she would be doing now that her war was over. He then realised that there were tears sliding down his face. What the hell? 'Buck up old chap,' he muttered to himself. He realised the hand that was holding his razor was also shaking. He sat down and closed his eyes for a moment. Then with a sigh he stood, finished his shave and went up to the quarterdeck to try and get some sleep in the cool night air. He knew the symptoms of the 'twitch', they all had it to some degree but he was the Commanding Office and it was his job not to show any weakness so he would just have to grin and bear it.

The next day got worse. Neville died. It was yet another ramrod. The weather was poor but they made their target. They were tearing over a Jap airfield shooting up some hangars and taking fire. Once committed to the attack, you could not manoeuvre to avoid ground fire, you had to concentrate on your own targeting. The Japs had been getting clever. They knew that their firepower was weak if spread around the field so instead they concentrated it in different areas each day. It was a game of chess because the British knew about it and so they always attacked from a different direction. Today was a bad day as the attack line John had chosen seemed to align with the direction the Japs had concentrated on and the Hellcats were taking heavy fire. By the time it was clear what was happening it was far too late, all they could do was concentrate on their own attack and get the hell out of it as fast as possible.

John caught a glimpse of a fireball to his left and for a split second saw the remains of a Hellcat tumbling in flames down the grass runway. And just like that his wing man of the last year had gone. Neville the gifted pianist and life and soul of the party who could sing any song including some really quite rude ones and never offend anyone with his winning smile. A damned good pilot, John had offered him a Flight Commanders position several times but he had insisted on staying as his wingman saying he felt far safer looking after his boss. Now just a burning smear on some god forsaken, bloody, island.

'Boss, pull up,' someone screamed over the radio.

181

Reality snapped back and he saw he was heading directly towards the remains of a hanger. He instinctively pulled back on the stick, the G force crushing him into his seat and the world went grey as he entered the low cloud cover.

Reflex took over, he concentrated on his instruments and levelled the nose of the aircraft, set a sensible power level and rolled the wings level at the same time. Damn, he was at three thousand feet now and it would be far too dangerous to try and get below cloud again while over the island, he knew just how low the cloud had been on their way to the target. Switching his radio to a particular frequency, he turned to take up a heading towards the fleet. He looked at his watch and did a quick mental calculation to estimate how far he had to go to open water. He then checked his fuel. There was plenty to get back.

The radio started to issue a series of chirps corresponding to the letter A. This was the rather clever homing system the fleet had come up with. Directional aerials on the ship sent out a stream of Morse code letters along specific sectors. If he wandered off course the letter would change telling him to turn back, that was if he was heading towards the fleet. If it went the wrong way, he was heading in the opposite direction. A small diagram was stuck to his dash to give him the letter sequence. Putting all thought of the past few minutes behind him, he concentrated on flying on instruments and watching his clock. It soon became apparent that he had a big problem, only minutes ago he had over half a tank of fuel now it was showing a significant drop. He realised that he must have taken a hit in one of his tanks. They were meant to be self sealing but that was never guaranteed. Looking out over his wings he could see no signs of obvious damage but that didn't mean anything. The results of ground fire was often not discovered until an aircraft was back on deck. However, he had no choice but to plough on and pray that his fuel lasted at least enough for him to bale out over the sea where a rescue sub or destroyer could pick him up.

Suddenly, he broke out into clear blue sky. He looked down and saw with relief that he was over the sea. Behind him, a bank of cloud was covering the island but the weather towards the fleet looked good. Maybe he would make it, he still had a quarter of a tank of fuel. He called the ship and asked for a priority recovery.

The controller on the ship acknowledged his request but warned him they were plotting a possible inbound raid some fifty miles away.

Radio chatter was building up, it was clear that the Seafires were off to intercept the incoming raid. John had to ignore it all as his fuel was getting drastically low. He saw the ship and lowered his hooks and flaps. The Batsman was waving him in. Suddenly the ship in front of him started to heel into a turn and he was given the wave off signal.

He knew if he didn't land now he would have to ditch. 'I'm committed, landing on,' he called over the radio and then concentrated on following the ship and trying to counter her heel. The Batsman stood again as he crossed the round down and gave him the cut signal. Because of the angle of the deck, he landed heavily on the port wheel and then was flung hard right as the aircraft righted itself relative to the now very sloping deck. For a second he saw the barrier looming and then the hook caught a wire and he came to a shuddering halt although he was angled at almost forty five degrees across the flight deck. He gave himself a second to catch his breath and then realised there was no marshaller and the barrier was still up. Looking at the masts he saw a red flag and people running for shelter. That was the signal for an imminent Kamikaze attack and here he was sitting in an aircraft on deck. Maybe he should have ditched after all. Without further thought, he ripped off his harness and parachute, jumped on the wing and slid to the deck. It was a fair drop from the wing's trailing edge to the deck and he stumbled as he landed and then started running hard. The door to the island was still open so he made for that. He saw Sean's face looking at him and gesturing him on. As soon as he reached the door he flung himself inside but before Sean could slam the door shut, everything went quiet and started to move in slow motion. He felt himself flying through the air and he saw the bulkhead approaching and then everything went black.

# Chapter 42

'Hello again,' the doctor said with a smile. 'You know you really don't have to spend so much time in here. Anyway, have another scotch.' And he handed John another glass of whisky.

This time John shook his head. 'How many?' He asked.

The Doc didn't reply straight away, clearly deciding on what to tell John. 'Seven on the flight deck and one in the island.'

'Who was that?' John asked dreading the answer.

'Lieutenant McGuire, one of yours I believe. I'm terribly sorry.'

Oh Jesus, that was Neville and now Sean gone in a matter of hours. 'What about my pilots?' John asked.

'No idea old chap they've all had to land on other ships while we fix this one. But I understand all those on the shore raids found somewhere to get down. Anyway you banged your head again, lucky that was it or you might have really hurt yourself. And hang on here's Wings he can tell you more,'

Wings came in and looked at John. 'Not want the scotch then John?'

John shook his head. Wings didn't hesitate and took the tumbler and downed it in one. 'Got any more old chap?' He asked the doctor, who turned and came back with another glass and then left them.

'How's the ship Sir?' John asked.

'Battered but still afloat. The engineers say we should be able to recover our aircraft quite soon and then it's some good news for a change, if you can call it that. It seems the Jap not only dented the flight deck but also managed to do something to our starboard shaft, shock damage of some sort, he was carrying a bloody great bomb. We're going to have to limp back to Sydney for a docking. So on that basis, you're grounded until we get back. It will probably take some time as we won't be going fast. Look John, I need you to take a break, don't argue I know what the twitch looks like. And you've got a concussion for that matter so the Doc and I both think you need a decent rest. Frankly, I can't afford to lose you at this moment so I want you to have some time off. I know about your wing man and AEO. You need to gather yourself up. I expect you will all

184

disembark when we get to Sydney and I want everyone recharged for when we go back. If we go back that is.'

'Why? Do you think the Japs are going to give up?'

'Well the Yanks have just about taken Okinawa so their big bombers will be able to target the mainland at last and between you and me there are rumours of some sort of massive bomb they've been developing, so who knows? It would well be all over before we are out of dock.'

John lay back, a massive headache was starting. He was suddenly very weary. Wings must have seen that he was wilting and left him to sleep but not before finishing his second scotch. Everyone had their own ways of staving off the twitch.

The journey back to Australia proved to be a tonic for almost the whole crew apart from the stokers down in the bowels of the ship who had to continue their labours just to keep the ship going. For the second time in only a short while, John found that being medically grounded wasn't a problem. On the day before the doc said he could be discharged, all his pilots piled in to see him. The resultant hangover almost caused him to decide he needed another day in sick bay. Neville and Sean were both saluted and then not mentioned again, although John knew he would be writing to their parents in short order.

The only flying they conducted were routine patrols and once they were close to Australia even they ceased. The flight deck once again took on a new role as the ship's sun and sports deck. The ship's company needed no encouragement to use it for recreation. A deck hockey tournament between various ship's departments and squadrons was fiercely fought over. The eventual winners were the stokers who magically managed to get a team together and were admired for their skill and almost Kamikaze like way of playing. A large screen was rigged on the side of the island to show films. On the day before they were due to arrive in Sydney, they had a 'sods opera' a particularly naval tradition. All the messes and departments put on a sketch. The rules were liberal and it was accepted that the sailors could use ship's officers as the target of their wit.

John's squadron had put on a parody of a George Fornby film in which for some reason John was depicted as the butt of all the main character's jokes. He didn't mind, as he said afterwards, he had the power of writing their confidential reports and he knew who had written the script.

During one hilarious sketch, the supply department had the Commander, who was well known as being rather straight laced judging a beauty pageant of sailors dressed up as girls. John turned to Tom. 'We are in a warship that's been fighting for months and thousands of miles from home. Where on earth do these chaps get all this female clothing from?'

'It's a mystery, I agree,' Tom said. 'But I suspect much of it was liberated from various ladies in Australia. The Ozzie girls have been rather affectionate.'

John grunted in acknowledgement as his thoughts turned to a rather pretty young Australian girl in particular. Then he thought about Heather and a pang of loneliness hit him.

Early the next day they entered Sydney and as soon as the ship was secured, they piped 'Hands to flying stations'. John had been declared fit to fly and so it wasn't long before he was airborne circling the ship and the city waiting for everyone to join up. They would then fly to their air station to the south and only thirty miles away. As he waited for the stragglers to join up he looked down at the harbour. There were four large white aircraft floating off to one side which he immediately recognised as Sunderland flying boats belonging to the RAF. Right, time for some fun.

When the last aircraft called 'aboard' meaning he was now in formation, John got on the radio. 'Squadron, slight change of plan, three columns in flights go. Follow me,' He gave them enough time to form three lines with him in the centre and then pushed the nose down. He levelled out a few feet above the water and aimed at the gap between two of the massive sea planes. He reckoned there was just enough room between their wingtips for a Hellcat.

For someone watching from one of the Sunderlands, it must have been an impressive sight. Ten Hellcats, in three columns shot between the gaps of the four machines at over four hundred miles an hour, the roar of their Pratt and Whitney engines deafening and spray from the slipstreams of their engines making rainbows in the sunshine. What was probably even more impressive was that the leading aircraft was upside down. John actually didn't know he was going to do it until the last moment but it suddenly seemed a good idea. As he rolled upright and climbed away, someone came on the radio. 'Nice one boss, guess that woke them up.'

For the first time, in what seemed ages, John's heart lifted and he suddenly felt happy again. Turning south he realised that he was looking forward to some time off in the sunshine and for a few days at least not thinking about the bloody war.

# Chapter 43

John's mood became even better after they arrived. The Squadron landed at was now known as the Royal Naval Air Station, Babbington. They were expected and as they were the first squadron back due to their early departure from the fighting they had their pick of the facilities. A hangar and office space were given to them and later that morning several buses and two lorries arrived with the maintainers. Now that Sean was no longer with them and as there hadn't been time to arrange a replacement, Sean's Senior Chief, an old and very experienced Chief Petty Officer called Simpson had taken over. He and John had a quick chat over what the aircraft needed and then he let Simpson get on with it. Unsurprisingly, the machines would all need some work and there were several modifications that could now be fitted. One of which was a water injection system that would give them several hundred more horsepower more when needed.

Also waiting for them was Commander Simon Peters who had driven down from Sydney.

'Nice fly past John, the RAF asked me to say it was most spectacular and asked if you would please not do it again,' he said with a smile. 'Now I've heard you've all had a pretty bloody time so I'm going to make sure you all get some leave as soon as possible but you will need to write up a report of proceedings and complete all the other paperwork before you can escape yourself.'

'Yes Sir, actually, it's already written, it gave me something to do while we were on the way back here. It will be with your Admiral's staff today I expect.

'Alright but would you give me a quick verbal report anyway, I've only got the bare bones so far.'

'Of course Sir. They've given me an office we'll chat there.'

Twenty minutes later John finished. Simon hadn't interrupted once. When John finally told him about the Kamikaze attack, he sat back in his chair.

'Goodness John, it's one thing to read the signals and look at the statistics but hearing it as a first hand account is something else. You all seem to have gone through hell and it will be the same for the other ships which will be back in a week or so. I'll do my best to ensure that everyone gets as much leave as possible.'

'Before what Sir? Will there be more of the same because frankly my people have performed magnificently but you can only ask so much.'

Simon sighed. 'Honestly, I don't know but we have to be prepared. One thing I do know is that it won't be until June before you are needed again. The fleet needs a solid maintenance period, so you should all make the best of your time here.'

There was the sound of a car drawing up and a door slamming. 'Oh and it seems someone is as punctual as promised. Just hold on there for a moment I have a surprise for you.'

Simon disappeared out of Johns's office leaving him mystified. He didn't have to wait long to find out what it was all about.

Impossibly, ridiculously impossible but nevertheless clearly true, there was Heather in the doorway.

For seconds John simply couldn't take it in. She was thousands of miles away, there was no way she could be here. Was this some sort of cruel joke and someone had found a girl that looked just like Heather? No that was impossible, no one had a smile like her. He found he couldn't move or breathe and just sat there gaping as his mind tried to reconcile where he was and what he was seeing.

'John are you alright? You look like you've seen a ghost. It is me.'

A dam inside him broke. A dam he hadn't even realised was there. Holding back emotions in front of everyone had built up enormous pressure over the last year and having to leave Heather behind was the first brick in the dam. But now that brick was gone and the whole edifice was crashing down. Without conscious thought, he was in her arms, smelling her hair and feeling her body tight against his.

'John, yes, it is me. Are you alright?'

He pulled back slightly and looked into her eyes, he knew there were tears in his. 'I am now. The last months have been awful without you. Hang on, how on earth did you get here? I know you were in England on VE day, it's just not possible.'

She smiled. 'Now, when you and your squadron did that spectacular and silly fly past in Sydney this morning who do you think was watching?'

The penny dropped. 'You flew a Sunderland out here?'

'Well not just me, there was a crew on each aircraft. When I heard they were sending some out here I leant on some contacts and got myself invited. The ATA is going to be wound down soon but we are still working hard. I've got a multi-engine rating and the RAF needed extra crew to fly such a long distance.'

John hugged her again and they shared a rather long kiss.

'OK that's enough,' Heather said, breaking contact. 'We don't want anyone catching us.'

'Why not? I don't bloody care,' John replied with a grin. Then he sighed. 'But of course, you're right. We are all going to get some leave and Commander Peters was kind enough to come out for an initial chat but I've going to have to call on the Admirals staff and God knows how much paperwork I'm going to get bogged down in. Where are you staying?'

'Oh, in a hotel in Sydney for the moment. I can camp out there until you get everything sorted.

'I think you mean we can camp out there. It should only be for a few days. Oh and Freddie should be back in a week or so. It will be like old times. Look, I've made some friends out here, I think I can arrange some time with them. They've got a fabulous house with plenty of rooms by the beach. I'll give them a call soon.'

'Sounds great and what about all your boys?'

A cloud passed over John's face. 'Heather we've had a rather busy time, I'm afraid half of them are replacements including Neville and Sean.'

She could see the pain on John's face. 'Still, I'll know some of them and you can introduce me to the new chaps.'

Ten days later, John and Heather were staying at the Andersons. Dick and Joanna had been adamant that they come and stay once they heard John was back and with Heather as well. Then Freddie had turned up much to Tracy's delight, the two of them seem to have really hit it off. The weather stayed fine and sunny but it was the end of Autumn and getting chillier. Even so, it was warm enough to sit on the beach.

John, Freddie and Heather were sitting in the sunshine on the veranda of the house enjoying the house and the peace and quiet.

Tracy had gone off somewhere shopping and the Andersons were in Sydney.

'What a contrast to only two weeks ago,' John said as he gazed over the tranquil blue sea.

'Who would have thought that, when we were playing around with that old biplane of your dads back in thirty nine, we three would end up here in Australia with everything we've done,' Freddie said. 'John and I were off to try and join the navy and you Heather were getting really cross because they wouldn't let girls fly.'

Heather chuckled. 'And here's me now with more types in my logbook than both of you combined.'

'Show off,' John said. 'But please tell me how on earth we are all still here?'

'Well, we're not, are we? Not completely.' Freddie said. 'You left your foot somewhere in the Mediterranean.'

'Good point Freddie. But Heather managed to get herself lost and had to escape from France, you and I Freddie have had our share of scrapes. I've lost count of the number of the King's aircraft I'm responsible for destroying. But we've been incredibly lucky. Can you remember how many of our flying course are still around?'

'You just have to put that behind you. All three of us have lost friends and colleagues but if you dwell on it, where would you end up?'

'Hopefully, it will all be over soon,' Heather said. 'And surely you two are due to be relieved anyway?'

John and Freddie exchanged glances, they had already talked to each other about this. Both had been offered jobs out of the front line and both had turned them down for similar reasons.

'Shall I tell her?' Freddie asked.

'Tell me what?'

'Look,' John said. 'Just before we went on the last operation, Freddie and I were offered the chance to stand down. We both refused. You may think we were mad to do so but we've formed our squadrons, worked them up and led them into the fight, we feel a duty to them. Not only that but we are probably two of the most experienced pilots left flying out here. We're needed. It's that simple.'

'Don't you think you've done enough?' Heather said in a sad voice. 'I understand, I really do but surely it's time other people took on the responsibility?'

'Heather, our ships are both due to be replaced soon,' John said. 'As I understand it by late  summer as there are new ones coming out to relieve us so we'll be heading home then.  It's one last push for us and in all honesty, I can't leave now.'

'Nor me,' Freddie said. 'Just a few more months at sea, in ship's not designed for the tropics, with lousy food but a bar full of booze and crazy pilots.  We have to see it through.'

'Just come back to me, both of you,' Heather said.

# Chapter 44

In late June, they sailed again. The largest fleet the Royal Navy had ever assembled; the fleet carriers, the Battleship KGV, warships of all sizes and a massive train of support vessels trailing behind to set up the logistic chain they would now need to operate off the main coast of Japan.

John had just about recharged his batteries. Having Heather with him was a complete tonic, not that he saw that much of her in the last few weeks ashore. He had several new pilots to train up as well as getting all the old hands back in the saddle. Several of his aircraft were declared write offs once they had been inspected and they were broken down for spares. Sean had finally been replaced by a taciturn Warrant Office called Smith who seemed competent enough but clearly didn't have Sean's innate ability to scrounge spares and perform minor engineering miracles. John realised just how spoilt he had been with Sean.

They re-embarked in the carrier two weeks before they sailed which gave the new chaps a chance to settle in. Before they did, John had an emotional farewell with Heather. She was due to set sail for England in a merchant ship just after he had gone back on board. He was able to wave goodbye to her as her ship sailed past his anchored carrier. She was too far away to communicate but as he waved he could hear her last words as they had parted the previous night. 'After all we've been through, don't you dare not come back to me.' He just hoped he could deliver on the promise he had made.

Two days after sailing, all the squadron Commanding Officers were once again in Indomitable's wardroom.

This time the Admiral had a few more words to say. 'Gentlemen this is the last lap. We are not going to act independently this time, rather we are going to be part of the overall invasion fleet on the right flank. Our job will be to harass the enemy both on the ground and in the air. There are estimates that there could be up to ten thousand aircraft on the mainland. They may well be flown by green pilots but we all know the damage they can do if they get through our defences. Now, someone may ask why we don't just leave it to the heavy bombers that can now reach the mainland. My answer to that is psychology. We all know how tough it was to take Okinawa, imagine what a full scale invasion of the Japanese islands will be like. We need to break their will in every way we can. So the bombers will bomb the large targets and we will harass the smaller ones. The more damage we can do before the soldiers have to go ashore, the less casualties we will have. Any questions?'

There were none.

'Oh and yes, before anyone says it, I still want you to get bloody stuck in.'

A ripple of laughter ran around the assembled officers.

Later that day, John called his squadron together to brief them. He stood at the front of the ready room about to speak when something very odd happened. His pilots occupied the front two rows of seats but suddenly he could see people seated behind them. There was Sparky his friend who had died during training and several RAF officers from his Battle of Britain days including James Smythe his Flight Commander who had died under odd circumstances. Then there were naval pilots he recognised but never really knew well from his time flying Wildcats and finally Neville and Sean. They were all looking at him and smiling. What the hell? He felt his legs go weak and he had to grab the side of the rostrum for a second. When he looked back up they had gone.

'You alright Boss? Tom asked. 'You look like you've seen a ghost.'

John could hardly say he had just seen a host of them. 'No SPLOT, just lunch repeating on me.' He forced himself to concentrate. 'Now listen up everyone, we have about three weeks before we go back into the fray and we are going to have an intensive work up period. The ship will be producing a flying programme starting tomorrow. I want you all to make the most of this. We will be practicing ground strafing and bombing against towed targets as well as air combat. We all need to get used to the new water injection system fitted to our aircraft and see how best to use that in action. So lots to do. The Senior Pilot will now brief you on the detail. I'll see you in the bar tonight.'

He went down to his cabin and sat down still feeling lightheaded. Coming back on board and being back at sea, it was like he had never left the ship in the first place. The constant noise from the machinery, the smell of food, diesel, rubber and sweaty bodies were just the same. If anything, the ship was even more overcrowded than before and the heat below decks was already building up, even though they were miles from the really hot latitudes. He suddenly felt desperately lonely, which was crazy in such a crowded environment. It was only three in the afternoon but he reached into his sock drawer for one of his illegal bottles of scotch. A large helping soon restored an air of calm. Maybe he shouldn't be drinking alone at this time of the day but what the hell, he knew what was coming.

That evening the bar became a bit of a riot. Dinner was reasonably civilised but afterwards, the lads from the Seafire squadron seemed in a combative mood and his chaps were more than happy to rise to the occasion. The game decided on was to see who could climb around the ante room without touching the ground. There were various hand holds; pieces of furniture and bulkhead fittings that made it possible. Possible for a sober athlete maybe but not necessarily for a rather tight Squadron CO as John found out when trying to leap from above the ante room fire place to the back of an arm chair. As he hit the deck there were cries of foul from his pilots who seemed convinced he had been interfered with and a more robust game of mess rugby was initiated. At that point, John decided that discretion was the better part of valour and retired to the bar for a top up.

Wings was there propping the bar up and handed John a scotch as he arrived. 'I thought you were going to make it old chap, getting old?'

'Must be but I swear that chair was moved.'

'Well your chaps obviously thought so, I just hope they are in a fit state to start tomorrow.'

'They will be but it's good to be able to let our hair down, God knows when we will get the chance again.'

'Too true John, too true.'

# Chapter 45

The next weeks were hectic. The fleet had new ships, there were new carriers and new aircrew. Their own ship had many new sailors and John's squadron had four new pilots. The first week was spent allowing individual ships to work up their deck crews and squadrons. One big change was that the Seafires were all now fitted with long range fuel tanks and would no longer be limited to fleet defence. Ranging aircraft in the right order was going to be even more complicated. So during the first week, they practiced just that making sure the right machines were in the right place at the right time. Once airborne, John and Tom split the squadron into two, one half would attempt to fly like they knew the Japanese did and the other half would attempt an ambush. The new water injection system proved its worth allowing for a swift attack and an even swifter climb away. John was fairly impressed and more than happy that they would be able to cope with any Jap fighters they encountered. They then went on to low flying strafing attacks on splash targets towed by the ships. Analysis and past experience had made it clear that anything but a low level attack was going to put the aircraft into more danger and reduce the amount of time they had to fire their guns and aim and drop their bombs. Flying at over three hundred knots at less than fifty feet was an art in itself and John made sure they all practiced whenever they could.

Back on the ship, they studied maps of the terrain especially the main island of Honshu. There was good intelligence available to pick out potential targets. They also had briefings on survival should they end up on the ground. The consensus was that they would be treated harshly. There were enough horror stories circulating already. John let everyone make their own decisions as to what to take with them just as they had done previously. Privately he decided that trying to resist or evade would be almost impossible. Unlike Sumatra or the Sakishimas, Japan was very crowded and trying to hide would probably be impossible. He didn't say so to his chaps as it was a very personal decision.

Another key issue was operating with the Americans and coordinating flying operations. Many of the procedures the Americans used were new to them and they needed to fit in seamlessly. This included forming up over the fleet and even more importantly getting back to it. There had been several occasions when a Japanese aircraft had been able to tag onto the back of a returning formation, especially in bad weather and then make a surprise attack. So in the latter weeks, these procedures were all practiced carefully.

Only a few days out from arriving in their operating area all the British aircraft were launched to fly past the American ships. The reason was to give the ships, especially the guns crews, experience of what the British aircraft looked like. John wasn't too worried about this as his squadron were flying American aircraft, albeit with slightly different markings but it was probably the first time many Americans had seen a Seafire or Firefly. Having done their flypast the squadron climbed to ten thousand feet to await recovery instructions. The sight was breath taking. The weather was good and the visibility was excellent. The blue sea was covered in ships as far as the eye could see. From that height, they were just little grey warships trailing white wakes but the firepower they represented was simply phenomenal. Did Japan really think it could hold out against such military might? Would they have attacked Pearl Harbour if they had realised it would result in such retribution?

'Silly sods are in a right pickle.' Neville said

'Aren't they just,' John replied and then he realised he was talking to someone behind him which was impossible. He swung his head around but obviously he was on his own. Had someone just used the radio? Maybe he had spoken out loud while he was thinking, then hit the transmit button by mistake and someone had replied. Yes, that must have been it. The radio then interrupted telling him it was time for them all to recover to the ship and he had other, more pressing things to think about.

On the sixteenth of July, they prepared to attack. The atmosphere in the ship had been getting more tense, day by day. The old hands knew what to expect, the newcomers had heard all the stories. It wasn't just the aircrew. The fighting at the Sakishimas had made all the sailors realise that it was an all ship affair not just for the few who flew off the deck every day. They all knew how much of a fight the Japanese would put up to defend their home islands. No one was in any doubt that it would be a fight to the death. It didn't help that with a supply chain now over four thousand miles long, getting reliable food supplies was proving difficult and they were all mainly surviving on canned food and this was before they had even entered the fray.

The tension stopped at five o'clock the next morning when everyone was too busy to worry anymore. The whole massive fleet; all the carriers and ships turned into wind and started launching aircraft. It would have been an impressive sight had it been light enough to see. The largest maritime aerial armada the world had ever produced. Corsairs, Hellcats and Avengers from all the ships along with Seafires and Fireflies from the British ones. They flew straight into dreadful weather.

John's squadron had been tasked with a Ramrod to an airfield about twenty miles to the west of Tokyo. They never found it. As they crossed the coast of mainland Japan for the first time they could see very little. As they progressed inshore, the cloud base dropped and it became clear very quickly that they would never make it as far as the airfield they were after. The Met man had warned them that this might happen and all squadrons had been briefed on what to do if they couldn't attack their primary target. John turned them all around and made for the coast. 'Targets of opportunity' was the fall back option and that meant anything that looked remotely like a military facility or logistic infrastructure like railways or factories. He ordered the squadron to split up into flights and go hunting and led his three aircraft down the coastline towards Tokyo. It didn't take long to see a harbour appearing in the gloom. Not only that but there appeared to be a warship tied up to the outer breakwater. That would do. Leading his flight into a shallow dive he opened up with his machine guns and then dropped his two bombs. As soon as he had flown clear, he turned hard out to sea and looked to see what his two pilots managed to do. They were two of his new intake and this was their first real attack. He quickly realised he would need to have words when they returned to the ship. Harry in the first Hellcat managed to fire too late and then proceeded to bomb the sea, way beyond the harbour. The locals were going to have a lot of fish to eat that evening. James in the other Hellcat didn't manage to even drop his bombs as he was desperately trying not to hit the sea. It was quite clear that he had got carried away in his dive and ended up far too low. Even so the Japanese warship, which John could now see was some sort of destroyer was clearly on fire. They must have been caught completely by surprise as none of her guns had even managed to fire back. Presumably, at least one of his bombs had done the job.

'Right you two clots,' he called over the radio. 'Calm down and go around and do it properly this time. Just remember your training.' He knew he was breaking his 'never go back and attack again' rule but there was no real threat here and it was too good an opportunity to get his two new pilots some real experience. While he circled overhead just below the cloud and kept an eye out for either Japs or other roaming allied aircraft he let them have another go. This time Harry managed to score some good hits with his guns and James even managed a half decent attack with his bombs. They left the ship half capsized and blazing from stem to stern.

With most of their ammunition gone he called them to join up with him and they headed back to find their ship. That was it for the day as the weather socked in completely.

Later in the bar, there was much excited chatter from the pilots as they recounted their exploits to each other. John and Tom let them get on with it.

'Not the most auspicious start,' Tom said. 'I overheard in the operations room that we are going to head down the coast a bit tonight to try and find some better weather.'

'Not auspicious no,' John agreed. 'But it was good for the new chaps. At least they all got to fire their guns and drop their bombs.' And he told Tom about James and Harry's performance. 'So they learned a good lesson. Next time it won't be so easy I'm sure but I'd rather start off this way than go straight into a major firefight.'

'Good point,' Tom conceded. 'One thing I'm sure of it won't be like this every day.'

# Chapter 46

It wasn't. The next day the weather was much improved and John's squadron was tasked to try to attack the airfield they couldn't find the previous day. The fleet had moved down the coast a little and the transit to the target was going to be longer but not difficult now that they could see where they were going.

They roared over the land at low level keeping a wary eye out for enemy aircraft but none were seen. The target was over the top of a forested ridge which was easily identifiable. As soon as they crested the top they could see what they faced and it was clear that they were expected. A hail of ground fire met them but as usual, they were now committed and all they could do was slam throttles fully forward, select targets and go for it. One thing John immediately noticed was that, unlike the Sakishima airfields, there may have been plenty of guns around this one but the gunners were clearly not in practice. Despite the fireworks display, very little of the shooting seemed accurate. Looking ahead, he could see several hangars and a line of twin engine bombers parked up outside. It was yet another mistake caused by inexperience. The aircraft should have been dispersed around the field but it was too late for them now, he thumbed his trigger and blasted his six guns down the line of parked aircraft. In the middle, he dropped his bombs. The rest of the squadron followed him. Some went for the hangars and some continued down the line of aircraft. As soon as he was clear he turned hard and looked back. The airfield was a mass of flames and smoke. 'Well done chaps,' he called on the radio. That's it, no going back. Time to go home.'

The whole squadron made it back to the ship in one piece although several aircraft had some minor damage. John called all his pilots into the ready room before they went off to make their individual combat reports.

'Well done everyone. That was an excellent attack. I counted at least ten aircraft destroyed on the ground. However, don't get complacent. Their gunners were inexperienced and there were no enemy aircraft to contend with. It won't stay like that. Now, we are providing air defence this afternoon. Three aircraft at all times, so make your reports and grab some food, the day isn't over yet.'

Just then one of the ready room phones rang and Tom reached over and answered it. 'That was Commander (Air) Sir he asked for you to go and see him in Flyco.'

'Did he say what he wanted?' John asked.

'No, just that he wanted a word with you.'

Thanking Tom, John made his way up the island ladder to Flyco. He didn't know why but he had a vague sense of dread, something had happened.

'Ah, John,' Wings said when he appeared in Flyco. 'Come with me will you please?'

Wings led John to the small Captain's day cabin at the rear of the bridge and closed the door when they were inside.

John started to speak but Wings cut him off. 'Read this John.' And he handed him a piece of paper. John looked at it. It was the summary report from all the British ships after the morning raids. He couldn't see what Wings clearly wanted him to see.

'The last paragraph,' Wings said.

John's eyes dropped to the bottom of the paper and it was like a knife had been thrust into his heart. The paragraph was titled 'Losses' and the first name was 'Lieutenant Commander F. St John-Stevens, CO 1855, missing.'

'It says missing Sir. Do we know any more?'

'Yes, they were conducting a Ramrod on an airfield near the coast to the west of here. Witnesses say he went around and made a second run, nobody knows why but another of his pilots had been shot down on the first attack. His aircraft was hit and although he was able to turn back, his aircraft crashed before he could reach the shoreline. It didn't catch fire but no one was seen to get out. Sorry John, I know you two go back a long way. He could have survived we just don't know.'

John felt completely numb. He should be used to losing people by now but Freddie? That was the problem with these bloody Ramrods. There was no skill involved. It was pure luck if you were hit or not. Freddie was the best pilot John knew but skill just didn't enter into it when attacking the ground. And then apparently he went back, he broke the golden rule, that just wasn't like him.

'Thank you Sir,' John said in a dull tone. 'We're on air defence this afternoon. Please excuse me while I get ready.'

Wings gave him a hard look. 'We all lose friends John but hopefully this will all be over soon. Put it behind you like you've done many times before. I don't want to lose you as well.'

John just nodded and went back to the ready room.

The afternoon happened on automatic. John flew the first of their sorties but if you asked him what he did, he wouldn't have been able to say. He was so devastated he didn't even find his sadness turning to anger as it had done many times in the past. Mind you, had a Jap pilot been foolish enough to take him on, he wouldn't have lasted a minute.

He didn't socialise at all that evening. He knew it was bad form but he just needed some time to himself so he sat in his cabin with a whisky and thought back over all the good times he had shared with Freddie. All of a sudden his motivation, his desire to see things through seemed to be melting away. As he took a last gulp of scotch before attempting to get some sleep knowing it was another early start tomorrow, he realised his hand was shaking. 'Yes a definite case of the twitch,' he said to himself. 'but who cares?'

He lay on his bed fully clothed and closed his eyes. Did someone say 'we do' just before sleep took him?

The next day and the ones after that seemed to merge into a waking dream. Eat, sleep, fly, get drunk and repeat. It was like the Sakishimas all over again. But worse. He lost two more pilots on Ramrods but some time into the second week they got their chance to be fighter pilots again. As they transited at low level to a new target or maybe one they had hit before, he couldn't remember or even care less, someone called bandits above them. Sure enough, eight Zekes were attempting an attack. The Japs had the advantage of height and surprise. They didn't seem to know it. After calling 'tally ho' and slamming the throttle fully forward with the water injection on to start a climb, John deliberately pulled to one side and let his chaps have a go at them. Only one Zeke survived and he disappeared trailing smoke. The chaps were all delighted. He went through all the motions with them but inside felt nothing at all.

In fact, in later years John had great trouble remembering the three weeks up until the sixth of August except as a sort of dream. His log book told him he flew nearly every day that they were in theatre and not away refuelling and replenishing. There were numbers relating to flying hours, places attacked and aircraft destroyed on the ground and several in the air but it was as if someone else was doing the flying and he was standing back as a spectator.

Then everything should have changed. The Americans wiped out the city of Hiroshima with an atomic bomb.

# Chapter 47

The news swept around the ship like wildfire. At first, no one knew what it meant. Then when it was explained there was amazement and jubilation. Surely no country would be stupid enough to carry on with a war that they clearly couldn't win?

John and Wings were propping up the bar that evening discussing exactly that.

'They can't carry on surely?' John said. 'And it's not just this amazing bomb, I hear the B29s have been carpet bombing with incendiaries and destroying massive areas of the country. Why don't they bloody well just give up?'

Wings sighed, 'You tell me John but it appears they are not going to stop. This ridiculous military philosophy of theirs means they just can't surrender.'

'So what then? We keep attacking, losing our people until there's no one left?'

'I reckon so, at least for the short term.'

So they did just that with Ramrods and aerial sweeps and attacks on targets of opportunity. John had to write another letter of condolence to grieving parents when Harry was shot down. They had been attacked by some Jap fighters and it seemed that his radio must have failed as he didn't react to the shouted warning. The squadron took its revenge but it was yet another hollow victory.

On the ninth of August, the Americans did it again and wiped out the city of Nagasaki with another atomic bomb. The reaction in the ship was muted this time as no one was convinced that the Japanese wouldn't literally fight to the last man woman and child rather than surrender.

The next day, they were still flying, although a large part of the British Fleet left to go back to Sydney. They needed sort themselves out so that they could come back for the final invasion later in the year. Invincible stayed as it was planned for her to go back to England in a few weeks anyway. So they kept flying and attacking and dying.

It was crazy, they had been told that the Emperor was attempting to negotiate a surrender. On the twelfth, they were told that surrender terms had been offered to the allies and then almost immediately afterwards that the Jap military refused to agree and had vowed to fight on. So they kept flying. It was a sort of madness, it was almost as if the Allied Command didn't want to stop. There was a sort of logic to it. 'If you want to keep fighting then so will we' but was it really worth the cost? Many didn't think so including John but it was not their decision.

Three days later John and his squadron were conducting yet another attack near Tokyo. The devastation on the ground was almost complete. It was so bad John wondered if another atomic bomb had been dropped and no one had noticed. They were half way through the sortie when the command to return to the ship came over the radio.

John circled the carrier while his men landed one by one and then it was his turn. As the barrier dropped to allow him to taxi forward he could see that the deck crew were in a strange mood. As he unstrapped and slid down the wing, Tom came up to him.

'It's over Boss. The bloody Japs have surrendered. The war is over.'

The words washed over John's head for a moment before they sunk in. No more killing, no more dying, no more letters to grieving parents. He suddenly felt water on his cheeks and realised he was crying. Then he realised that Tom would see him like that and felt embarrassed except he then saw that Tom was in tears as well.

'Oh God,' he choked. 'Oh thank God.' He grabbed Tom's hand and the two men just grinned like idiots at each other.

There was a party in the wardroom that night.

John had his first real night's sleep for weeks. No ghosts visited him. But there was still work to do.

The very next day they changed from fighters to angels of mercy. Their job now was to scour the countryside and identify the prisoner of war camps that littered the area. Then they would do their best to drop supplies to provide help before they could be properly liberated.

For the first time in a very long time, John lined his Hellcat up on the deck to fly a sortie that would not end up in death and destruction for someone. A sortie where, hopefully, no one was going to try and kill him. It was a surreal experience, although they all knew that some Japanese were still attempting resistance and so they would all have to be careful.

They were all flying individual sorties now to cover the largest area as quickly as possible. John had been allocated a search area towards Tokyo along the coastline and then returning five miles inland. The ship was only a few miles from the coast now and within minutes he was starting his search. He had decided to stay at about two thousand feet to get the best visibility but still see details on the ground. There was going to be a large area to cover and time would be important. There was very little intelligence about conditions in the camps but what there was, wasn't good.

He flew along the coast for an hour and was about to turn inland and return when something in the distance caught his eye. At first, he thought it was some sort of farm. There were rough looking buildings in an open area surrounded by low scrub quite close to the shoreline. There was something written on the roof of one of the buildings. As he got closer he could make out the letters 'PW' and then he could see some more letters written on the sand on the beach. Pushing the nose down to descend and get a better look, he soon saw people waving frantically at him. He roared overhead waggling his wings and entered a tight turn to see what was on the beach.

'Brits 75 Yanks 50 DU 30 and then the letters SOS.' He immediately understood that they were telling him how many were there and of what nationality but what the hell did the SOS mean? Suddenly a red flare shot up from the camp and as he looked a party of people carried something down to the sand and waved at him. It was a body. It could only mean one thing but what the hell did they expect him to do about it? He had a first aid kit on board but there was no way he could drop it to them with any guarantee they would be able to retrieve it. He looked carefully at the shoreline, the sand looked firm but that could be deceptive at this height. He knew that what he should do was head back to the ship and make a report but the people on the ground were military, some were quite possibly aircrew. He made a decision. He'd been risking his life for months to kill people, he would do the same now tory to save someone.

He flew away for half a mile and then turned back towards the beach, throttled back and lowered his flaps and wheels. This would be tricky and he had to do it just right. He knew there was only a gentle breeze as the sea was quite calm. As he descended through two hundred feet he slowed the aircraft right down. He could feel the stall starting as a gentle shuddering through the airframe but he let it build up and used the power of the engine to literally hold the machine in the sky. He was on the wrong side of the drag curve now and he knew if he made any sudden increase in power it would result in a torque induced stall. The beach was coming up fast now and when he was only a few feet up, he shut the throttle and pulled the stick back into his stomach and prayed. They hit with a remarkably gentle thump but decelerated fast as the wheels dug into the sand. The risk of them digging in too hard and flipping the machine onto its back was what he was really worried about but it didn't happen, with the Hellcat coming to an abrupt halt as it lifted its tail and then dropped back.

He unstrapped and climbed out to be greeted by what looked like a group of human skeletons. Most were dressed in rags although some still had the remains of military uniforms. However, a couple looked almost normal and one of them came up and greeted John. He had bruises all over his face and a slight limp but at least he looked well fed.

'Lieutenant Scott Thompson, 1839 Squadron, shot down a week ago. I'm afraid my friends here haven't been looked after very well.'

John shook his hand. 'John Hunt 1854. Yes, I can see that. I'll get your position reported back to our ship. As you are on the coast I'm sure they can get boats to you pretty quickly but why the SOS and who is this?' John asked as he pointed to the stretcher the men had been carrying.

'We had a bit of a fight on our hands last night,' Scott said. 'When news of the surrender came in, some of the guards decided they didn't want any of us to go home and had a go at us with their swords. They came off worse I'm glad to say and then the officer in charge of the camp intervened and put a stop to it but this chap was hurt and frankly, without him we probably would have had a lot more people in trouble or dead. He took a knock to the head and he's lost a lot of blood. We have a doc at the camp and he reckons he needs urgent medical care. When we heard your plane in the distance we decided to try and get you to come and pick him up. I flew Hellcats as well and know that you can cram two people into the cockpit although maybe I'd better not say how I know that.'

John let the remark pass although he could guess.  He had heard of several girlfriends back in Australia getting an unofficial ride on the lap of an amorous pilot.  Instead, he went over to the casualty.  There was a blood soaked bandage over half his face and the rest was quite bruised.  John pulled the bandage back.

'Hello Freddie, let's take you home.'

# Chapter 48

'You stupid bastard. You went back. You broke the golden bloody rule. What were you thinking?' John asked. He was in the ship's sick bay, sitting next to Freddie who had finally regained consciousness after two days in a coma. John had rushed down to his bedside as soon as he had heard that Freddie was awake.

'And hello to you too old friend,' Freddie replied with a weak grin. 'And how the hell did I get here? The last I remember was some bloody Jap guard swinging a sword at me. Mind you I had just kicked his friend rather hard in the bollocks. Now that was fun.'

'I found you. Your campmates had put a sign out on the beach while I was flying to try and locate the camps, as we all are. I had the enormous pleasure of having you on my lap, once we got off the ground that is. Getting airborne wasn't exactly easy and believe me a deck landing with a big fat lump on your lap is not easy either.'

'Ah yes, some of my chaps did that back in Oz until I put a stop to it,' Freddie said. 'Mind you, I do wonder how many children have actually been conceived inside a fighter's cockpit at ten thousand feet. Anyway, thank you old friend.' He held out his hand and John shook it.

Just then the Doctor came over and shooed John away. 'I'll come and chat again as soon as the doc says I can.' John said as he left, with a lump in his throat.

Flying continued for another week and then the ship was ordered back to Australia for a package of maintenance before heading home. This time, they kept the aircraft below decks. On the way to Sydney, the flight deck was once again turned into a sports and recreation deck. A large canvas swimming pool was set up and once again a deck hockey pitch was marked out. There was no flying, there was no threat anymore. It was something everyone was having trouble getting their heads around.

John, Tom and Freddie had taken up a sun bathing spot next to the island. Freddie had been released from sick bay the previous day with strict orders to take it easy and lay off the booze. Something he was studiously ignoring.

'You still haven't answered my question you silly sod,' John said.

'Which one was that old chap? You seem to have so many.'

'Why did you break the rule? Why did you go back?'

Freddie leant back and closed his eyes. 'Madness is the answer. I'd just lost my wingman, he pranged in hard and I saw which gun emplacement had done it. There was no way I was going to let those bastards get away with that so I went back and shot the buggers to hell.'

'And then they shot you in the process,' John said.

'Probably, I'm not sure really but someone certainly did. And yes it was a bloody silly thing to do but that's easy to say now. All I can say was that I felt it was the right at the time.'

And how did you manage to need my help after that? You know, you could have waited for a normal rescue.' John asked.

'Ah well after I got out of the crash I had already decided to give myself up. Foolishly, I thought they would treat me better if I did. Anyway, after a couple of soldiers gave me a damned good kicking they threw me into that camp. You saw how badly treated most of them had been John but Scotty and I were relatively fresh. We were told about the surrender but it was clear that some of the guards weren't that happy, particularly two of the buggers who were notorious for being absolute bastards. Most of the chaps couldn't have put up any fight at all but Scotty and I decided not to go down easily. We found some old wooden boards made some rudimentary clubs and hid behind the doors to the main sleeping hut. The bastards waited till it was dark. When they paraded in, shouting in Japanese, Scotty and I took a swing at them. He missed his chap so I kicked the bugger between the legs and then the lights went out. Simple really.'

'Bloody hell.' Tom said. 'That was either very brave or damned stupid. I think I'll settle on brave if you don't mind.'

'Thanks Tom,' Freddie said. 'But it was either that or let those sods and their swords loose on a bunch of starved prisoners. No choice really.'

The three men fell silent for a while.

Tom broke the silence and asked. 'So what happens now, does anyone really know?'

'Well, nearly all the aircrew out here are reserve or volunteer reserve so I guess they'll go back to doing whatever they were doing before the war.' John said. 'We certainly won't need a fleet this massive in peacetime.'

'And are you going to apply for a permanent commission John?' Freddie asked. 'You always were a bit anchor faced.'

'If you had asked me that a year ago I would have said yes. But now? No, I've had enough. Peacetime flying will be dull and safe and that's a good thing but who's to say this won't happen again and I couldn't take that. All I want to do now is go home, jump into bed with my wife and do silly, stupid mundane things that definitely do not involve the Royal Navy, stinking overcrowded ships and really lousy food. What about you Freddie?'

'Oh, I know exactly what I'm going to do. I'm going to go back to Sydney and I'm going to propose to Tracy and marry her. Then I'll drag her back to a rather large country house and farm in England where she will learn the beauty of being a farmer's wife and mother to a large batch of unruly, badly behaved children.'

John was speechless for a minute. 'Good God, I never thought I'd hear those words from your lips Freddie. The world really must be changing.'

A month later they sailed for England. It would take several weeks and no one seemed sure what their lordships wanted or had planned for them. On the second day out, Wings called John to his cabin and handed him a signal. John read it carefully.

'Any problems John?' Wings asked. 'It's your squadron after all.'

'Well, it seems to be pretty mean spirited of the Yanks but there again we only had the aircraft on lend lease so at least they are offering us the opportunity to buy them.'

'Or send them back or scrap them,' Wings said. 'It seems to me that politics are rearing their ugly head already. And as you can see their lordships have already decided what to do with your machines. You won't really be a CO of anything after today.'

'That's alright Sir, I already expected something like this. Oh and this means I will no longer be responsible for the chaps behaviour in the bar on the way back.'

'Hah, good try old chap, I'm damned sure the Commander won't see it that way. And what about you? What are your plans?'

'All I want is to go home and before you ask, no, I will not be asking to extend my commission. I've going to do something totally different and please don't ask me what that is because I haven't a clue.'

'Fair enough. Well I'll see you on the flight deck at sixteen hundred.'

By four that afternoon most of 1954 squadron were drunk. The officers had been in the bar since lunchtime and many of the sailors had been illegally hoarding their tots. A blind eye was turned by everyone. Ten Grumman Hellcats were ranged on the stern of the flight deck. They were in two rows of five aircraft. John, Tom and the rest of the pilots were seated to one side along with his engineers. The rest of the ship's company were further forward watching.

Chief Petty Officer Simpson came over to John and saluted. 'Permission to carry on Sir?' he asked.

'Carry on Chief,' was all John said.

Simpson nodded and walking to the rearmost two aircraft, he signalled to the men standing around them. They unfastened the lashings holding it to the deck and then together as a team pushed both aircraft off the stern of the deck and into the sea where they hit with a splash and immediately started to sink. The deck crew immediately walked forward to start on the next row

'I suppose I should be upset to see such valuable machines, ones that only a few weeks ago were so important and kept us alive, being simply thrown away,' Tom said to John. 'But I'm not. Funny that.'

John simply nodded. He was looking at the ghosts that thronged around the aircraft. As each fighter fell into the sea, some of them simply faded away. When the last two machines were about to slip over the stern the last two ghosts, Sean and Neville, seemed to wave at John and then they too, quietly, ceased to exist.

# Epilogue

John put the newspaper down and looked over at Heather. 'If you thought I was wrong to leave the navy darling, just look at this.' He waved the paper at her over the breakfast table. 'It's all happening again and in just about the same bloody place. A British carrier Task Force is now engaged in operations off Korea. If I'd stayed in, I could be there doing it all over again.'

'Well you're not and thank goodness for that. It was just as bad for me you know. Even if the press seemed to ignore what you were going through out there, I knew.'

'Yes it was bloody awful for all of us, I never intend to do that again. Now are we going to Freddie's this afternoon? A good party is what we need and let's face it he does do good parties.'

'I think Tracy has a bit of a hand in organising those you know and it is her pregnancy we're going to celebrate.'

John caught an odd tone in Heather's voice but didn't say anything. Despite several years of normal married life after the war had ended, there had been no sign of offspring. It was getting to the point that he was going to have to suggest they both went to see a doctor to try and find out what wasn't working.

That afternoon, they drove up to the country house that belonged to Freddie's parents. It had been requisitioned during the war but was now back in private ownership. Freddie and Tracy had taken over the farm house that his parents had used when they had been required to move out of the big house. However, the gathering was going to be on the lawn in front of the old place. Just close family and friends. This was going to be Tracy's second child. They already had a very cute and very spoiled two year old called Rachel and were hoping for a brother for her to play with.

Freddie and Tracy greeted them when they arrived and within minutes Heather had been whisked away to talk girl talk somewhere, leaving the men together. They chatted for a while and then parted to mix with the other guests. Heather suddenly appeared at John's side.

'John, can I have a word for a minute please?'

'Of course, what is it?'

'Not here, come on down to the pond.'

Mystified, John followed her along a short path to the large duck pond at the bottom of the lawn.

'Remember this place?' Heather asked with a smile.

'Well yes, we all used to play here as kids. Why on earth are you asking?'

'Remember a certain night when we started to play more grown up games?'

John certainly did. It was the first time he had suddenly appreciated Heather for the beautiful girl she really was rather than an annoying younger playmate.

'And remember what we got up to later that night?'

'Are you trying to make me blush? You won't you know. Come on, what's this all about? Is there something you're not telling me?'

'Yes there is. I was waiting to find out for certain and that's why I went off with Tracy when we got here. I rang the doctor and he confirmed it. So this isn't just a party for Tracy, It's for us as well.'

He stood there for a second as the realisation hit him. She didn't need to say anything else as he hugged her and lifted her off the ground and then just as quickly put her down again. 'Sorry I'll have to be more careful from now on.'

'Oh don't be so silly but are you happy?'

'Good God, how can you ask that? I'm absolutely delighted. And we can go and tell everyone else I guess and have a few extra drinks to celebrate two events rather than one.'

That night as they lay in bed John turned to Heather. 'Names? Any ideas?'

'Well if it's a girl, I rather like Lucy but if it's a boy you decide.'

'Hmm if it's a boy, I will expect him to join the navy and become a famous pilot like his dad and the name I've always liked is Jonathon.'

You can read the Jon (Jonathon) Hunt series of books on Amazon starting with 'Sea Skimmer' here:   amazon.co.uk/Sea-Skimmer-Jon-Hunt-Book-ebook/dp/B004X6ZIP4

## Author's Notes

Much of this story was once again based on my father's career. As I said in my previous book 'and the pilot can't swim', after service in the Mediterranean, he returned to England and in 1943 was promoted to Lieutenant Commander (Acting) and formed up 1839 Squadron flying Hellcats, initially in Northern Ireland. So a sub lieutenant in the summer of 1940 to CO of a squadron in three years. I would hope a lot of this was because of his skill as a pilot and as a naval officer but sadly it was almost certainly also because he was still alive! By that point in the war, the need for naval aviators was rapidly growing and the number of experienced pilots was falling.

He took the squadron out to Trincomalee but had a very bad accident there. As the last aircraft to land on the deck, ahead of the barrier was very crowded, either the number four arrester wire failed or his arrester hook broke. Either way rather than crash into the crowded deck he ruddered the aircraft over the side and very nearly didn't survive. A few months later he was relieved. I suspect it was a similar situation to the one that I put John into when he was in Australia and Father either took or was told to take the option to stand down. Either way, I'm damned glad he did as I probably wouldn't be here to write this.

I've tried to keep to real time lines with the narrative but compressed the story with regards the Hellcat and Corsair story. Although I give John and Freddie a starring role in assessing the aircraft, the facts about the machines are true. The US Navy turned down the Corsair as a fleet fighter for the reasons I give and it was only when the RN made it work that they reconsidered. It is of note that the only naval aircraft to fly in the Korean War that was also in WW2 was the Corsair. The Hellcat, whilst not quite so good in performance was responsible for shooting down more Japanese aircraft than any other type.

The chapter I've titled 'Interlude' is a mix of several meetings between Churchill and the US navy staff but the final outcome was decided by Roosevelt and Churchill despite Admiral King's misgivings. It is fact that the Americans lost no territory to the Japanses whereas we lost Hong Kong Singapore and large swathes of territory including much of Burma. Had we not stopped the Japanese there we might also have lost India.

The chapters about flying a Hurricane into rocket propelled wires designed by Barnes Wallace are true and as accurate as I can recall from my father's account of him doing the flying, including nearly losing one wing.

Operation Tungsten was a success. In reality, Tirpitz was so badly damaged she could never have gone to sea again. Quite why the Barracudas dropped their armour piercing bombs too low is something I've not been able to discover but I suspect it was felt to be too high to be accurate enough. It was a shame though as once again the RAF PR machine was able to grab all the glory when they dropped their Tallboy bombs on her and turned her turtle.

Trincomalee was a massive naval base for a while but once Australia accepted the need to host the fleet the major effort moved there. Mind you, the Australian government were initially quite reluctant even if the general population were all for it (including many young ladies).

The attack on the Palembang oil refineries was both a wake up call for the aviators and also a lesson in what their new role was going to be. Losses were high and arguably the damage was not that significant but one thing it did do was make the Americans realise that the Brits meant business.

Now you know why the book has its title, I can confirm that Admiral Vian's only words to his aircrew were those four words 'Get bloody stuck in'. It sums the man up in many ways. A non-aviator but a fighting admiral who had to balance aggression with the need to conserve his fighting capacity.

The stories of being partially blinded by a piece of a Kamikaze skin and having to fight off two Japanese guards after the surrender are based on true events.

The attack on the Sakishias, half way through the campaign there by the fleet capital ships happened as I described along with the damage caused by Kamikazes in their absence. A gamble that didn't pay off, it generated much resentment with the aircrew.

Some figures at the end of the Sakishma campaign, Operation Iceberg:

The fleet spent 62 days at sea with 8 days at Leyte for replenishment, they flew over 5000 sorties in over 23 days of strikes. They shot down 42 enemy aircraft and over 100 on the ground. They lost 42% of their original aircraft and 41 aircrew, that's about 10% of the total. 44 men were killed in the ships with 83 wounded and every carrier was hit by a Kamikaze at least once.

Aircrew losses during the final weeks of attacking the mainland were three times higher.

When they sailed again to attack the Japanese mainland they were all expecting a long bloody campaign followed by an invasion probably in 1946.

The atomic bombs were obviously the final straw but carpet bombing by B29s had already wiped out most of the Japanese infrastructure. Maybe that would have been enough to get them to surrender without the need to use the bombs but we'll never know.

The army's campaign in Burma was known as the 'Forgotten War' but also mainly forgotten was the British Pacific Fleet's operations. Press coverage was poor, partly because of the distances involved in getting information away from the action but also, dare I say it because the navy didn't really have any interest in good PR. Now, if the RAF had fielded the largest fleet ever put together with the largest British aviation firepower ever flown and it had the successes and losses that were experienced – we would never have heard the end of it!

Finally, the Americans did insist on lend lease aircraft being returned, paid for or destroyed and many now litter the sea bed around Australia. Quite why they had to be so small minded is something I don't really understand but with the war over, politics was now taking centre stage.

Printed in Great Britain
by Amazon

16002726R00127